Through the Mists of Time

Historical/Time Travel Romance

T.A.Moore

Books

Disclaimer

While inspired by actual events, this novel is a work of fiction.

Front, Back Cover Art and Interiors by Laura Givens

Edited by Sharon Stevens

LIC in Progress

LBF Books
Pittsburgh, PA 15216

FIRST PRINTING

Dedication

To my brother, Frank Barnett Jr. (1949-1981), who introduced me to the world of books and instilled me with a love of history.

Acknowledgements

Thank you to Indiana Writers' Workshop, for your critiques, encouragement and continuing examples of professionalism. This book wouldn't have been possible without all of you and I'm forever blessed to be counted among your members. Thanks, Pat, for taking me under your writerly wing and drawing me into the fold.

Author Endorsement:

"T.A. Moore is at the top of her game with 'Through the Mists of Time.' With a delightful mix of some of the best-loved genres in Romance, this sensual novel is a treasure trove of originality, an honest-to-goodness must-have!"

-K.L. Nappier, author of Voyagers, Full Wolf Moon and Bitten

Through the Mist of Time

T.A.Moore

"If you were the one
suffering the fires of love,
you would be in
more of a hurry
to see Venus.
I love a young
and handsome boy;
I beg you,
spur on your mules.
You've finished your drink,
let's go;
take up the reins
and shake them.
Take me to Pompeii
where my sweet love
is waiting."

-from graffiti found
during the excavation
of Pompeii.

Prologue

Pompeii, Italy
79 A.D.

The soft breeze entered through the bedchamber window and moved like a lover over Christos' naked body. A low moan escaped his lips as he turned onto his stomach. The breeze continued upward, over his thighs, and across his shoulders, stopping to tease the thick black hair curled at the nape of his neck.

Christos stirred, kicking away his rumpled bedding. He turned his face toward the window. Could it be she was here again? He opened his eyes drowsily. Ah, yes. She was here.

The finely woven linen curtains that flanked the window danced around her where she stood, casting an ethereal quality to her form. How she came to be in his room, night after night, he had no idea, but she continued to appear before him just the same. Always when he was asleep, always when he was alone.

Long golden brown hair cascaded down her arms and to her hips, concealing her breasts where the strands fell. The hair lay across her belly almost bidding him to lower his gaze to her sweet gate. Ah, but he was hard pressed to remove his eyes from her gentle face. She wore only jewelry as she stood there - a necklace with a single large emerald and dangling earrings that matched. The gems echoed the color of her eyes and they sparkled and winked in the moonlight, teasing him, daring him - to touch.

He ground his hips into the mattress, his loins aching with desire as he stared at her. He would've reached for her, tried to make love to her then and there, but knew it would do no good. He'd tried to touch her before, but she always managed to elude him during these nocturnal visits.

Christos' eyes drifted closed for a moment and he felt the breeze again. When he opened them, he found that this time it wasn't the breeze, but the woman's fingers moving over him. She leaned above him, her hair brushing against his skin, and delicately ran her nails across his back and down his thighs. Oh, but she was a treasure, this woman of the night. He sighed, savoring the delicious feel of her touch. He had stopped asking long ago from whence she came and now only enjoyed her nearness.

Then the touching stopped and, all too soon, she was moving away from his side. Though knowing it would do no good, he still reached for this restless spirit that haunted him in the night. But all he caught was the night air as she drifted toward the window, a sweet smile on her lips. What was this game she was playing with him?

He found his voice. "Please. Wait," he whispered, his words urgent. "You must tell me this time. Who are you?"

She turned to him and smiled. He thought his heart would break from the kindness he saw in those emerald eyes, now darkened by the shadows of the room. "I am yours," she answered simply. Her voice carried the sound of garden chimes in the summer and soothed the fever that had begun to build inside him.

Christos let his breath out slowly. "You say you are mine, but I know you are going to leave again." He pushed a black curl off his forehead and sighed. "Will you ever stay or will you only continue to pass through my chambers on your nightly journeys?"

"The next time you see me will be in the flesh," she murmured. "You have my word."

He watched in silence as she turned to face the window. Her body, bathed in the silver moonlight, glowed for a moment, then slowly vanished into the darkness.

At her disappearance, Christos awoke with a start. "By the gods," he cursed under his breath, the tension tight in his belly. How long would he continue to dream of her, this beautiful, nameless entity that followed him into the arms of Morpheus? Was it possible to desire a ghost, for truly that's what she must be?

"How soon 'til you return to me, my sweet one?" He closed his eyes, his words a soft prayer. "How soon?"

Chapter One

London, England
April, 1865

"Why dost thou cry?"

Her tears fell freely, clinging to her long dark lashes for a brief moment before spilling down her soft cheeks. "I cry because there is no love in my world."

He gently cupped her chin, forcing her to look into his deep brown eyes. "Nay. 'Tis not so. One as gentle and beautiful as thee will always be loved."

"And who shall love me?" Even as she asked the question, she knew she was being much too bold, much too daring. Her heart threatened to break under the burden of her sorrow.

He smiled warmly. "Can thou sayest with all honesty that thou dost not know?"

"I must hear the words aloud, so my heart will know 'tis not a lie."

"Then thou must listen carefully, for there shall be no misunderstandings between us." He traced the outline of her lips with his eyes. "I love thee, Caroline, and will spend the remainder of my days making thee happy."

Caroline caught her breath as he pulled her close, his strong arms locking around her. "And I love thee, Damon," she whispered against his lips as they pressed their bodies together.

Valerie Sherwood Brooks fell back against the soft goose down pillows and sighed as they enveloped her within their soothing embrace. She held the book up in the air, just over her face, and reread the last line again and again until she could close her eyes and see the words still pictured in her mind.

"And I love thee, Damon."

Valerie closed the novel gently and hugged it against her chest as if it would steady the rapid beating of her heart. Oh, but these new romance novels were just marvelous with their tales of love. A woman would truly be blessed to be loved so by such a man.

She glanced at the gold watch suspended from a delicate chain around her neck. She sighed. It was getting late. With one last longing look at the novel, Valerie leaned over the side of her bed and tucked it between the bed frame and thick feather mattress.

She pushed it as far past the edge as she could reach. Past where the snowy white linens were folded around the striped ticking, all the while being careful not to bend the red chipboard cover or wrinkle the heavy yellowed pages.

For an instant, guilt grabbed at Valerie's conscience. If Mama should find out what she was reading she'd be in trouble for certain! Then she shook her head, dismissing the thought. No, she wouldn't let herself even *consider* the consequences. After all, she was eighteen and old enough to know of such things that happened between a man and a woman. She straightened her shoulders. Old enough to already be married and starting a family of her own, for heaven's sake!

The last thought clutched at her stomach and her shoulders sagged forward. Valerie took a deep breath, forcing the melancholy back to where it resided in the hidden depths of her mind. Never mind Mama *or* marriage. Tonight she would not allow such thoughts to upset her good humor. She had just finished reading a perfectly marvelous romance story and would take the elation she felt when the lovers reunited with her into her dreams.

Rising slightly, Valerie leaned over and lifted the globe from the clear glass hurricane lamp on her night table. Being careful to shield the flame with her left hand, she blew out the fire and replaced the globe with a quiet clink and scrape of metal against glass. She settled back onto the pillows and pulled the creamy satin comforter up around her neck, shifting about until she was comfortable.

Suddenly, a voice bellowed out from the street below, breaking the stillness of the night. Valerie realized too late that she had left the window ajar. She tossed back the covers and pushed herself to the edge of the bed, first one foot, and then the other, hit the thick needlepoint wool rug with a muffled thump. She reached for the dark English oak cane that was propped against the rose velvet side chair and grasped it with her left hand, the top well worn and comfortable in her grip. Valerie took a step with her right foot, then dragged the lame left foot behind her, leaning on the cane for support. Finally, she reached the window and pulled it shut.

Once back to the bed, Valerie again laid the cane against the chair and let her body sink into the mattress. She snuggled as far down as she could under the covers without her feet hanging off the end and closed her eyes. As her breathing grew steady, Valerie drifted into a deep sleep, images of a man with curly black hair and dark blue eyes filling her dreams.

* * *

"Valerie! Valerie!"

The high pitched screech broke the heavy veil of sleep and went straight through to her bones. Valerie's eyes flew open only to find her little brother staring right at her, his face so close she could see where the sleep still clung to his dark lashes.

"What in heaven's name do you want?" she grumbled.

"Mama said it's time for you to get up. She said you're a sleepy head and I should come and get you for breakfast," he explained matter-of-factly as his eyes darted about his sister's room.

"Please, Reggie. I'm not ready to wake up just yet. Tell Mama I don't want any breakfast this morning." Valerie rolled over to face the wall, pulling the comforter up over her shoulders.

Reggie stood next to the bed for a few moments longer, considering his sister. Then, he spied where the dust ruffle was stuck between the mattress and the bed frame. Ever so gently, so as not to disturb Valerie, he slipped his small hand into the opening and pulled out the novel. The book fell open somewhere in the middle and his eyes grew wide as he started to read. "Papa's going to beat you for certain!" he exclaimed.

Valerie flung back the covers and whirled around. "Give that to me!" she demanded, grabbing for him. But he was too fast for her and darted toward the door, stopping just short of the portal. Her eyes focused on the boy, Valerie fumbled for her cane. "I said give that back to me, you little lizard! You have no right coming into my room and taking my things!"

"What's going on here?" Jacqueline Brooks peered into Valerie's room. "What have you got there, Reg?" she asked, ruffling his hair.

Victorious, Reggie handed the book over to his mother. His success made him feel bold. He wrinkled his freckled nose and stuck his tongue out at Valerie.

Valerie glared at her brother as she stepped carefully over the pile of tossed bedding to where he and their mother were standing. "It's nothing, Mama. Just a book." She reached for it, but Jacqueline wouldn't give it up. Valerie sighed, rolling her eyes. This wasn't going to be easy.

"I can see that. But what sort of book would have you calling your brother names?" Jacqueline opened it and Valerie could see her expression change from one of amusement to dismay. She slammed the book shut. "Really, Valerie, you shouldn't be wasting your time reading such nonsense."

"Yes, Val, you shouldn't be wasting your time reading such nonsense." Reggie mimicked his mother, with a decidedly haughtier tone added to his version.

Both women turned to the boy and eyed him. He took a step backward. "I-um, I think I'll go get dressed now." Reggie turned and ran down the hallway, his white cotton nightshirt whipping behind him.

Valerie looked at her mother and they both smiled. "The little lizard." She walked back to her bed and sat down on the edge. Jacqueline followed.

"You should be concentrating on your studies, young lady," her mother admonished, patting Valerie's hand. "Your schooling is nearly complete and it won't do well for you to start easing up now. How will you gain entrance to Queen's College and earn your teaching certificate if you let your studies go?"

Valerie's emerald eyes met Jacqueline's. She stood and went to the window, pulling back the heavy burgundy velvet curtains. She fingered the long single braid that hung over her shoulder, the rich chestnut colored hair glinting with golden highlights in the morning sun. Staring at the street below, she took a deep breath and let it out slowly.

"Please, Mama, reading romances will not harm my school work in any way. It's just, well, I know I won't ever marry." Valerie looked up quickly. "You can't say it isn't so, Mama. I may be crippled but I'm not blind. I've seen how people look at me."

She glanced toward the window. "How men look at me." She sighed, then turned to her mother. "Truth is, I've thought about little else for quite some time now. And I believe I've made peace with this fact." She hugged her arms about her. "Oh, don't you see, Mama? I only want to dream a little."

Jacqueline reached out and pulled her daughter to her in a hug. It would do no good to argue. She knew in her mind no man would want a crippled wife, but in her heart she wanted to believe there was someone out there for her only daughter. Someone who would see past the useless foot and into the warm and loving soul she possessed. She released Valerie and carefully put the book down on the bed. "Well, then, you have my permission, as long as your studies don't falter."

Valerie smiled. "They won't. I promise."

Jacqueline stood and smoothed the wrinkles from her cotton day dress. "And whatever you do, don't leave this out for your father to see. He'll be beside himself if he finds out what you've been reading."

"I assure you I'll keep it out of arm's reach from now on." She narrowed her eyes. "Short and stubby eight-year-old boy arms' reach to be exact."

Her mother laughed as she walked out the bedroom door. "Now, don't dawdle getting ready for breakfast," she called over her shoulder. "Your father wants to talk to the entire family before leaving for the bank today."

"Did he say what it was about?"

"You know your father, Valerie. Everything's a huge secret with him that doesn't usually amount to much of anything." Jacqueline turned around and raised a finger. "I will tell you one thing, though. He hasn't stopped smiling since he came home last night."

Chapter Two

Valerie pulled open the doors of her large oak armoire and rummaged quickly through the rack of dresses hanging there. Stopping at a blue moiré one, she pulled it off its wood hanger, balanced on her right foot, and slipped it on over her chemise. She struggled to button the back, reaching first one arm, then the other, behind her in innumerable contortions. She stopped for a moment and leaned on her cane, out of breath.

"Here now, Miss, let me help ye."

Valerie straightened, then rubbed her shoulders where they were already beginning to ache from the strain. "Thank you, Lucy. I fear I'd have sent an arm out of place if you hadn't shown up just now."

"Ye should have called fer me," the servant gently scolded. "I was jest helpin' yer brother get himself ready fer the mornin' meal." Lucy buttoned the cuffs of the dress then stopped when, out of the corner of her eye, she spied a stiff pile of fabric resting on the floor. It looked exactly like someone had kicked it out of the way in order to hide it. "What's this all about?" She nodded toward the mess. "It best not be what I'm thinkin' it is," the older lady warned.

Valerie's eyes caught Lucy's in the mirror. "You'll not lecture me today, Lucy. I've had quite enough of those contraptions and I will not wear it." Valerie glared at the heavy, whale-boned corset. "The bloody thing *had* to be created by a man. A woman *never* would think of putting herself into something like that. Why, I wouldn't be a bit surprised to discover it was used as some sort of medieval torture device."

Lucy gasped and her finely lined skin paled. "Miss Valerie! Yer language!" Then her eyes narrowed. She drew herself up and stuck a thin bony finger in the younger woman's face. "I won't have ye talkin' like a common trollop, I won't! Why, I've raised ye since ye were but a wee babe and never thought I'd live to hear such talk. I won't have it, I tell ye. I won't!"

Valerie raised a hand in surrender. "Forgive me, Lucy. I apologize to your dear sensibilities." The servant merely looked at her as if she'd heard the same apology a thousand times before.

Valerie squirmed under the scrutiny. "But I still won't wear it." She stuck out her bottom lip as she watched Lucy's reflection in the mirror. The woman took a deep breath and mouthed a silent prayer as her aged but still deft hands fastened the buttons of the dress.

"It's just not proper," Lucy muttered under her breath. "Not proper at all not to wear yer corset. What's to become of the world if young girls quit wearin' their under things? I'll be havin' a talk with yer mum, I will." She finished fastening the dress and took a step back. "There, now. Ye're as pretty as a picture. Why, I bet ye'll have at the very least ten swains callin' on ye today."

Valerie forced her smile to remain in place. "Do you really think so, Lucy? It would be such a nice change to be visited by *young* men. I get so tired of old Master Hobbs, constantly beating his baton on the table. I suppose he thinks Reggie and I will learn faster if he keeps up that constant racket."

Valerie drew herself up, hand on hip, and lowered her voice an octave. Brandishing her cane in the air, she bellowed out, "Pay attention, girl. Heaven above knows you women haven't got a shilling's worth of brains in your head and it is my unfortunate task to have to try to force some learning into yours. Listen to what I say, I'll try to speak slowly, and if you pay strict mind, you just may learn a thing or two."

Lucy put her hand over her mouth, stifling a laugh. "Show some respect, child. Master Hobbs is yer elder."

Valerie leaned on her cane, considering the picture she presented in the mirror. Pity she hadn't been born a man. Walking sticks were all the rage right now and she'd fit right in. She turned around. "Of course you're right, Lucy." Her eyes sparkled with humor. "What ever could I have been thinking?"

* * *

"Gather 'round, family. Gather 'round," Frederick Brooks instructed as he summoned everyone to their places. He stood at the head of the table, one hand tucked into his weskit pocket while the other tapped on his crystal water glass with a small silver butter knife. He watched with pride as they seated themselves -

Jacqueline to his left, Valerie to his right and Reggie at the opposite end of the long narrow table. Such a fine family indeed. An adoring wife, a healthy son to carry on the family name, and a daughter who was as intelligent as she was beautiful. He drew himself up and cleared his throat, running a finger along the stiff celluloid collar.

What's this? he thought as everyone continued to chatter around him. Why, they weren't paying him the least bit of attention. Well, this wouldn't do. No, it would not. Frederick cleared his throat again, only louder this time. He tugged at his suit jacket anxiously. This wasn't going at all according to plan. Not at all. These people he called his own were supposed to be transfixed by his presence, in awe of the head of the household. At least, that's what all the gentlemen's journals said.

Frederick cleared his throat a third and final time. "See here, all of you. I would like your attention. That is, I *demand* your attention."

Jacqueline patted his hand where it rested on the edge of the table and smiled benignly. "Why don't you sit down, Freddie? Your tea is getting cold."

Valerie hid her own smile behind a sweet roll. Poor Papa. He was just too much of a dear for any one to be afraid of him. True, his size commanded respect from those less than six foot in height, but he was too gentle to do any real damage. She leaned forward and rested her elbows on the table.

Valerie started to take another bite of the roll when it was snatched out of her hand. She immediately looked up.

"Thank you for your attention, my dear." Great Aunt Mabel held the roll in front of Valerie's nose. "Now, proper young ladies do not eat with their elbows on the table, do they?"

Valerie leaned back in the chair, considering the older lady. Dear Aunt Mabel. She was nearing seventy and, since coming to live with them several years ago, had taken on the assignment of personally seeing to it that she and Reggie learned proper manners. "Aunt Mabel, I'm not a child any more and I've learned quite well from you," Valerie reasoned. "I'd like my breakfast back now."

Mabel straightened her shoulders and Valerie feared for a moment that the black cotton dress would pop its bodice seams.

"Proper young ladies always ask for something politely. I believe you forgot the 'p' word."

Oh, Aunt Mabel was in a mood today. She must not have slept well or something. Valerie decided to enlist Jacqueline's help. Surely Mama could explain that she didn't need any further instructions. "Please, Mama, tell Aunt Mabel to let me eat in peace. I've learned my manners well enough and I'm hungry."

Jacqueline glanced over at the two women. She smiled at her aunt. "I believe you need only do as you're told if you'd like to eat today, daughter. Keep your elbows off the table and your tone polite and I believe Aunt Mabel will leave you be."

Valerie sighed, resigned to her fate. There would be no help here this morning.

Jacqueline turned to the older woman. "Isn't that right, aunt?"

Mabel nodded and her black mourning cap bobbed on her head. She smiled, obviously pleased. "That's exactly what I've been saying all along."

"See here, now, I have something to say!" Frederick bellowed. "Everyone pay attention this minute!"

With the outburst, Mabel eyed Frederick for a moment, her glare imperious, before returning Valerie's roll and moving to her place at the table.

Relieved to be left alone for the time being, Valerie turned her attention to her father. His face was quickly turning a most unbecoming shade of red, making his eyes look like they were ready to pop out of their sockets. "What is it, Papa? Mama said earlier you had something you wanted to discuss."

"Yes, Papa," Reggie chimed in. "Why haven't you told us yet?"

Frederick rolled his eyes in a prayer to heaven as he pulled a neatly folded piece of paper out of his inside pocket. He shook it out, then turned it around for his family to see.

Valerie leaned forward and studied the missive. Her eyes widened. It was a boarding notice for the clipper ship, *Fast Alice*. Currently docked on the Thames River, it would be sailing for China in less than a week.

"Are we going to China, Papa?" she whispered.

"China?!" Reggie screamed and jumped out of his chair. "Please say we're going to China, Papa! I want to see me a real live panda bear!"

"China, Frederick?" Jacqueline asked quietly. "Is this the surprise?" Suddenly turning pale, she clutched at her stomach.

"No, no. You've got it all wrong." Frederick took a deep breath then let it out. "No one said anything about China. Did you hear me mention the word at all?"

"Well, no, Papa. But you did hold up the paper and say this was our surprise," Valerie ventured. "And it *is* a boarding notice for China."

"Indeed, I did hold up this very piece of paper. However, we are not going to China." He sat down and carefully placed a linen napkin on his lap. He looked around the table. "We are going to Italy."

"Italy?" Jacqueline rubbed her forehead. "This is all too confusing, Frederick. Please, just tell us exactly what you have in mind."

Frederick scanned the faces around him. Pleased he now had their undivided attention, he began, "As you all are aware, I have several important clients at the bank. One of them in particular, Sir David Smythe, has some vested interests outside of England. He'd like me to loan him money to pursue those interests. In order to do this, I need to investigate his proposal to determine whether or not I should give him a loan."

"Yes, dear, but what does this have to do with Italy?"

"Smythe's latest interest is archeology. Seems he'd like to help finance the excavations at Pompeii. News of it has been in all the papers lately." He took a bite of his sweet roll, glanced at Valerie, and winked. "Surely *you've* heard of it."

Pompeii? Oh, Papa was teasing her. Of course he knew she had heard of it, even before Master Hobbs and his classes on Roman culture. Just the word itself conjured up images in her mind of robed men and women strolling some ancient street lined with fluted columns; a forum marketplace filled with vendors of sundry items; the gods and goddesses of Rome sitting high on Mount Olympus as they played games with the fates of mere mortals.

"Pompeii," Valerie repeated the word quietly to herself, letting it roll off her tongue, savoring the pronunciation. All of her studies had been directed toward the antiquities, but to get a chance to actually visit the site of one of these places was beyond even *her* imagination. She smiled at her father, her eyes twinkling. "You're playing with me, Papa."

Reggie cleared his throat and, from his perch on the arm of a heavily carved dining chair, declared, "I don't want to go to Italy or this Pompy place. If I can't see a panda bear, I'd rather spend summer at Grandmother's village, like we always do."

Valerie looked at her father quickly, terrified Reggie's comment would make him change his mind. She held her breath while he considered his son.

After what seemed like an eternity to Valerie, he spoke. "No, Reggie, we won't be visiting Grandmother this season. Smythe's business is much too important to throw away on a childish whim. He owns the clipper ship and has already made arrangements for it to make a detour to the Bay of Naples for us." Frederick leaned back in his chair and smiled grandly. He reached out his hand for Jacqueline's and she placed her damp, shaky one in his.

"And, by the way, Aunt Mabel," Frederick continued, his eyes fixed on Jacqueline's aunt. "I was concerned about your ability to travel so I've made arrangements for you to stay with Jacqueline's sister while we're away. She said she's looking forward to spending some time with you."

Mabel snorted, a decidedly unmannered gesture, Valerie thought. The older woman pursed her lips, drawing all the wrinkles on her face together around them. "Oh, I'm *certain* she is." Pressing her hands against the table, she pushed herself to her feet. "Won't you *please* excuse me? I feel one of my 'spells' coming on."

Frederick simply smiled and nodded, ignoring the older woman's gibe. He then turned his attention to Jacqueline as she spoke.

"You know the ocean makes me nervous, Freddie," she commented quietly, fidgeting with the edge of the white linen tablecloth.

He squeezed her hand. "I have every confidence you'll do just fine, dear. As a matter of fact, I'm certain you'll all make fine sailors." Frederick regarded his daughter. "You've been much too still about all of this, Valerie. I'd have thought you'd have plenty to say on the subject, given your interests."

Valerie opened her mouth, then closed it as tears threatened. To be presented with this opportunity was the greatest gift of all. To be able to actually see and touch the ancient streets where so many people lived, worked, and perished centuries ago – why, it was a dream come true. She stood and, using the chairs around the table for support, made her way to her father. Reaching him, she threw her arms around his neck. "Thank you so much, Papa. I can't wait to leave!"

Chapter Three

"Ahem, ahem." *Tap, tap, tap.* "I said 'Ahem'." Master Hobbs continued to rap his baton on the library table.

Reggie scurried into the room, yanked out one of the wood chairs and plopped down. With a quick hand, he pushed a thick lock of brown hair out of his hazel eyes and grabbed a pen and inkwell. He straightened his shoulders and sat upright, expectantly, as if he'd been there for hours.

Hobbs took a deep breath and let it out slowly. "And will your sister be joining us today?" he asked, his voice a pitch higher than usual.

"Yes, sir!" Reggie answered enthusiastically. "She definitely will be, sir!"

Hobbs shook his head. The blasted girl was *always* late. Why he should be assigned to educate a woman was beyond him anyway. Certainly, the girl had a propensity for the ancient languages but she, like all women, belonged at home, not competing in a man's world. It was a good thing her parents paid well or he would have given up the assignment long ago.

He kept one eye on the entry to the library as he pulled a small pewter flask out of his coat pocket. He stole a glance at Reggie who was busy twirling a piece of string around his finger until it turned purple, then sneaked a sip of the brandy. It burned all the way down. Good stuff, he thought, just as Valerie appeared in the doorway. He quickly tucked the flask away before anyone was the wiser. He smiled, his mouth a tight line under his thick bushy mustache.

"Good *afternoon*, miss. How nice that you decided to join us today."

Valerie tilted her chin and looked down her nose at the man. At five foot six, she was tall for a woman and Old Man Hobbs was a good head shorter than she was. She walked into the room, commenting casually as she went past him, "Hmmm. Actually, it's only eleven o'clock, still morning, I believe." She glanced at him out of the corner of her eyes. "A bit early for liquor, though, don't you think?" She deposited herself gracefully into the pressed back chair near Reggie, straightened her skirts, and hooked her cane on the edge of the table.

"I really don't know what you're talking about," Hobbs sputtered, a dark blush working its way up from his neck.

Valerie watched in amazement as it continued upward, covering first his face and finally his shiny bald head. Reggie snickered and Valerie pinched him hard on the arm. He yelped.

"All right now. I've had quite enough of all your antics." Hobbs stared hard at his charges. "Your father has informed me you will be traveling to Italy next week."

"Does that mean we'll be finishing our lessons early this year?" Reggie asked, his voice holding a definite air of expectation.

Hobbs frowned at the boy. Reggie squirmed. "I mean, if that were the case, we'd miss you very much, sir."

"No doubt." Hobbs walked around the podium until he was standing directly in front of his students. "Quite the contrary, Master Reginald. We will be reviewing your Latin verbs as well as some basic Italian phrasing to help you get along while you're there." He waved the baton. "Of course, if you meet anyone who's worth their salt, they should be able to speak English quite properly." He smiled smugly and returned to his place behind the podium. "When you two return, we will continue where we left off on our usual lessons and your studies will be extended for the period of time you're gone." Hobbs pulled a kerchief out of his sleeve and wiped at his brow.

Reggie slumped down in his seat and pouted.

"Easy, Reg." Valerie patted her brother's shoulder. "The time will go by quickly."

"That's easy for you to say. You'll be done with your studies after this session." He stuck his tongue out at Master Hobbs while the teacher's attention was focused on his lesson book.

Valerie giggled. Reggie relented and smiled broadly, displaying more gum than teeth.

"If you two are quite finished comforting each other, I'd like to begin." Hobbs glared at them imperiously, his small glasses pinching the end of his nose.

Valerie wondered for a moment how the man was ever able to breathe, then folded her hands neatly on the table in front of her.

"Please do, Master Hobbs. As you yourself have pointed out, it is getting rather late in the day. I'd have thought you would've begun long ago."

Hobbs gripped his baton in his hands so tightly it threatened to snap. "Conjugate 'to give pain to' in Latin for me, young lady."

Valerie recited the answer without hesitation. "*Dolere, dolui, dolitum.*"

"To be weary of."

"*Pertaedet, pertaedere, pertaesum.*"

Hobbs leaned forward, his knuckles white. "Tell me the Latin word for 'troublesome'."

"*Laboriosus.*"

Reggie stared wide-eyed as Valerie leaned back in her chair. She looked directly at Hobbs, an eyebrow raised, awaiting his commentary.

Hobbs purposefully placed the baton down on the table. Valerie watched as his sight jumped from one row of books in the library to another. He scanned the room as if he were memorizing each and every title and continued to avoid her gaze. She guessed he was trying to compose himself.

Tugging at his lapels, Hobbs pulled them tightly together under his chin. "All right, miss. I suppose you've proved yourself. Just remember what people say about show-offs. *No one* likes them." He sniffed. "Now, if you don't mind, I'd like to review some Italian."

Valerie decided to ignore the man. Did he really think she was so stupid she wouldn't understand what he was telling her? Well, she didn't like him all that well, either. As far as she was concerned, he was simply a means to an end in order to get her education and enter Queen's College. "Oh, please do, Master Hobbs. Unlike Latin, my Italian *is* in need of practice."

"Well, I'm happy to see you can admit when you don't know something after all." Hobbs smiled again, but the gesture never reached his eyes. "Now, in order for you to get along in a foreign country, there are certain specific phrases you should know."

Reggie raised his hand, bouncing up and down against the hard wood seat.

Hobbs raised an eyebrow. "Yes, Master Reginald?"

"I know! I know!"

"What exactly do you know, sir?"

Reggie let his arm drop to the oak-veneered table in a loud thud. "The words. That's what we're talking about, isn't it?"

Hobbs waved a hand as he used the other to page through the book of Italian phrases. "Impossible. You can't know the Italian words because I haven't taught them to you yet."

"Let him give it a try, Master Hobbs," Valerie urged, her eyes drifting to the bulging pocket where the teacher had stuffed his flask. Hobbs' eyes followed hers. He looked up quickly when he realized her meaning.

"Reggie used to try and read an old book of mine written in Italian and it's quite possible he may surprise you." She smiled at the teacher. "What harm can it do?"

Hobbs took a deep breath and let it out slowly. "All right, all right." He grasped the edge of the podium with his fingertips and leaned forward. "Translate 'good morning, Sir'."

"Um. Um. Wait a minute, I'm thinking." Reggie scrunched his face up. "I've got it! *Buon giorno, Signore.* Now, ask me another one."

"Hurry up."

Reggie grinned. "I remember that one. *Si sbrighi.*"

Hobbs' fingertips turned white as he squeezed the podium. "How about 'leave me alone'?"

"*Mi lasci in pace.*" Reggie leaned back in his chair, crossed his arms over his chest, and smiled proudly.

Valerie patted him on the head, ruffling his hair. "Good job, Reg."

"I have one question, young man. Exactly what type of book did you read?"

Reggie shrugged his shoulders. "I don't know. It was about a little boy who got in everybody's way by screaming 'wolf' all the time. That's all."

Hobbs threw his hands up in the air. "Of course. What else?" he whispered, shaking his head. "I honestly don't understand you children. You come to lessons late, barely pay attention, then sit here completely full of yourselves, reciting ancient and foreign languages. You're both much too smug for your own good and

I've had quite enough for one day." He pulled out his pocket watch and checked the time. "It's late and I will now conclude this lesson. Tomorrow we will study the Italian language in greater depth." He looked at Reggie. "If that meets with your approval?"

"Of course it does." Reggie leaned forward and rested his chin on his arms. "What a silly question!"

"Of course it does," Hobbs muttered. He eyed the boy for a moment, then scooped up his books and exited the room, fishing in his pocket as he stomped off.

Reggie let out a cheer as soon as he heard the front door slam. "What are you going to do with the rest of the afternoon, Val?" he asked.

"Mama said something about shopping for the voyage but I honestly don't know why. I have plenty of good dresses that would be quite appropriate for traveling and walking around an ancient site." She shrugged. At this point she didn't really care if she had new clothes or had to wear a corset and flour sack. She was going to see Pompeii.

Chapter Four

"Is this really necessary, Mama?" Valerie winced as the seamstress missed the fabric of the dress and stuck her instead.

"Well of course it is, dear. We can't be running off to Italy in last season's clothing, now can we?" Jacqueline took a step backward and admired the fine picture her daughter presented. The dress nipped in just right at the waist before billowing out and the apricot satin was the perfect shade to complement Valerie's fair complexion. "Besides, with this shop just opened and offering clothing practically ready-made - why, it's a godsend, that's what it is. Given your father's short notice, we'd never get our new dresses made in time the old-fashioned way."

Jacqueline pulled a bolt of lace down from the trimmings shelf as she talked. "Here now, don't forget to add this to the cuffs. It's just the touch this dress needs," Jacqueline told the shopkeeper.

"Yes, mum." The woman curtsied and took the creamy tatted fabric. "I'll make sure Susie doesn't forget to put it on the dress." She tucked it into a large willow basket filled with mother-of-pearl buttons, silver and gold thread, and crocheted gloves Jacqueline had already selected.

"Might I say, mum, your daughter is the picture of loveliness." She frowned and lowered her voice. "Pity about her leg though, isn't it? Was she born that way?"

Valerie stiffened. Jacqueline's eyes caught hers in the mirror's reflection. "Um, no. She was involved in an accident. But she gets along just fine, thank you." Jacqueline avoided her daughter's eyes. She picked up a soft yellow dress made of finely woven cotton from where it lay on a side chair.

"What do you think about this one, Valerie?" she asked, her voice strained.

Was it anger or resentment her mother was hiding? Valerie couldn't be certain. She knew how difficult these remarks from seemingly well-meaning people must be for her mother. And she secretly suspected her mother blamed herself for the accident that had left her crippled. But who could say for sure that if Mama had stayed by her side she wouldn't have dashed out in front of the carriage? After all, she was only six when it happened. The doctors said she'd never walk again, so she considered herself very lucky in the fact she could get by with the use of a cane.

"It'll be fine, Mama," Valerie answered, hoping her mother would understand the double meaning behind her words.

"Very well." Jacqueline turned to the shopkeeper. "We'll take these two as well as that green damask over there. This is just so exciting to be able to select an item that's practically finished." She tapped her chin with a finger and scanned the rack of dresses. "Let's see now. Oh yes, that dark red one as well. The color will look quite smashing on you, Val. We'll be needing the appropriate undergarments also. Some of those new-fangled crinolines that aren't so wide in the front will do nicely."

The shopkeeper curtsied again. "Yes, mum. How soon did you say you'd need these to be ready?"

"No later than Saturday." Jacqueline put on her bonnet and tied the ribbons in a neat side bow. "Do you think you can have them in time? We'll be leaving for Italy on Sunday."

"Saturday, you say?" The woman drew herself up and smiled broadly. "Why, I'll have them to you on Friday if you'll tell your friends about me. But I must say I'm a bit surprised," she added. "I didn't think they'd set sail on the Lord's Day."

"That's what I thought, but it seems the captain is the one to set the schedule and he prefers to leave then. Some sort of old sailor's superstition, according to my husband." Jacqueline turned to her daughter. "Are you ready to go?"

Valerie nodded as another seamstress removed the sleeves she had been fitting. "Let me get my things." She slipped her blue velvet purse over her hand and pulled on her beige gloves. As they exited the shop, Valerie leaned toward her mother. "It's almost tea time. What do you say we stop here at Rennie's and have a cup?" She gestured toward the wood and leaded glass entry next to the dress shop.

But before Jacqueline could reply, Valerie steered her through the door of the teashop and directed her to a table near the front window. "My goodness, Val, let me catch my breath!" Jacqueline laughed.

"I'm sorry, Mama. You looked like you were going to say no." Valerie's smile faded. "I just needed a moment to collect myself and thought this would be the perfect place." She glanced around the room. Almost all of the small round tables were filled with patrons. Watercolor pastorals in silver leaf frames hung in groupings on the wall. Large mauve cabbage roses floated across the golden fringed tablecloths and candles were already lit at each table. The candlelight reflected against the gilded wallcovering and lent the room a warm, elegant glow, like a cozy parlor. Valerie took a deep breath to calm her nerves. "I don't think I'll ever get used to people talking about me like that."

A tall, thin man dressed entirely in black approached the women. Jacqueline ordered a pot of tea and a plate of lemon cakes from the server. When he left, she looked at Valerie. "The woman didn't really mean any harm. She was only trying to be nice."

"It's all right to be nice, Mama. But for heaven's sake, I was standing right there. She talked about me as if I were on the other side of the world!" Valerie raised her voice and the couple at the next table eyed her.

"Really, Val, lower your voice."

Valerie sighed. "I'm sorry, Mama. It just amazes me sometimes that people can be so unfeeling."

Jacqueline blinked hard as tears threatened. "No, no. I'm the one who's sorry. I should have told her to mind her own business. I won't let you down again. I promise."

The server returned with their tea and cakes. Jacqueline poured each of them a cup and Valerie took a sip of the strong beverage. It was good and hot and warmed her insides, chasing away the ill feelings that had started to accumulate this day. Soon she'd be out of London and sailing across the sea, bound for Italy. She looked out the window at the passersby. Even though she sometimes wondered what it'd be like to be someone else, someone who wasn't crippled, at this moment she wouldn't trade places with any of them.

"Tell your future, young miss?"

Shaken out of her reverie, Valerie glanced up. An old gypsy fortuneteller was standing at their table. Though Valerie had seen her in Rennie's reading for other patrons, the woman had never approached her. She stood quietly with a smile on her weathered face, fingering the beaded fringe of her bright red shawl, as she waited for an answer.

Jacqueline took one look at the old woman. "No, thank you."

Valerie leaned across the table. "Please, Mama. It'll be fun."

Her green eyes glittered with excitement. "Who knows what our future might hold?"

"I told you that you've been reading too many of those romance novels." With a wave of her hand, Jacqueline relented. "Oh, I suppose if it means that much to you."

Eager, the gypsy pulled an empty chair up to their table and took Valerie's teacup from her. She swirled the contents around then poured them back into the pot. Jacqueline grimaced, but the old lady ignored her and continued with the ritual. Peering into the bottom of the cup, she began to talk. "Look there!" the gypsy exclaimed, a large smile spreading across her face.

Valerie leaned over and wrinkled her nose as she studied the residue. "All I see are some tea leaves."

"It's not just tea leaves, miss. It's the way they're arranged in the cup that's important."

Jacqueline's eyes caught Valerie's. They smiled at each other. "Really? What does mine say?"

"I see a ship. You'll be taking a journey soon."

"How did you know that?" Valerie asked, her eyes wide.

"I wouldn't be much of a fortuneteller if I didn't know such things, would I?" The gypsy nodded her head and her large gold hoop earrings bobbed up and down. The woman's earlobes were stretched beyond repair by the heavy jewelry and Valerie feared for an instant they'd break through the thin layer of skin holding them in place. "Hmmm. Well now. This is good. I also see a heart. Of course, that would be a symbol of love." She winked at Jacqueline. "Ah, but what's that?"

"Where? What else do you see?" Valerie's attention was riveted to the bottom of the cup. "What were you saying about love?"

"There's a lightning bolt – here - running through the heart. That's a love that'll break your heart." The gypsy looked up, her coal black eyes filled with great sadness. "I'm so sorry, little one."

Valerie leaned back in her chair, considering what the woman had just said. A love that would break her heart. It might seem awfully impractical to even consider such a thing as true, she thought, but at least there would *be* a love. "Do you see anything else in there?"

"Well, there is something different here, something I've heard of but never seen before." The gypsy tilted the cup for Valerie to see. "See that line going through the ship?" She pointed to the symbol and Valerie nodded. "There's more than one journey in store for you, child. A crossing of some great chasm." She shook her head. "Like I said, I never seen anything like it before. Only heard stories from fortunetellers long dead."

"Is there anything else about love?" Valerie asked, more interested in hearing about the man in her future than about any traveling she might do. After all, in her mind he didn't even exist up until this moment.

The gypsy put the cup down. "I see nothing more today." She took Valerie's hand into hers, growing serious. Their eyes met. "Be careful, and may God keep you safe."

Valerie felt a nervous twinge in the pit of her stomach. There was something entirely too spooky in the way the woman was looking at her. Slowly, she withdrew her hand from the other woman's. "Thank you for the reading, ma'am."

Jacqueline laid a shilling down on the table. "I believe that will be all."

The old woman picked up the coin and turned it over and over in her palm, the metal flickering with the reflection of the candlelight. "Do you want to know what the leaves say for you, dear lady?" she asked.

"Thank you, but no. I already know what the fates hold for me. You see, I'm married and have a wonderful family." She reached across the table and squeezed Valerie's hand. "I've realized my dreams. It's now my daughter's turn to realize hers."

Chapter Five

The Brooks family pushed their way through the thick crowd of people surrounding the docks and shipyards along the Thames River. The bustle of travelers pushed tightly against each other, crowding their way to whatever ship would carry them onto their respective destinations. One couple, obviously very wealthy, seemed to have the only breathing room as several servants fanned out before them, parting the crowd like the Red Sea. Once or twice, a child in tattered clothing tried to approach, dirty hands outstretched, looking for an offering. All they received was a swat on that same hand which sent them yelping back into the assembly.

Valerie nudged Reggie. "Maybe we should send Lucy on ahead as *our* lookout." She squeezed the handle of her cane and displayed an evil smile. "Or perhaps I could use this to clear the way."

Reggie giggled, then hollered out himself when someone stepped on his foot. "Where's our ship?" he cried above the din. "I'm tired of all these people."

Valerie had to agree; the mass of people pressed in on all of them. She tried to glance around as her family walked but the activity was a blur. Aside from the throng of passengers, one sailor after another scurried by, each intent on his mission ashore before returning to his ship. One such sailor paused in his duties for a moment and stared at Valerie until his companions, laughing, grabbed his arm and pulled him along. He continued to watch her over his shoulder, grinning.

Valerie smiled at him shyly. How romantic the life of a sailor must be, sailing the Seven Seas on the crest of a wave, she thought. Then, suddenly self-conscious, she tucked a lock of stray hair back into her bonnet and nervously smoothed the skirt of her brown traveling suit.

"What do ye think ye're about, young lady?" Lucy whispered harshly in her ear.

Valerie jumped and the smile vanished. "Nothing. Nothing at all." Lucy took her arm and helped her along as they hurried to catch up with the rest of the family. Closer to the ships, the crowd was beginning to clear somewhat. Valerie watched as passengers laden with heavy luggage wandered about, searching for whatever ship they had booked passage on. Thank goodness, she thought, Papa had the foresight to courier their luggage on ahead of them. She couldn't imagine trying to carry it while maneuvering about in this mob.

They turned a corner on the wooden dock and the smell of decaying fish and bilgewater filled the still air, assaulting Valerie's nose. She pulled a scented handkerchief out of her reticule and held it to her face. A loud horn sounded from the harbor, followed by another. "Can you see the ship yet, Papa?" she called to her father above the racket.

"I think it's just ahead, to the starboard." He adjusted his hat. The horn stopped and he lowered his voice a few notches. "That translates as 'to the right,' you know."

"Really, Freddie, how long are you going to keep throwing out those silly ship terms you picked up during the last week? You must have told us a hundred times what 'starboard' means," Jacqueline snapped, her agitation growing the closer they came to the water.

Frederick stopped in his tracks and turned to face his family. They all but slammed into him. "In an effort to educate all of you on the nature of this journey, I saw fit to teach you a few definitions you'd be able to use once aboard the *Fast Alice*." He looked them each in the eye. "Are you going to be so ungrateful as to say you've heard enough?"

Reggie covered his smile with a hand and pretended to be coughing. Valerie elbowed him in the head, then feigned innocence. "Stop it, Val!" he commanded.

Valerie shook out her hanky. "Oh, no, Papa. We've quite enjoyed your lessons. Are they over now?"

"Can we please be going?" Jacqueline begged as another sailor hurried by. He bumped her arm and she dropped the willow basket of needlework she was carrying. Reggie lunged for the sewing and caught it just before it hit the walkway. "I'm getting a terrible headache. And my stomach doesn't feel well at all."

"All right, all right." Frederick raised his hand in surrender and scanned the docks until he spotted the clipper. "There she is."

He pointed toward a fairly new ship about fifty feet further down the dock.

Valerie felt her stomach catch at the sight of the *Fast Alice*, fresh from her last voyage around the Cape to China. Her sails were in various stages of being hoisted and several members of the crew were climbing the mast and riggings. *Here is the chariot that will propel us to Pompeii*, she thought.

"Come along, everyone," Frederick bade with a wave.

Reaching the ship's berth, Valerie stood in awed silence, the surrounding clatter and odors lost to her. She watched as a light misty fog rolled along the banks of the Thames and greeted them, the morning sun just beginning to burn through it. From somewhere in the distance a low whistle could be heard as the trains pulled out of their station. Valerie was glad Sir David owned a ship instead of a train. Though the steam engine would be the quickest way to Italy, it just didn't carry the romance of a clipper fighting the crested waves, doing battle with the elements.

Valerie stopped halfway up the gangplank and scanned the waters beneath her. They enveloped the bottom of the clipper, only reflecting back that portion of heavy black and varnished mahogany wood that floated above it. She continued up the plank, holding the thick rope handrail for support and being careful not to catch the tip of her cane in one of the gaps between the weathered boards.

"Valerie!" Reggie ran up beside her.

"Do you always have to scream when you talk, Reg?" Valerie asked. "You scared me half to death."

"No one listens to me if I don't," he reasoned.

"Trust me, we'll listen just as well, if not better."

"Well, I'll think about it." He skipped along behind his sister and the walkway listed first to the right, then to the left. "We are going to have the most wonderful adventures, aren't we?"

"I certainly hope so. Please, stop shaking the walk. You'll send me tumbling head first into the water for sure."

"I'm sorry, Val," Reggie said as he slowed down. "Tell me, do you think the volcano - what's its name? Suvio? - will *interrupt* while we're visiting?"

Valerie laughed. "First of all, it's called Vesuvius. And second, it hasn't *erupted* for a number of years. So, I think we'll be quite safe."

"Welcome aboard, Miss." The captain stood at the ship's rail and bowed low, his neatly combed and parted gray beard touching his chest. "It's a pleasure to have you aboard my *Alice*. I'm Captain James Marcus." He held out his hand and assisted Valerie onto the deck, Reggie scrambling up behind her. "Johnny - he's the steward here - he'll show you and your family to their cabins." He gestured to the small, bird-like man to his right, then extended his hand to assist Jacqueline and Frederick as well.

Lucy hung back, staring at the ship with a growing uncertainty. "What's the matter, Lucy?" Valerie called to her.

The older woman frowned. "Never left the land afore. Not sure I wants to now." She sniffed.

"Don't be a goose, Lucy. This ship is perfectly safe." Valerie flexed her knees, pretending to bounce up and down. "See? I haven't fallen through."

Lucy carefully handed the carpet bags she was carrying onto the deck. She crossed herself, took a deep breath and stepped over the low railing. The steward took her hand.

"I'm very happy to have you aboard, Miss."

Valerie's eyes grew wide when Lucy giggled. She could hardly believe it, nor would she have if she hadn't heard it herself. She watched in quiet amusement as Johnny worked his charm.

"It's not often we get such lovely ladies of your maturity and bearing on ship. I must say, I'm looking forward to seeing you around." He bowed low.

Lucy placed a gloved hand on her chest. "Why, Mr. Johnny, ye do go on, don't ye?"

The captain stepped forward, carefully elbowing Johnny out of the way. "I hope all of you will join me for dinner at my table tonight."

Frederick shook Marcus' hand. "Thank you, Captain. We'd be honored. You haven't seen Sir David Smythe yet, have you? We're to be traveling with him."

"Yes. As a matter of fact, he and his son are on the other side of the deck, seeing to some last minute details." Marcus pointed to his right.

"Mrs. Brooks, if you'll excuse me. I'll meet up with all of you later. I need to discuss a few matters with Smythe." He turned to the steward. "I'd like you to go ahead and take my family to their quarters."

With a curt bow, Johnny scooped up Lucy's baggage. "Be careful with it," she admonished, shaking a finger in his face. "The lady's beauty cream is packed tight in there along with a few other things I shan't be discussin' in mixed company."

"Ah, but I can see you won't be needing any needing any beauty cream." Johnny winked, then motioned with a nod. "Let's head over there. We'll need to go down the booby hatch to the suites."

"Booby hatch?" Reggie echoed.

"Yes-sir-ree. That's what we call that hole in the deck. It's where the stairs leading to the lower levels are. Stick by me, boy, and I'll have you talking like a real sailor in no time."

"You will? May I, Mama?"

Jacqueline eyed the hatch carefully. "Um, well, I suppose it wouldn't do any harm."

Reggie jumped and hurried to the hatch, scrambling down the heavy teak steps. Jacqueline went next, followed by Lucy. Valerie stood poised at the opening, not certain what to do next. She sighed. She was thankful her family didn't treat her as an invalid, but at times like this, they always seemed to forget that she might need a hand. True, she had to maneuver up and down stairs in their house, but they weren't nearly as steep as these were.

"Mama? Lucy? I think I'll be needing some help," she called, but they had already walked on ahead.

Hesitantly, she placed her right foot on the first step. Next, she lowered the cane, pulling her left foot down behind it. Valerie smiled, victorious. She tried it again, only this time, she lost her footing and started to stumble. Her mouth opened in a scream just as a firm strong hand caught her arm.

"Careful, Miss. You could have broken your neck."

Valerie turned around and looked up. A man stood above her, but she couldn't make out his face. The sun shone brightly behind him, sending a golden halo out around his head. A god. That's what he is, she thought. A great Roman god.

"Can I help you to your quarters?" he asked, his hand still on her arm.

Valerie quickly composed herself. "Uh, no. No, of course not. We haven't been properly introduced." She glanced down. "But I do appreciate your help."

The stairs were wide enough that he was able to maneuver past Valerie. He stepped down a level below her and she could now see his features. A strong square chin, deep blue eyes, dark blonde hair. Why, he looked just like she'd imagined Damon, the hero in her romance novel, would have appeared!

"Would it make a difference if I said your father sent me over here to help you?"

"I beg your pardon?"

"I'm Thomas Smythe, David Smythe's son. I was talking with Sir Frederick when he saw your distress. He asked that I lend you a hand."

"I - I see. I suppose it would be acceptable for you to help me then." She let him guide her down another step. "I'm Valerie Brooks," she whispered.

Thomas smiled, and his teeth shone white against his tanned skin. Valerie took a deep breath and her heart skipped a beat. "How did you ever hurt your ankle?" he asked politely as he continued to help her down the stairs.

Hurt my ankle? she repeated the words in her mind. For heaven's sake, he didn't know she was crippled. A whole new world of possibilities opened before her. "It, uh, it was a riding accident. Yes. That's it. My horse, Rexford, threw me."

"Your horse threw you? Well, then, I'd say you were lucky to only have injured your foot."

"Very lucky," Valerie answered with a frown. "That evil animal could've killed me, behaving the way he did."

"There, now. You've made it down the stairs." Thomas squeezed her arm intimately before releasing her, sending a shiver through Valerie.

"Valerie! Where have you been?" Reggie ran toward her, screaming as usual.

"Go away, you little lizard," she whispered harshly. Turning again to Thomas, she smiled sweetly.

"And who might this young man be?"

Reggie grinned, drawing himself up. "I am Reginald James Brooks, at your service, Sir."

"Well, it's a pleasure to make your acquaintance." Thomas shook Reggie's hand.

"Mama said it's time for you to unpack, Val."

Valerie caught Thomas looking at her, a definite smile playing about his eyes. "I'll be along soon," she replied tersely.

"She said you had to come *now*!" He stomped his foot. "I'm not going to go back there without you. I'll get into trouble for sure if I don't have you with me."

"Sounds to me as if you should be going now, Miss Brooks. Will I see you at dinner?"

"Perhaps. We'll be seated at the Captain's table. Do you know where will you be?"

Thomas smiled again. "At the captain's table as well."

Valerie blushed. Of course he'd be at the captain's table. After all, his family owned the ship. "I'm so sorry. I should have known."

"Nonsense. I wouldn't expect someone as lovely as you to litter your brain with such trivial things." He took her hand and kissed the back of it lightly. "Until we meet again."

Reggie tugged on Valerie's skirt and she reluctantly pulled her fingers out of Thomas' strong lean ones. She turned and let her brother lead her to their suite, taking each step carefully for fear Thomas would realize his mistake. She gripped the cane tightly, her hand still tingling where he had pressed his lips against her fingers.

Valerie fought the urge to turn around and look at him one more time. She knew with certainty that she could lose herself in those deep blue eyes. What was it the gypsy had said? A love that would break her heart? Well, as far as she was concerned, that prophecy would simply not come true. She absolutely wouldn't allow it.

Chapter Six

Valerie followed closely behind Reggie as he led the way to their suite of cabins, stepping carefully over the raised thresholds that defined the long corridors.

"How much farther, Reg?" she asked as she turned sideways, struggling to squeeze her wide crinoline through the narrow passage.

Reggie stopped and looked from one cabin door to the next, studying them intently. He opened his mouth, then closed it again. He turned around, looked at the door behind him, and scratched his head.

"What's the matter?" Valerie asked, beginning to suspect her brother hadn't the faintest idea where he was taking her. "For heaven's sake, Reggie, you don't know where our rooms are, do you?"

No sooner had she spoken than Lucy poked her head out through one of the doorways. "Why Miss Valerie, there ye are. I thought I heard yer voice. Yer mama and me were startin' to get worried about ye."

"See? I knew our rooms were right here," Reggie answered, his smile smug.

Valerie shook her head and rolled her eyes. She gave her brother a shove. "Why don't you go and try to find *your* room now?" She turned to Lucy. "Which room is Mama's?"

"She's in the next cabin over. This here's my room. Want to take a look?" Lucy asked, her voice holding an air of expectation.

"Of course I would," Valerie replied. Sticking her head into the small cabin, she looked around. Though small, the servant's cabin was nicely appointed with oak paneling on the walls, oriental rugs on the floor and even a tiny porthole window. Everything Lucy had brought aboard was already neatly put away, from the hair brushes and curling irons she'd tucked into the holders on the wall, to the plain black servant's dresses hanging from a pegboard.

"It's lovely, Lucy. I thought you weren't going to like being on ship, but it seems to me as if you've made yourself comfortable," Valerie observed with a smile.

Lucy glanced down and Valerie thought she saw a faint blush flit across the lined cheeks. Lucy smoothed back a stray lock of curly gray hair. "I just wanted everything to be nice while I was here. Thought it'd make me feel more like I belonged."

Valerie put her arm around the maid's shoulder. "Well I think it looks just wonderful."

"Oh, now, don't be patronizin' me, Miss." Lucy shook off the compliment. "Off with ye. Yer mother's been wonderin' after ye."

Valerie ducked out of Lucy's small quarters and opened the door next to it. There, she found her mother in a much larger cabin, the dark oak paneling more ornate with crown molding and chair rails. Even the oriental rugs were plusher, their crimson and blue colors reflecting the colors of the sea at sunset. Occupied with putting away their belongings, Jacqueline smiled absently at her daughter.

Valerie immediately shut the door, hoisted her skirts, and untied the fasteners to the metal hoop crinoline she was wearing. "These things are no better than a corset," she commented as it dropped to the floor, collapsing upon itself. Valerie stepped out of the garment, then looked up at her mother. "Why don't you have Lucy put everything away for you, Mama?"

"I thought it'd be nice to give her some time to get her own belongings organized. Besides, I needed something to keep my mind occupied," Jacqueline explained. She gestured at the metal heap on the floor and frowned. "You know you should keep your undergarments on during the day, child."

"Undergarments? Ha! More like a bird cage than anything if you ask me." Valerie wrinkled her nose. "I think it would be quite natural if a woman tweeted and whistled when she had the thing on." She grew quiet as she took in her mother's drawn appearance. "Are you still not feeling well?"

"No, not well at all, but I'm trying not to think about it. It just may take a while for my stomach and nerves to settle. I've never been able to abide sea travel and your father knows it," she replied, her voice tense.

"I have some news you may be interested in. It may even help you to feel better," Valerie said coyly as she looked out the small porthole window. On the decks below, the sailors were finished with their preparations and were busy untying the ship from the dock. Several onlookers stood on the shore, waving, as the *Fast Alice* pulled away from the dock and into the channel. She turned around and picked at a bunch of grapes left on the bureau as a bon voyage gift from the Smythes. Tossing one into her mouth, she sat down on the edge of the berth. "News about a young man."

Jacqueline turned to Valerie, her eyebrows raised. "Go on."

"Oh, Mama, you should have seen him. You simply would not believe how handsome he is." Valerie fell back on the bed, her arms spread out beside her.

Jacqueline crossed her arms in front of her, considering her daughter. "Really now? And just where did you meet this young man of yours? Were you properly introduced?"

"Well, somewhat. Papa sent him to help me down the stairs after all of you deserted me." Valerie leaned up on one elbow. "Just as he arrived, I started to fall. He came to my aid, as if I were a damsel in distress. I believe he rescued me from a certain death." She fell back to the pillows, her arm across her brow, and sighed.

"For heaven's sake, Valerie. I told you not to read so many of those romance novels. What happened to the intelligent young woman who came aboard with me just an hour ago?" Jacqueline dropped her arms and went back to putting their clothing away. She pulled open a small drawer built into the side of the cabin wall and tucked several pairs of stockings inside.

Valerie shrugged her shoulders then stood. She unlatched the trunk containing her new dresses and heaved back the heavy lid. There, amidst the blue tissue paper, were the new ready-made creations. "Which one do you think I should wear tonight? Mr. Smythe - did I tell you he's Sir David's son? - will be dining at the captain's table as well."

"So the plot thickens," Jacqueline commented. "No, you failed to mention he's the son of our host."

Valerie held up the dark red satin dress in front of her and studied the picture she presented in the wavy reflection of the mirror. Wrinkling her nose at the image, she hung the dress on a wooden hook and pulled out the green one. "What do you think, Mama?"

Jacqueline looked over Valerie's shoulder at the reflection. "What I think is that my daughter has grown into a lovely young woman."

"Oh, Mama, you know what I meant."

Their eyes met. "And you know what I meant. See? I told you all along there was a man out there for you. You only had to give it some time."

Valerie lowered the dress, her smile fading.

"What's the matter?" Jacqueline asked as she went about hanging the hairbrushes and toiletries along the wall.

"Well, there's something I need to ask of you. You *and* Papa." She limped back to the berth, a task belabored by the sway of the ship as it made its way out of the Thames and into the Sargasso Sea. The ship's horn bellowed and the cabin vibrated with the sound.

"You see, I have a bit of a problem. Mr. Smythe doesn't know I'm crippled. He knows I don't walk too well, but he thinks it's because I hurt myself."

Jacqueline turned around slowly, her expression closed. "Oh? And how did he happen to come to this conclusion?"

"I told him I fell off a horse. A horse named Rexford, to be exact." Valerie lowered her eyes, a slow pang of guilt building up inside her. The horn blew again and she felt like it was mocking her for her lies. She'd never really lied before, except to Reggie. But, of course, he didn't count.

"Listen to me, Valerie," Jacqueline began.

Valerie raised a hand. "I know, Mama. I shouldn't have done it, but it was *his* idea. What I mean is, he assumed I was only injured. The thought that I was crippled never even entered his mind." She shook her head. "I couldn't bring myself to tell him the truth. I wanted him to think I was whole."

"You shouldn't have lied, Val. If he is as special as you believe him to be, he'll accept you as you are. Haven't I convinced you of that yet?"

"Mama, I know you feel that way, but you need to understand that I see a different story in every young man's eyes I meet."

Valerie stood and smoothed her dress. She walked toward the mirror again, carrying her green dress over her right arm. She pulled up her skirt in the front and stuck her left foot out. As long as she kept her shoes on, no one could really tell what was wrong. They couldn't see the misshapen toes and where her heel had pulled itself up.

"Once they find out I'm crippled, I know they laugh, or make fun of me. I've heard them when they think I'm not listening, just like the lady in the dress shop. Or - and I believe this to be the worse - they stop talking to me as if I've vanished from sight. Just because I can't walk like the other girls, I cease to exist in their minds."

Jacqueline reached for her daughter, but Valerie held back. "Tell me you won't let him know. Please, Mama. You have to promise me."

Jacqueline let her arms drop. "I won't lie for you, Val. If he asks me, I'll tell him, and so will your father." Then she smiled, a mischievous glint in her eyes. "Of course, if the subject isn't broached, then there will be nothing to say, will there?"

"And you'll tell Lucy to mind her own business?"

"Lucy? Mind her own business?" Jacqueline laughed out loud. "And where did you get the notion Lucy would ever mind her own business where you - or any of us for that matter - are concerned?"

Valerie sighed. "I see your point. Well, I'll just have to make certain the two of them are never alone together."

"You know you'll have to tell Mr. Smythe yourself sometime, don't you, Val?" Jacqueline asked, her voice low.

"I know. And I will, when the time is right." Valerie took a deep breath and let it out slowly as the events of the day caught up with her. She suddenly felt so small and alone. She held out her arms and her mother embraced her. Mama was warm and soft and smelled of lavender, like all mothers should. And she wouldn't tell if she wasn't asked, like a best friend who kept your innermost secrets.

Chapter Seven

Lucy darted back and forth between the adjoining door to her cabin and Valerie's. "The curlin' iron's heatin' up in the coal bucket in the hallway. Can ye imagine they have a man who tends it fer ye? Somethin' to do with not wantin' anyone to burn down the ship." Lucy shook her head. "Such luxuries! Anyway, it'll be hot in just a minute, miss."

Scooping up a thick lock of hair from Valerie's head, Lucy twisted it near the scalp, then slipped in a hairpin to hold it in place. She ran back out again and returned with the curling iron. Grabbing the end of the lock, she quickly wound it around the iron. Once released, she repeated the action several times with the other sections of hair until the iron was cooled off.

"There, now, ye're as pretty as a spring bloom." Lucy admired her handiwork, tucking in a loose strand here and there. The elegant upsweep was accented with a pearl comb in the back, pushing long corkscrew curls over to dangle impishly in front of Valerie's green eyes.

Valerie smiled as she looked at her reflection. "You do fine work, Lucy. It looks just like this magazine picture." She held the drawing next to her face so she could compare herself to it, pursing her lips into a serious pout like the woman in the portrait.

"Well, this thick hair of yers was made for the 'do. Now it's time to get ye in yer corset." Lucy lifted the heavy garment from the berth.

Valerie's eyes narrowed as they swept over the dreaded article. She didn't argue, though. She had to look her best for Thomas Smythe and if it meant wearing a corset, she'd do it. Valerie stood and held her arms above her head. "Do what you will with that cursed thing," she muttered, taking a deep breath and holding it.

Lucy stared at Valerie for a moment, clucking her tongue. "I told ye about that language, didn't I?"

Valerie didn't answer, but only pretended her attention was diverted by some commotion outside the cabin's porthole window.

Lucy shook her head and wrapped the corset around the younger woman's midsection, pulling the ties tightly in back. Satisfied the laces were just as they should be and a perfect hourglass shape was achieved, she worked the strings into several small knots, tucking the ends into the top. "There. Ye can breathe now."

"Thank goodness." Valerie exhaled loudly. But, as soon as she relaxed her stomach muscles, a sharp whalebone poked her in the side. "No wonder fainting couches are so fashionable these days." She squirmed. "The corset all but guarantees a woman will faint dead away at the slightest agitation." Valerie tugged at the top, pulling it into place around her breasts. "I suppose it's a good thing that I'm not quite as well endowed as some other women. I fear this hideous garment would greatly decrease the chances of feeding my children should I ever be blessed with any."

"Miss Valerie, I have heard just about everythin' from yer mouth. I don't know where ye've been learnin' to talk so, but I won't tell ye again to stop it." Lucy shook her finger. "A proper lady wears her undergarments without complainin', even if she finds them uncomfortable. As a matter of fact, proper young ladies do *everythin'* without complainin'."

She held out the steel hooped crinoline and pulled it into place as Valerie stepped into it. "I'll be havin' a talk with yer mother if ye give me any more trouble about it." She lifted the bottle green silk dress from its hook and slipped it over Valerie's head, being careful not to damage her coif. The dress fell into place in a soft cloud. "Am I makin' myself clear?"

"Lucy, after all the years you've been with this family, I never thought I'd see the day you'd threaten to run to Mama about me." Valerie shimmied into the dress, pushing her arms into the long fitted sleeves. "I must say I'm surprised at you."

"Surprised at *me*?" Lucy looked at the girl, her eyes wide. "*Ye're* surprised at *me*?"

"That's what I said." Valerie presented her back to the older woman, a smile tipping her lips. Lucy couldn't stand it when Valerie acted like she was disappointed in her. It serves her right for making me wear this bloody corset and birdcage, she thought. And yes, I said bloody and I meant it.

"If ye just do as ye're told, I'll not be needin' to pull yer mother into this. To tell the truth, I'd rather not since she's not feelin' well anyway." Lucy spoke quietly as she fastened the buttons of the dress. "So it'll be yer conscious that'll be the worse off if'n I have to disturb yer mother, not mine." Finished, she turned Valerie around to face her, looking her over with a practiced eye. "Ah yes, ye look just like yer mother did when she was yer age. And a bonnie lass she was. Yer father was right lucky to have caught her."

Lucy scanned the wall until she found the rectangular antimony jewelry box where it was tucked into a railed shelf. Retrieving it, she pulled out an intricately woven gold chain with a round cabochon emerald hanging from it. An antique piece, Valerie's father had given it to her for her sixteenth birthday. "I think this will look real fine. What do ye think?"

Valerie leaned over and gave the servant a quick hug.

Lucy puffed herself up, straightening her crisp white apron. "What was that fuss all about?"

"For asking me what I thought. I do believe it's the first time you ever did." Valerie let Lucy hook the pendant around her neck. Next, she took a pair of matching earrings from the box and clipped one to each earlobe.

"I can see ye'll be havin' yer hands full with the young men this night." Lucy smiled and handed Valerie her best cane, the ebony one with the carved silver grip.

"Maybe I shouldn't use this cane. I don't want any harm to come to it." Valerie reached for her old cane where it was leaning against the bureau. Thomas may wonder why she had such a nice cane for a temporary injury.

"Nonsense. Ye're much too dressy to be carryin' that old thing. Besides, ye'll be needin' all the help ye can get to chase away the hordes of men. They'll all be a-courtin' ye before the evenin's over. Providin' ye mind yer tongue, that is," Lucy said as she began to straighten the cabin. "Gentlemen don't take to opinionated women, you know."

Valerie smiled as the image of dozens of men standing in line to speak with her filled her mind. She forgot about the cane as a rush of anticipation ran through her with the memory of Thomas Smythe's lips pressed against her fingers. Of course, it didn't matter how many men there were around her tonight, Thomas was the only one she was interested in. She twirled the cane in her hand. "We shall see, Lucy. We shall see."

* * *

The Brooks family made their way single-file down the narrow wood paneled corridor leading from their quarters to the main reception area below deck. Frederick was in the lead, followed by Jacqueline, then Valerie, with Reggie skipping along behind them all.

"Hurry up!" Reggie demanded. "I'm starving!" He shoved at Valerie's backside, pushing her into their mother.

"Stop it, Reggie. You'll knock all of us down," Jacqueline scolded. "It's hard enough to maneuver through this passage what with the sway of the ship and all without you causing more trouble."

Valerie swung her skirts behind her, running the stiff steel crinoline into Reggie's shin. He fell flat on his bottom and Valerie smiled. "Lizard," she hissed.

Reggie jumped up and started for Valerie just as they arrived at the grand salon. At the site of the massive room, he froze in his tracks, as did they all.

Here, the narrow passage opened into a large expanse of a room, opulently furnished with upholstered banquettes and heavy velvet curtains. Valerie's gaze swept the space, taking in each and every detail. The walls were painted a streaked dark red overlaid with fantasy scenes of King Neptune and his court. Mermaids and dolphins in shimmery shades of green and gold seemed to float right off the wall and into the room itself. She took a step forward and ran her hand along the back of one of the heavy blue tapestry-covered seats which were wrapped around a support column. On each side of her, seating was arranged neatly into small conversation groups, from one end of the room to the other.

Reggie ran over to one of the chairs and all but leaped into it, bouncing on the firm cushion.

"Here now, Reg. Take it easy son," Frederick admonished. "You'll crash the seat right through to the hull."

"Do you really think I could, Papa?" Reggie asked, his eyes wide. Quickly, he stood. Gripping the arms, he readied himself to bounce down again. "Hey! This chair doesn't move." He tugged at it, but it wouldn't budge.

"Of course it doesn't move. The seating is fastened in place in case of a storm," his father explained.

Valerie left her family and made her way over to one of the murals, her cane creating a soft thumping noise against the carpeted deck. She studied the representation of the birth of Venus, a typical rendering of the maid arriving on a mollusk shell, escorted from the sea by several angels.

"Beautiful, isn't it?" The deep voice startled her and she felt her stomach catch.

Valerie turned around, then smiled as she took in the image of the man before her. Dressed from head to toe in a crisp black suit, only the fine white linen shirt and creamy ascot he wore broke the darkness. "Yes, it is. Good evening, Mr. Smythe."

Thomas bowed his head slightly, a satisfied grin on his lips. For a brief moment, he reminded Valerie of a cat that was about to corner its prey, then she shook the picture from her mind, her musings interrupted by her father's voice.

"Good evening, David, old man." Valerie turned her attention to the gentleman Frederick was greeting. He looked exactly like an older version of Thomas.

"There's my father," Thomas said. "Come, I'll introduce you." Valerie slipped her gloved hand around his arm as he led her toward the gathering. He leaned near her as they walked. "I must say I'm very grateful to Father for forcing me on this trip. If I hadn't come, I never would have gotten to meet someone as lovely as yourself."

Valerie inclined her head, blushing. She felt positively light-headed in Thomas' company. Never in her life had a man paid such close attention to her or spoken to her so.

"Valerie, come here, child," her father bade. "I'd like you to meet someone."

"Sir David, this is my lovely daughter, Valerie." Frederick introduced his daughter with a smile.

Valerie curtsied as best she could, catching a slight frown on David Smythe's face as she did.

"That's not really necessary, young lady. I can see it takes a great deal of effort on your part."

She froze, embarrassed he would call attention to her malady, then straightened. "It's a pleasure to make your acquaintance, Sir David," she offered with a tight smile.

The elder Smythe nodded. "I see you've already met my son," he observed. "Have you two been properly introduced or did he simply force his company on you?"

"Actually, sir, Papa sent him to my aide when I needed assistance going down the stairs earlier today."

"He helped you down the stairs, did he?" Smythe murmured, eyeing his son. "Well, that's just like him, a perfect knight in shining armor."

Valerie was about to agree when a man wearing a short white jacket entered the salon. He cleared his throat loudly. "Dinner is served," he announced.

There weren't many passengers on the ship, as its main purpose was to carry cargo from England to China, but the ones who were there crowded toward the dining room. Smythe caught his son's arm, then motioned for Frederick and his family to go without them. "We'll catch up with you in a moment," he explained. Frederick nodded and they went on, Valerie trying to catch a last glimpse of Thomas as she entered the other room.

As soon as the Brooks' were out of sight, Smythe leaned toward his son, making certain he had the younger man's attention. "See here, boy. I'll not have you spoiling this business deal by compromising Brooks' daughter. This loan is too important to the expedition."

Thomas looked at his father, a demeanor of innocence portrayed on his face. "Be assured, Father, I haven't a clue as to what you're talking about."

"Oh, you know perfectly well what I'm talking about. I won't have a repeat of that scene you caused back in Liverpool after your dalliance with the Count's girl. Besides," he began, his eyes following Valerie's painful trek to the dining room, "the girl's got something wrong with her."

Thomas shook his head, aggravated. "It's only a sprain. Do you really think I'd waste my time on a cripple?" His eyes met his father's. "You've taught me better than that, you know."

Smythe's face hardened. "I suppose you *are* much too vain to be seen with a permanently damaged woman. Mark my words, though, you lose this loan for me because of your behavior and I'll take the money out of your sorry hide."

Chapter Eight

Valerie was utterly amazed by the ingenuity of the shipbuilders as she entered the dining room. Wide velvet covered booths were built into both sides of the clipper under a double row of narrow windows. In place between them were dining tables long enough to seat eight or ten people at each one with stark white tablecloths covering the wood. Anchored to the table legs and opposite the booth was an upholstered bench, all fastened neatly in place in case of a storm. Over the tables hung heavy dark oak racks designed to hold wine glasses and bottles. Every last detail of the room assured a satisfying meal in even the roughest of seas.

Frederick stopped one of the waiters. "We're to sit at the captain's table this evening. Can you point us in the right direction?"

"Certainly, sir. It's the large one at the other end of the room."

"Come along, family." Frederick motioned with a wave of his hand. "The table's over here." He straightened his jacket and squared his shoulders proudly as he led his brood past the other passengers.

"What's Papa doing?" Valerie whispered to her mother. "He acts as if he's in command of Her Majesty's army."

Jacqueline laughed quietly. "I haven't the faintest idea." She put her hand on Valerie's arm. "Tell me, Val, was that the young man you spoke of earlier?"

Valerie nodded, a smile curving her full lips. "What did you think? Wasn't he everything I said he was? Why, even his own father called him a knight in shining armor."

"Indeed he did." Jacqueline frowned, remembering the note of sarcasm contained in the comment. She was surprised her daughter didn't catch it as well. "I've noticed there are plenty of young men on board, though. Have any others been introduced to you yet?"

"Why no, Mama. But I'd just as soon that none of the others bother me now. Mr. Smythe may get annoyed if they showed me any attention."

"Valerie, don't you think - "

"Good evening, Madam." Captain Marcus interrupted Jacqueline. "So happy you could join me this evening."

The steward peered out from behind the captain, his long gray hair tucked neatly into a queue. "Where is that lovely Lucy of yours? Is she coming later?"

"Of course not, Johnny," Jacqueline replied. "She's dining in the kitchen with the other servants."

"Well, if you'll all excuse me, that's where I should be as well. I'll go see to her comfort."

"I'm certain she'd like that very much," Jacqueline offered as the Captain helped her to a chair. Next, he seated Valerie a few seats away from her mother.

"Sorry about Johnny," he muttered to his guests. "Seems the man's smitten with your maid." He motioned to Frederick. "Sir Frederick, won't you sit next to me? I've reserved the seat on the other side for Sir David. I understand you two are business acquaintances?"

"We are. Reggie here can sit on my right if you don't mind. I think it's time for him to start learning a bit about the banking trade so he can follow in his father's footsteps some day." Frederick smiled and rumpled Reggie's hair as the boy took his seat.

"Of course, of course." The captain caught sight of Thomas and his father. "Over here, men," he gestured as they approached. "Young Mr. Smythe, I'd like you to seat yourself next to this lovely young lady, if you don't mind."

Thomas smiled at Valerie. "I'd be honored."

"And you, Sir David, please take the seat at my left." The captain claimed his seat between Frederick and David. "There, now." He scanned the faces at the table. "Everyone's hungry, I pray?"

"Yes, sir!" Reggie answered enthusiastically. "I'm always hungry." He leaned back in the booth with a grin, satisfied he'd made his presence known to all. He caught Valerie looking at him and stuck his tongue out at her. She wrinkled her nose, then quickly turned her attention to Thomas.

"So, will you be visiting Pompeii with us, Mr. Smythe?" Valerie asked as the server poured her a glass of red bordeaux. She took a small sip of the dry vintage then coughed, not accustomed to the wine. She held her napkin to her mouth, then wiped the tear from her eye. "Excuse me, it must have gone down the wrong way."

"No excuse needed." He leaned forward and whispered, "The tear in your eye makes their green depths glimmer with a vibrancy to rival the emerald you're wearing."

Valerie rested her elbows on the table, and gazed into Thomas' eyes. "Oh, please, Mr. Smythe. You're much too kind."

"Ahem." Jacqueline cleared her throat and stared pointedly at Valerie's elbows. Valerie glanced down. Horrified, she quickly pulled them away. Before she could say anything else, the first course was served.

In the center of the table, the server placed a tureen of seafood chowder. He dipped a silver ladle into the thick, creamy soup and, starting with the ladies, offered each a half bowl full. After everyone was served, Reggie peered into his bowl. "How come it's not filled all the way to the top?"

"If we happened to hit choppy waters, and your bowl was filled to the brim, it'd spill all over you," the captain explained.

Reggie considered the explanation. Then, satisfied it made perfect sense, scooped up some soup and slurped it off the spoon, loudly smacking his lips.

"Really, Reggie," Jacqueline scolded. "Show your manners, boy."

Reggie smiled, and the chowder pushed out the hole in his mouth previously occupied by his front teeth. "Sorry, Mama." Valerie rolled her eyes at her brother.

Once everyone was finished, the server quickly took the bowls from in front of the guests and piled the table high with the main courses of leg of mutton and beefsteak pie. He left for a moment and returned with mustard potatoes, creamed onions, and loaves of steaming hot bread. The aroma of warm yeast mixed with onions filled the dining room.

"It - looks - wonderful," Jacqueline whispered, clutching her stomach.

"Are you all right, Mama?" Valerie asked as her mother grew increasingly pale.

Jacqueline placed a hand to her mouth. "I think I'll be fine in a moment. Just a touch of *mal de mer*. That's all."

"Perhaps you should go lie down, Mrs. Brooks," Frederick offered. "I can have Lucy bring you a plate later. You may feel like eating after you've had a nap."

"Well, if you wouldn't mind?" She scanned the faces at the table.

"Of course we don't mind," Captain Marcus said. "Sea sickness is, unfortunately, a common occurrence among our passengers. You go on ahead and I'll personally make sure your maid gets you a plate."

"Thank you, Captain. I do appreciate your gracious hospitality." Jacqueline stood and excused herself from the table, but not before sending one of her "behave yourself" warning glances Valerie's way. Valerie's eyes grew wide and she quickly turned her attention to her plate.

"It'll be good to be back in Italy. I so enjoy the countryside," David Smythe began. "The area around the site is most lovely, as you'll all soon see."

"Have you traveled to Italy often?" Valerie asked, forgetting her dinner in favor of information concerning their destination.

"Not nearly enough. For the time being, I only go as necessary to visit the excavation. There's this gentleman in charge there whom I keep in contact with, name's Fiorelli," Smythe explained. "Most fascinating person. Two years ago, he devised this clever method of preserving the bodies of the ancient people who were killed during the eruption."

"Why, I've never heard of such a thing," Valerie interjected. "How in the world could someone do that?" She looked at everyone. "After all, the eruption occurred almost eighteen hundred years ago."

Smythe waved his hand and took a drink of wine. "I know. I felt the same way until I saw it myself last year. During the digging, when the workers hit a hollow spot in the ground, a small opening is made and plaster is poured into it. The next day, the volcanic ash is chipped away, usually revealing a perfect cast of the object that had once occupied the space under it - be it man or beast. Even casts of food and furnishings have been taken." He shook his head. "The detail is so great, you can see the poor souls' expressions as they lie dying, captured forever in a plaster statue."

Valerie leaned back into her chair. A chance to see what the Pompeians looked like was a special treat she hadn't counted on. Were they tall? Did they have classic Roman features, as she had seen on sculpture of the period, or were they different? "Can you see anything else there? I mean, have you uncovered many other finds?" She leaned back in her chair. "Can you imagine what it would be like to have actually lived during the time before the eruption?"

Smythe chuckled and looked over at Frederick. "Your daughter has quite an appetite for knowledge, doesn't she?"

"Yes, she has. The girl has always shown a keen interest in the antiquities and hopes to be teaching the subject soon."

"Teaching? Frederick, forgive me for saying so, but someone of your stature certainly wouldn't need to put his child out to work."

Frederick straightened. "It's Valerie's choice."

"Valerie's choice? Well, I can see you're much more modern in your thinking than I. If it were my daughter, I'd be busy finding a husband for the dear thing."

Valerie's eyes darted back and forth between the men. She twisted her napkin under the table. Please don't say anything, Papa, she pleaded silently. They don't need to know anything about my foot.

Smythe wiped his mouth with his napkin and leaned toward Frederick. "Besides, whoever said a female should be making her own choices? They just don't have the capacity for serious thought."

"See here now, David," Frederick began, "there are obvious reasons at play as to why my daughter wishes to teach."

Valerie blanched. Dear Lord, he was going to spill the story about the accident and the doctors and her crippled foot. She pushed herself a short distance from the table, ready to leave.

"Of course there are. But there's plenty of time to talk of this later, if you like. Where are my manners?" Smythe grinned, then took a bite of bread. "We should be discussing less delicate matters over dinner."

Valerie let out her breath slowly and relaxed a bit. That was much too close. Papa would have explained everything about her right then and there. Thank goodness Sir David decided to change the subject. Perhaps if she left, they'd forget all about the conversation. "Papa, I'm not feeling well. Would you mind if I went to my cabin?"

"Certainly not, dear. Will you be all right?" he asked as he pushed his plate away.

"I'll be fine in the morning. It's just been a long day." She began to stand, and Thomas quickly rose and helped move her chair out of the way.

"If you like, Sir Frederick, I'll see Valerie to her room."

"Well, if it wouldn't be any trouble?"

"No. None at all." He looked at his father. Smythe frowned at his son. "No need to worry. I'll be back in a few moments." Thomas tucked Valerie's hand into the crook of his arm as he led her from the dining room. The cool night air blew in through the open windows of the grand salon as they walked toward the corridor. Valerie shivered and Thomas drew her even closer. His body felt firm and warm through the thin silk of her dress.

"You didn't really need to leave the table, Mr. Smythe. Although I do appreciate your help, Reggie could have seen me to my room." Valerie glanced at him out of the corner of her eye. Oh, but he was quite smashing indeed, this rescuer of hers.

"Nonsense. I would have insisted, anyway." He held her hand as she stepped over the threshold and continued to hold it as he walked in front of her through the narrow passage.

"Here's my room." Valerie reluctantly let go of Thomas' hand and pulled the key out of her reticule. She handed it to him and, as he took it, his fingers caressed hers and she shivered again. He pushed the door open, then bowed low.

Valerie inclined her head and felt a warm blush color her cheeks. "Thank you, Mr. Smythe. As I said, I do appreciate your kindness."

"I have to admit it was entirely selfish on my part." He lightly caressed her cheek with the back of his hand. "I wanted to spend a few moments alone with you."

"Mr. Smythe. I - I don't know what to say," Valerie murmured.

"You needn't say a word, for if you did, you may choose to deny me the sweet pleasure of your lips." Before Valerie could speak, he pulled her to him and lowered his mouth to hers.

His lips were hot and moist. Valerie knew she should push him away, but the delicious tingle stirring in her belly was too wonderful to let go.

Slowly, he raised his head. "Forgive me. I'm a cad."

"Yes, you are," she replied, her voice low. With a smile, she stepped into her cabin and gently closed the door behind her. She leaned back against it and hugged her arms around her. She'd just had her first kiss. And it was everything she had ever imagined it to be, and more. "Heaven help me," she whispered to the darkness. "I think I may be falling in love."

Chapter Nine

"Lovely day, isn't it, Lucy?" Valerie peered over the ship's brass railing and out into the expanse of deep blue-green sea. The sharp bow of the clipper, true to its name, cut through the water without effort, sending white capped waves crashing along either side. She turned her face to the warm sun and it dried the spray that had splashed her cheeks.

"Yer in an awfully good mood this mornin'," Lucy observed.

Reggie ran up to Valerie's side and she bent over and hugged him. His eyes widened and his body grew stiff. He struggled to wrestle away and when his sister released him, he stumbled backwards. "What was *that*?!"

Valerie shrugged. "Just a simple hug. You're my brother." She tweaked his nose. "It is allowed, you know."

Reggie eyed her for a moment before running off again, yelling behind him, "Wait 'til I tell Mama! She's going to think you're sick!"

"And I think I might be agreein'," Lucy added.

"Oh, really now. What's the matter with you two? You would think you'd never seen me in a good mood before."

"Good mood is one thing. Stark ravin' mad is another." Lucy drew herself up and crossed her arms in front of her. "Spill it, girl. I want the details, I do."

Valerie turned back around and stared out into the sea again. A gull dipped low on the side of the ship and rose again, a squirming fish in its mouth. "I haven't the faintest idea what you're talking about. There's absolutely nothing to tell, Lucy."

"I'm not believin' it."

Lucy's eyes narrowed and Valerie felt the older woman studying her. Well, she would just ignore the servant. Perhaps she'd go away if she did. Valerie sighed. Then again, she probably wouldn't. She turned to face her just as Thomas was approaching.

"Good morning, ladies," he bade.

Valerie smiled and cast her eyes downward, feeling her cheeks grow hot. She glanced at Lucy, who was still studying her.

"Ah, I think I see the cause," she observed.

"The cause of what?" Thomas asked, still smiling.

My, but he looked gorgeous in his white linen suit and yellow ascot, Valerie thought. His straw hat was tipped rakishly to one side, shading his eyes. She caught her breath. "Nothing. Lucy here is just being a silly goose, that's all."

"May I escort you for a walk around the deck?" he asked, extending his arm.

Valerie reached for it as Lucy stepped between them. "There'll be no touchin' and feelin' goin' on while I'm around, thank ye very much." She glared at the pair. "Ye want to walk, fine, but I'll be only a few paces behind ye."

"Lucy, please," Valerie began.

Thomas laughed, interrupting her. "Of course, Miss Lucy. We would welcome your company."

Lucy smiled, satisfied. She waved her hand, shooing them ahead of her. "Go on with ye, then. And don't forget, I'm followin' ye."

Valerie stayed close to the railing as she and Thomas began their walk. The ship hit a wave, and listed to the right. She grabbed the rail, steadying herself. Thomas gripped her elbow, then quickly let go when Lucy intervened.

"She's fine, she is. Don't ye be babyin' her," Lucy scolded.

"He was just being nice, Lucy." Valerie eyed the maid. What would it take to make her to go away? "Don't you need to be with Mama? She still isn't well, you know."

"Yer mama can wait a few more minutes until I see ye back safely inside."

Thomas coughed and Valerie suspected he was really laughing and only needed to cover it up. "How is your ankle today, Miss Brooks?" he asked, composing himself. "Better, I pray."

"Ankle? What are ye talkin' about?" Lucy looked from Thomas to Valerie.

Well, this just wouldn't do. Lucy would most certainly tell all she knew once prompted. For goodness sake, she'd tell everything she knew even if she weren't prompted! Valerie increased her pace as they continued to walk, her cane thumping loudly against the teak deck. Maybe they could outrun the woman.

Thomas stopped and turned around. "Her sprain. I'm truly amazed the horse didn't do any further harm. Why, I knew a man whose entire leg was crushed when he was thrown."

Lucy looked at Valerie, eyebrows raised. "Oh, did ye now?"

Valerie felt her stomach roll over as panic worked its way up into her throat. "Yes, Lucy. Isn't that the most horrible story you've ever heard?" She watched Thomas' expression while she felt herself go pale. At least he didn't appear to understand Lucy's mood. "Thank you for asking, Mr. Smythe. It's feeling much better, but I fear I'll be needing this cane for quite some time to come." She had to get the maid away from Thomas before she told everything. Valerie glanced around, frantic, looking for any excuse. "There's the hatch. Lucy, would you be so kind as to help me to my cabin. I fear the sea has upset my stomach again."

"Has it now?" Lucy stepped forward and began to help Valerie down the steep stairway. "My own stomach's a-churnin', too. Ye never know what might make ye sick."

Valerie looked at Lucy and saw the disappointment glaring in the older woman's eyes. "Sometimes there's no easy explanation," she whispered.

"Will I see you later?" Thomas called after her.

"Perhaps," Valerie answered with a smile. "Perhaps you shall."

* * *

"I can't believe how you behaved, Lucy! I am so embarrassed!"

"Ye're embarrassed? Ye weren't the one who had to witness such lies." Lucy picked up Valerie's dress from the night before and folded it neatly. She wrapped it in tissue and placed it back in the younger woman's trunk, then closed the lid before speaking again. "I can't believe ye lied to him like that." She shook her head, clucking her tongue. "Well, at least I know now why ye're in such a good mood."

"*Was* in a good mood. You spoiled it for me," Valerie pouted. She lifted her skirt and untied the crinoline. It hit the carpeted floor with a muffled twang. Lying across the bed, she added, "You have to promise me you won't tell Thomas about my foot."

"Oh I do, do I? And just why didn't ye tell him the truth in the first place?" Lucy waved a finger at the girl. "Lyin'll get ye nothing but trouble, that's what my own mum always said."

Valerie sighed. Why was everyone so dead against her little charade? It wasn't like she was hurting anyone. "Never mind, Lucy." She rested her head on her arms. "I'm sorry I got you involved."

Lucy's expression softened. She knelt down on the floor next to the bed and smoothed Valerie's hair. "I understand why ye did it. Ye just need to make it right."

"I know. That's what Mama said, too. And I will." Valerie closed her eyes. Her head had begun to ache with a dull throbbing. "Eventually."

Chapter Ten

Valerie sat with her family in the grand salon of the *Fast Alice* and watched as the passengers began to gather for their last dinner together before reaching shore. The past three weeks had flown by so quickly, she felt as if she'd never catch her breath. Almost all of her days had been filled with Thomas' company. He was so attentive and kind and, when no one was looking, he had actually stolen a few more kisses. Without thinking, Valerie touched a finger to her lips, remembering the warmth he had generated with his touch. She smiled. Well, maybe stolen wasn't exactly the right word.

"I see that young man of yours coming this way," Jacqueline whispered. She was still so pale and gaunt from the sea sickness, but had insisted on joining everyone for their last night aboard ship.

Thomas approached and bowed low to the ladies. "Good evening, everyone." He adjusted his jacket. "May I say you both are looking quite ravishing this night?"

Valerie giggled. She felt so special in his company. This is what it's like to be in love, she told herself. Thomas offered his arm and, standing, she accepted it.

"Mama? Papa? Do you mind if we get some punch before supper?"

Frederick pushed his reading glasses against his face and glanced up from his book. "I think I'll join you." He removed the spectacles and tucked them inside his jacket pocket.

Reaching the refreshment table, Thomas poured each of them a glass of the fruity concoction. As she began to drink, Sir David walked up alongside them. He shook Frederick's hand and bowed toward Valerie. After their first meeting, she had decided she wouldn't again curtsy to the man. She simply nodded her head.

"Good evening, Sir David," she bade.

Smythe picked up a glass of punch and took a long drink. "So, tell me Frederick, have you managed to find a husband on board for the girl?"

Valerie all but sputtered her punch. She looked at the man, aghast. "I - I beg your pardon?" she asked.

Frederick interrupted. "Well, it would seem this son of yours has monopolized all of her time." He nodded toward Thomas. "I don't believe there's been a chance of anyone else getting to know her." He smiled at Valerie. "I must say, though, it's been wonderful for her confidence to have this boy pay such close attention to her."

"Really, Papa. We don't need to discuss this, do we?" she pleaded.

"She has trouble finding suitors, does she?" Smythe's eyes swept over her. "As comely as she is, I would think you'd have to keep the doors barred against the men."

"Well, no one else has seemed able to look past her injury like Thomas here has," Frederick explained.

Valerie frantically looked from her father to Smythe to Thomas. This wasn't going well at all. They were much too engrossed in the conversation and she knew exactly where it was leading. If she didn't do something fast, Papa was going to explain about her foot right here in front of everyone. Right in front of Thomas. Really, she had wanted to tell him the truth these past few weeks, but it just never seemed to be the right time.

She placed her hand on Thomas' arm, calling his attention away from the talk. "I'm not feeling too well. Would you mind escorting me above deck for a breath of fresh air?" Valerie asked quietly.

"Of course." He turned to their fathers. "Miss Brooks has asked me to take her above deck. She's not feeling well," he explained for her. "Would you mind, Sir?"

Frederick waved his hand. "No, go right ahead. But dinner will be served soon. Don't be late."

Valerie allowed herself a small sigh of relief as they made their way up through the hatch and out into the cool night air. With her hand on Thomas' arm, they walked to the front of the ship and watched the glistening spray as it shot up near the bow of the clipper.

The half moon cast its glow on the water and it rippled with the movement of the dark, shadowy waves. Valerie leaned on the railing, her curls blowing off her face. "It's so beautiful out here, isn't it?"

"Mmmm. It certainly is."

Valerie felt her stomach catch. Thomas was so close, his breath tickled the back of her neck and sent a shiver down her spine. She turned to face him.

Thomas lifted a hand and caressed Valerie's cheek. He let it drop to the back of her head and gently pulled her to him.

"Would you take advantage of me while we're alone?" she asked, breathless.

"Absolutely." He smiled, moving ever closer. Gently, he tipped her chin until her eyes met his. "I fear I'll never grow tired of your sweet, sweet kisses."

Thomas' lips touched hers, gently at first, and she melted against him. The butterflies in her stomach unleashed and surged through her. She felt for certain she would faint. Valerie leaned her hands on Thomas' shoulders for support as his kiss grew more insistent. His hands moved over her neck, her shoulders, and down her arms. Everywhere he touched her, she was on fire.

His hands caressed her waist and moved upward, over the thick whalebone that shaped her waist, and stopped at the edge of the square cut neckline. Thomas let his fingers tease the lace edge and dip beneath the fabric.

Valerie stiffened. "Thomas. Please. You mustn't."

"Don't tell me this isn't what you've been wanting because I won't believe a word of it," he whispered into her ear. "This is why you really asked me up here, isn't it?"

Valerie's mind whirled at the accusation. What in heaven's name was he implying? That she somehow was to blame for his behavior?

Thomas continued to speak softly. "Your lips were made for mine, Valerie. Let them do what they will." He kissed her ear, then her chin, then his mouth followed the path his fingers had just taken and moved along the delicate flesh of her chest.

This wasn't right. Everything was happening much too fast. Valerie struggled to catch her breath.

"Valerie!" Reggie scurried across the deck, screeching her name, and ran right into the pair. The momentum knocked Thomas and Valerie apart, and her to the floor. Thanks to the crinoline, her skirt went up over her head. Embarrassed beyond words, she struggled to her feet as Thomas gave her a hand.

"Sorry, Val, but Papa said I should come and get you. It's time to go in for dinner and he thought maybe I could help you down the stairs."

"I don't need any help, thank you." Valerie ground out the words. "Haven't you helped enough already?"

"But your foot," he pleaded.

"Your foot should be getting better soon, shouldn't it?" Thomas asked as he dusted off his trousers. "After all, it has been nearly three weeks."

"Y - yes. It will probably be back to its old self in a day or two. Run along Reggie." She shooed him with her free hand. "I'll catch up with you in a minute."

"But Val, your foot isn't going to get better. The doctor said it wouldn't ever get better."

Valerie closed her eyes and prayed to heaven. Please Lord, make it so Thomas didn't hear those words. But when she opened them, she knew he had. The humor in his eyes was gone and only the smile on his face remained. She thought of the cat again.

"What is the child talking about, Miss Brooks?" he asked, his voice growing ever more cordial as he spoke. "I thought you said it was only a sprain."

She took a deep breath. Like it or not, 'eventually' had arrived. "Well, I'm sorry I didn't tell you sooner, but it isn't 'only a sprain.' I was hit by a carriage when I was very young and my foot was - it was," she swallowed hard. "Crippled." Valerie looked at him. Overcome with a sudden desperation, she pleaded, "It doesn't matter to you, does it?"

Already, she could see the distance growing in his expression. "Of course not. Why should it?"

Though he'd said the words she had hoped to hear, she didn't believe him. His heart wasn't in them. Valerie felt like she'd been punched in the stomach, the wind knocked out of her. Why *should* it make a difference? she asked herself, trying to understand. But no answer came.

"I've asked myself that very same question, Mr. Smythe." She turned to her brother and put her hand on his shoulder. She blinked hard as tears stung her eyes. "Reggie, I believe I'd like you to help me down the stairs after all. Would you mind?"

Reggie straightened, sensing his sister's distress. "I wouldn't mind at all." In a brave move, he scrunched his face into a horrible mask and stuck his tongue out at Thomas.

Valerie turned her back to the man and left him standing near the railing. This time, though, she didn't feel an urge to turn around and look at him. In less than a month, her knight's armor had tarnished; her Roman god's feet had turned to clay.

Chapter Eleven

Valerie entered her cabin and pushed the door quietly shut, thankful she had a room separate from her parents. Leaning against it, she paused for a moment and struggled to catch her breath between the sobs that threatened to break through. It had taken all her willpower to sit through dinner with Thomas ignoring her. What had he been thinking the few times his eyes met hers? Probably about how he'd wasted the entire voyage on a cripple.

Her gaze skipped haphazardly around the room as she tried to steady her emotions. Valerie straightened and tugged at the back of her dress, all but ripping the buttons from the facing, until the bodice hung down around her waist.

"Damn," she cursed. "Forgot the bloody crinoline." Valerie undid the laces and let the steel cage drop, the dress following closely thereafter. She grabbed her cane from where it was propped against the wall and stepped out of the pile of clothing. Her foot caught in the folds of the fabric and she tripped. Valerie stumbled to the floor and didn't even bother to try and get up. She lay down and gave in to her sorrow.

A few moments later, Lucy appeared at the doorway between their rooms, carrying an oil lamp. "I thought I heard ye come in," she began, her voice trailing off at the sight of Valerie in a heap on the floor, crying, her clothes twisted around her. Lucy put the lamp down, bent over and helped the young woman to her feet.

"What's troublin' ye, child? I've never seen ye carryin' on so." Lucy used the corner of her robe to wipe away Valerie's tears.

"I'm all right, Lucy. Please. Leave me be." Valerie sat on the edge of the bed, tears still streaming down her cheeks.

"I'll not leave while ye're in such a sorry state." Lucy put her hand on the young woman's shoulder, stooping to look her in the eye. "It was that young Mr. Smythe, wasn't it? He's the reason ye're so distressed." Lucy studied her charge. "What'd he do to ye?"

Valerie quickly glanced up. "Nothing."

Lucy narrowed her eyes. "Ye answered much too fast fer me to believe ye."

"Please, Lucy, just go to bed. I really don't want to talk about it right now."

"Can I get ye some nice hot tea, then? It'll be good for what ails ye."

"No, thank you," Valerie whispered, her throat tight. "I'd just like to get some rest now. We can talk in the morning, all right?"

Lucy straightened. "I understand, girl. I'll leave ye be if ye promise ye'll call me if I can be helpin'."

Valerie nodded, wiping her eyes. "Thank you." As Lucy turned to leave, she called after her, "Lucy, please don't say anything to Mama. I don't want to bother her with this." She forced a smile. "Besides, I'm certain I'll be fine in the morning."

"Well, if that's what ye want. But I can't help feelin' yer mother'd like to comfort ye."

"Perhaps when her health is better," Valerie offered, staring after Lucy as she left the room.

As soon as Lucy was gone, Valerie laid down on the narrow bed. She felt terrible and was furious with herself for feeling that way. She took a deep breath to steady her nerves and was stuck in the side by a corset stay. Turning this way and that, Valerie wrestled the ties until it finally loosened. She pulled it off and threw it down on the floor with her other clothes. "Well, that's the first and last time I wear a bloody corset for some man," she vowed.

How could I have been such an idiot? she asked herself, embarrassed beyond words, a tight knot growing in her stomach. She should have known how he would react to her disability. Why had she been foolish enough to believe he would be different from any of the other men she had ever met? For heaven's sake, in her vivid imagination, they were already wed and had a full brood of offspring. The old gypsy's words echoed in her mind – *a love that'll break your heart.* How could she have known?

Her heart hurt, deep down inside her chest. Valerie rolled over and started to hug the pillow against her when her arm brushed against something. She felt the familiar shape as she pulled it out. It was the romance novel containing the story of Caroline and Damon. *This* was what was responsible for making her hope for a love of her own. With a disgusted sneer, Valerie threw the book, slamming the volume against the wall. Well, there'll be no more of that, she swore silently, steadily retreating inward. She would use this trip to further her knowledge so her teaching could be enhanced.

And as for love? Well, she'd not put herself into such a vulnerable position again.

Chapter Twelve

The morning sun was just beginning to work its way into the small porthole window of the cabin when Valerie was awakened by the cries of the sailors on the deck above.

"Land ho!" one shouted.

"Italy!" another answered.

Valerie tossed back the covers, grabbed her cane, and hurried to the window. Balancing on one foot so she was standing on tiptoe, she could see of the sandy shoreline in the distance. She smiled broadly, her heart pounding with excitement.

It would be good to get off this ship, considering what had transpired between Thomas and herself the night before. She had tossed and turned all night, finally falling asleep when the black night sky began to turn indigo on the horizon.

She continued to stare at the shore without seeing. Earlier this morning, in that hazy place between waking and sleep, Valerie had come to realize that it wasn't Thomas' reaction that had bothered the most. No, instead it was her wanton response to his touch and the feelings it had invoked inside of her. To think she'd just let him kiss and fondle her like that. She shook her head. And she hadn't even tried to stop him. Worse yet, she had to admit that she'd enjoyed his attention. Guilt rippled through Valerie's being and clutched at her heart.

She pushed herself away from the window, forcing the tension away, promising to react differently if ever a similar situation presented itself.

Valerie took her brown traveling suit down from its hook and rapped on Lucy's door. There wasn't time to feel sorry for herself right now. Besides, it wasn't an emotion she cared to be experiencing. Today, she was finally going to set foot in Italy, the land of ancient peoples and ancient civilizations. The land of Pompeii.

* * *

"Let me help you, Miss Brooks," Johnny offered. He held his arm out and Valerie took hold of it. Gently, he assisted her in climbing over the lowered railing and onto the wooden ramp leading from the ship to the shore. Reggie ran up behind them.

"Wait for me, Val!" He tossed a small canvas bag over her head. The bag landed with a loud thud on the walk.

"Careful!" she scolded, ducking just in time. "What have you got in there? Cannonballs?"

Reggie sighed impatiently. "Of course not. Everyone knows cannonballs are much too heavy to be carried around for everyday use." He placed one hand on the rail and, before Johnny could help, vaulted over the side and landed next to his belongings.

"What's in it then?" Valerie asked, straightening her skirt.

"Rope and knots and wax and some pitch and -- "

Valerie raised a hand and laughed. "Never mind. I get the picture." She started to disembark the plank when she caught sight of Thomas Smythe heading down the walkway. Well, he was the last person she wanted to see! Valerie grabbed Reggie's arm and yanked him along as she started walking.

"Where's Mama and Papa?" she asked, scanning the crowd at the end of the plank. Lucy was busy saying goodbye to her dearest Johnny, the first beau Valerie could remember her ever having. "Have you seen them, Reg?"

"Miss Brooks. How nice to see you today."

She winced. She could hardly avoid a direct greeting out in public. Valerie stopped and turned slowly around. She smiled, a hard glint in her eye. "Pity I can't say the same thing about you."

"I beg your pardon?" Thomas asked, a shocked expression on his face.

Good. He'd been caught off guard. "I believe you heard me quite plainly." She hit her cane hard on the wood walk beneath their feet, then raised it up between them. The carved Jack-in-the-Woods head stared threateningly down at Thomas, its eyes slanted in an evil grin. "We may have to travel together, but if you don't keep your distance, you'll get to know Jack here intimately." Valerie looked him in the eye. "Do we understand each other?"

Thomas straightened, an angry flush covering his cheeks. "I don't see what you're so upset about. After all, *you* lied to *me*, you know."

"Be honest just for a moment, Mr. Smythe. Are you going to say you'd have been interested in me if you'd known I was crippled?" She looked him in the eye. "Well?"

He shifted his weight from one foot to the other. "I see Father up ahead. I have to go now."

Valerie stepped in front of him. "I asked you a question and I believe I deserve an answer."

"You want an answer, do you?" Thomas snorted, shaking his head. "What do you think? Of course I wouldn't have been interested. You may be quite lovely, Valerie Brooks, with your bright green eyes and shining auburn hair." He lifted a hand as if to touch the curls, then let it drop to his side. "But the simple truth of the matter is that crippled foot of yours makes you, how shall I put it -- undesirable." He shrugged his shoulders. "That's just the way it is."

Valerie looked past him and out into the distance, suddenly grateful for the cool Mediterranean breeze. Tall cypress trees dotted the rocky landscape above the shore, bowing away from the direction of the ship as the wind caught their upper branches. She took a deep breath, tears stinging her eyes. "Thank you for your honesty, Mr. Smythe."

He nodded and walked on. Valerie stood motionless for a moment longer as the crowd of passengers pushed past her. A single tear trailed down her cheek. "Thank you very much."

Chapter Thirteen

The long winding road leading from the Bay of Naples inland was well rutted and strewn with rocks of every size. The carriages carrying the Brooks and Smythe families moved slowly, the drivers taking their time, choosing the proper path in order not to throw a wheel.

Valerie peered out the small window. The grey dirt of the road contrasted sharply with the cool green of the surrounding countryside. She fell into an almost hypnotic trance as the landscape unfurled before her, watching in silence as the coaches moved steadily past groves of silvery olive trees, arbors of grape vines, and scattered ruins of places whose names were long forgotten by modern man. Even Pompeii had ceased to be called by its Roman name for a while and was referred to by the locals as only *La Civita*, The City. It wasn't until the excavations began in earnest earlier this century that the original name had been rediscovered.

She caught her breath as her gaze shifted to the horizon. There, in the distance, loomed Mount Vesuvius. What remained of its peak was surrounded by low lying clouds; the sky near it, gray and misty.

"Look, Papa," Valerie whispered. She gestured toward the mountain. "It's Vesuvius. Isn't it magnificent?"

Frederick glanced in the direction she was pointing. "Yes, quite lovely," he mumbled before returning his attention to the account books he had brought along.

How could he be so flippant when presented with such a beautiful sight? "Papa, you didn't even look," she gently scolded.

"Valerie, your father is busy. You mustn't bother him right now." Jacqueline shifted on the hard wood seat and straightened her hat. "Tell me, how are things going with you and young Mr. Smythe?"

Valerie quickly glanced at her mother, who was studying her much too intently. Would Mama be able to tell she had been kissed and -- and touched? She fought to school her expression into one of mild disdain, ignoring the guilt that still nagged at her.

In what she imagined to be an uninterested gesture, she shrugged. "I decided I didn't really care for him after all."

Jacqueline raised an eyebrow. "Really now? What happened to the 'knight in shining armor'? You had me convinced he was the man of your dreams, Val. Why, I even began to wonder if we'd be planning a wedding after we left Italy."

Valerie frowned. She had actually thought the same thing herself. Until last night, that is. "Remember the fortune teller, Mama?" she asked quietly.

"You mean at Hazel's?"

She looked at Lucy and Reggie out of the corner of her eye. Good. Lucy was asleep and Reggie was busy trying to remember how to tie the sailor's knots Johnny had taught him. "Do you recall what she said?"

Jacqueline's cheerful expression fell. "You mean 'a love that will break your heart'?

Valerie nodded and returned to studying the countryside. "Who'd have thought she would be so accurate?"

"I'm so sorry, dear. If only I hadn't been so ill with the *mal de mer*, I would have known." Jacqueline leaned forward and squeezed her daughter's hand. "You should have come and told me earlier."

"Why don't ye tell yer mother what happened?" Lucy's eyes flew open. "Ye promised me ye would."

Valerie jumped. "For heaven's sake, Lucy, you scared me half to death. I thought you were sleeping."

Lucy waved her hand. "Just restin' my eyes, I was."

Jacqueline looked from Lucy to Valerie. "What are you both talking about? What happened?"

"Nothing really, Mama." Valerie forced a smile. Letting go of her mother's hand, she leaned her head back against the cushioned board behind her. "Lucy happened into my room last night when I was upset, that's all." She shrugged again and held her hands up in the air. "What can I say? Mr. Smythe turned out to be nothing like I had imagined."

"She came to her cabin in tears, she did," Lucy fussed. "Why, I never seen the girl carry on so."

"I want to know exactly what he did to make you cry," Jacqueline demanded. "Frederick, are you listening to this?"

Valerie shot Lucy a disgusted look. Lucy smiled back, her eyes wide and innocent as a newborn babe's. Could the woman ever keep a secret? She sighed and answered her own unspoken question. Only when it suited her.

Frederick nodded from behind the bank ledger he was still studying. "Yes, dear."

"Frederick, this is serious. Mr. Smythe may have compromised our daughter."

Frederick slammed the book down on his lap. "What are you talking about?" he bellowed, thumping his fist on top of the volume. "I'll have him flogged!"

Valerie shook her head. Papa only listened when it suited him. "You're jumping to conclusions, Papa."

"No, he's not," Reggie piped up as he tossed the rope aside. He was obviously more interested in the conversation now that it had taken a turn against his sister. "I saw it! He kissed you!"

"He kissed you?" Jacqueline shrieked. She pulled off one of her gloves and fanned her face. "Thomas Smythe forced himself on you? What else did he do?"

"Mama, please."

"Don't 'Mama, please' me, young lady. How could you have allowed yourself to be placed into such a position?" She fell back against her seat and the glove went limp in her lap. "Well? Aren't you going to answer any of my questions?"

Frederick and Lucy leaned toward Valerie, elbows on knees, waiting for an explanation. Valerie looked from one to the other as her mother came forward as well. Reggie was the only one indifferent to her plight. Having had his say, he once again returned his attention to tying knots. She glanced out the window. Was there no escape from these people she called family?

"It was just a peck, on the cheek," she lied. For heaven's sake, if they really knew what had happened she'd probably be forced to wed the hateful man. "And it was only last night. Reggie came to help me down the stairs for dinner. That's when he saw Thomas kiss me." She watched her brother as she spoke, hoping he'd keep out of the conversation. She didn't need any more of his help at all.

"I certainly hope that's why you decided you didn't like him any more. The nerve of that man." Jacqueline fumed. She looked at her husband. "It's our fault, Freddie. We're much too free with the girl."

"Well, I'll be having a talk with Smythe about his son's behavior." Frederick picked up his ledger again. "And I want you to stay away from him from now on, Valerie. He's apparently only after one thing."

"Frederick! How can you be so insensitive?"

"Well, it's true, dear. I was a young man once myself. I know how they are." He returned his attention to Valerie and stared hard at her over the top of his reading glasses. "Is that understood, young lady?"

Valerie let out a sigh of relief. Thank goodness her family was more forward in their thinking than most. They could have decided right then and there to lock her up for the remainder of the trip if they had so desired. "I understand, Papa. I promise it won't happen again."

* * *

"Look! There it is!" Reggie yelled.

Valerie awoke from the light sleep she had fallen into. Earlier, the carriage had finally hit semi-smooth ground and the sway of the vehicle had rocked her to the place of dreams. She rubbed her eyes, then peered out the window. There it was. The city of the ancient Romans. The city of Pompeii.

"Beautiful," she whispered. In the near distance, the ruins themselves seemed to emerge from the very ground they had been built on. She knew the site had been excavated off and on for several centuries now. Those areas long ago exposed were most likely the ones covered in thick vines and weeds. Tumbling portions of a stone fence, the original paint now peeling and almost indiscernible, sprang up from the earth. Scattered on either side of the road were fragments of fluted columns, some with their decorative capitals still intact. Graceful Ionic, with tight swirls forming all four corners, were the most dominant. Simple Doric, straight and square, also appeared within the architectural mix. Valerie stared hard until her eyes watered, impressing the images on her mind.

As they approached the main entrance gate, they came upon the Necropolis, just as she had seen it illustrated in her history books. Large stone mausoleums, as far as Valerie could see, surrounded the town. Built of cool white marble, they now sat in stoic silence, illuminated to a soft orange by the setting sun. Here and there, a bench beckoned from a grotto to passersby. Come. Rest your weary bones and offer up a prayer for the dead.

Valerie caught her breath as the carriage passed through the stone and iron gate. There, to her left and near the remains of a small building, stood a statue of Dionysos, the god of wine. Balancing on the balls of his feet, he held high a goat skin and gestured as if he were pouring the entire contents down his throat. She studied the small structure next to it and decided the local vintner must have owned it, for he would have been most interested in invoking the help of this particular god.

"Look over here, Val!" Reggie motioned out his window.

She leaned over her father. There, lying in the dust thrown up by the carriage, were the cast images of several people, each preserved in the throes of dying. In one grouping, she could make out the forms of a man, a woman, and a small child. The man was raised up on one elbow, obviously still trying to save his family from the ash and pumice that had pelted the city. Near this group, a solitary woman laid, her head on her arms. She appeared to be only sleeping, waiting to be awakened. Valerie wondered how would she have reacted if in the same situation. Would she have died so peacefully?

Though Sir David had explained the process, she had no idea how life-like the statues would be. The folds of their clothing, the horrified expression on their faces as they must have realized what their fate would be, were exactly detailed. Valerie sat back, her eyes damp, a new respect forming for the large mountain in the distance. The god of the volcano had spoken here almost eighteen hundred years ago, sending thousands of people to their deaths.

Valerie was shaken from her thoughts as the carriage pulled to a jerky halt. Reggie threw open the door and toppled out and onto the ground. He jumped up, ran over to the remains of a stone house and began to climb up the wall.

Sir David was right behind him and pulled the boy down by his collar. "See here, now. You mustn't be doing that. You'll get hurt or damage the building."

"How can I hurt this place if the volcano didn't?" he asked, his eyes wide.

Smythe cleared his throat. Frederick walked up next to him. "What's the problem here?" he asked.

"The boy shouldn't be climbing all over the structures. Some of them may be unsafe," Smythe explained, his eyes never leaving Reggie.

"Run along, Reg, and help your sister out of the carriage. I need to talk to Sir David in private for a moment."

As Reggie scurried off, Frederick turned to his companion.

"What is it, Frederick?" Smythe asked.

"Your son seems to have put my daughter into a compromising position while on ship."

"Wh -- what?" Smythe sputtered. He rubbed the mutton chop whiskers on his cheeks with a nervous hand. "But I told him -- he wouldn't -- "

"Well, he did. And I want you to keep him away from her." Frederick straightened to his full six feet three inches and glared down at Smythe. "Do we have an understanding here?"

"Of -- of course, Frederick. I'm so sorry. I certainly hope this won't affect our business dealings." Smythe's voice had turned to a desperate plea.

Frederick extended his hand. "I don't see why it should. Business is business."

"Yes indeed. Indeed it is." Smiling, Smythe shook the other man's hand. "I know what I can do to help regain your peace of mind. I shall send Thomas on ahead to Naples. I've a friend there who can keep an eye on him."

"I think that'd be best, considering the situation," Frederick conceded. Both men turned to Valerie and Jacqueline as they approached.

Jacqueline looked at her husband, askance. "It's all taken care of," he explained. "Thomas will not be staying here with us."

Valerie felt as if five hundred pounds were lifted off her shoulders. If Thomas were to stay, she'd probably be guarded every moment by either Lucy or Mama. With him gone, though, she could explore Pompeii freely. And she knew exactly where she would start once he left the site. The City of the Dead.

Chapter Fourteen

"Sir David. Welcome back to Pompeii." A short, robust-looking man approached the visitors. He shook Smythe's hand, pumping it up and down vigorously.

Valerie peered over her mother's shoulder and decided this must be Guiseppe Fiorelli, the man in charge of the expedition. The man responsible for bringing the dead back to life. She had seen lithographs of him working amongst the ruins, and had come to expect someone much taller and younger. She laughed to herself. Artists always did seem to have a habit of subtly changing reality.

"Good to see you, Guiseppe. This is Sir Frederick Brooks. He'll be extending the loan to keep this little operation of ours running." He smiled. "If he likes what he sees, that is." He waved his arm behind him. "And this, of course, is his family -- Mrs. Brooks, Valerie, and Reggie."

Fiorelli bowed low. "So happy to make your acquaintances. Would you like a tour of the site before you get settled?"

Valerie stepped forward. "That would be just wonderful."

Jacqueline cleared her throat. Valerie glanced at her mother who was looking none too pleased at the moment. She should have asked permission. "May we go, Mama?"

Reggie jumped up and down. "I want to see the bodies. All of them." He tugged on Fiorelli's sleeve. "Are there any bones or skulls lying around? I'd love to see that too."

He laughed and patted the boy on the shoulder. "Maybe we can find a few for your inspection."

Jacqueline sighed. "I suppose it would be all right, but don't be gone too long." She looked at the sky. "It'll be dark soon."

Fiorelli whistled and motioned with his hands to the workers. Several of them quickly grabbed three chairs fastened to long poles. Reaching Valerie, two of them squatted down, balancing one of the seats on their backs. Fiorelli started to lend her a hand, when Thomas appeared, helping her instead.

Valerie froze just as she was stepping into the vehicle. "What are you doing here?"

He smiled. "Just coming to say goodbye, that's all. It seems your father would prefer I be removed from the site." He shrugged as she finished climbing into the chair. "I'd rather be in the city anyway."

"See here now!" Frederick bellowed from across the way. "Unhand that girl!"

Valerie and Thomas both turned in the direction of Frederick's voice. Thomas quickly pulled his hand to his side and stepped away from her. Dear Papa. He'd always be her only knight in shining armor from now on.

"Well, goodbye, then," Valerie bade. She squared her shoulders and opened her parasol. She really was better off without the man. Her shoulders drooped a little, though, when she heard the carriage door slam shut and the driver call to the horses.

"Are you all settled now, Signorina Brooks?"

"Si." She swallowed hard. "I'm more than ready."

"Buono." Fiorelli climbed into his own chair after securing Reggie into another one. "Are you certain you won't join us?" he called to Jacqueline and Frederick.

Frederick waved his hand. "Plenty of time for that later. Smythe and I need to talk business."

"And I need to see to the unpacking," Jacqueline added as the workers rose, carrying the chairs with Fiorelli, Valerie and Reggie in them.

The trio began their explorations in the opposite direction the Brooks' and Smythe's had arrived from. Heading down the dusty main street of town, bits and pieces of what remained of the houses yet to be excavated poked up through the ground. Here and there, painted finishes could still be seen. Red, orange, yellow, blue, green, and a great deal of red. The city must have been beautiful in its day. Valerie sighed. Even a few touches of gold leaf glinted in the waning sunlight.

"What's that over there?" she asked, pointing to a large building almost totally unearthed. The entrance was roped off and the newly installed wood door closed tight.

"Uh - a simple palace of pleasure." Fiorelli cleared his throat. "Nothing you need to be concerned with."

Valerie looked over at him and shook her head. "A what?"

"Oh, you know. A brothel."

"A brothel!" she repeated. "Really? Can we go in there?" She leaned forward as the men continued to walk, struggling to interpret the writing that covered the walls. "Mamia - is - good - for - sex. Only - twenty - *sesterces*? Is that right?" Her eyes grew wide as she realized what she had just read. For heaven's sake. Did people really write such things for the public to read? "I don't believe it," she murmured.

"You read Latin quite good, Signorina. I'm most impressed. But, perhaps you should keep your eyes to yourself until we leave this block of buildings. That inscription was mild compared to some." He gestured to the area around them. "Most of the brothels in town are here, as near as we can tell. And," he looked at her before continuing, "I'm sorry, but ladies are not allowed in them."

* * *

With the unpacking done and dinner long over, the small group had finally settled in for the night and rested now near a fire.

"Would you like to hear a ghost story?" Fiorelli asked Reggie.

"Yes, sir!" He sat up straight as a board. "Tell us now!"

"You see, when I took over the excavation of Pompeii, there were rumors milling about." He stared hard at the boy. "Rumors that the ancients were rising from the dead."

"Impossible!" Reggie slammed his fist down on his thigh as he had seen his papa do a hundred times before.

Valerie covered her mouth, suppressing a giggle. "Please go on, Signore. What made the people believe this?"

Fiorelli smiled and pulled a cigar out of his jacket pocket. He lit a twig in the fire and held it to the tip. After puffing hard enough to create a sizable cloud around his head, he continued. "Seems an old woman keeps appearing from out of the strangest places. I've never seen her myself but, one day, she'll be in the tombs. Another, in the bakery." He leaned forward and tapped the ashes from the cigar. "And she's almost always seen wearing the clothing of the Romans."

"Now, Guiseppe, that doesn't prove anything, does it?" Smythe asked, joining the conversation.

"No, but the workers are superstitious. They tell me she gives them the evil eye. They go around making the sign against the devil all day long." He held up his right hand with just his forefinger and little finger extended. "Like this."

Reggie held his hand up in front of him and tried to form the gesture. "Look. I did it."

"So you did. According to the men, there have been other signs, besides the old woman," Fiorelli began. "Some of the statues we've cast have turned up missing. Why in the world would someone want one? The locals believe they came to life and walked away. And another thing -- "

Fiorelli stopped talking as a low growl rose up from deep within the earth. Everyone froze and stared at each other, uncertain what to do. The rumble grew louder. The ground began to shake and list. A large boulder tumbled from the top of a pile of rocks and rolled near the group.

Valerie jumped to her feet, clutching her cane so tightly her hands went numb.

"What's happening?" she yelled over the sound. It felt as if the very earth was going to open up beneath her. She glanced about frantically as the ground trembled again, rumbling with a long, low pain.

Jacqueline reached for her daughter and hugged her to her breast. After a few moments, the shaking finally subsided.

"Well, my friends, in case you haven't figured it out, that was an earthquake," Fiorelli explained, his voice quiet. "We've been experiencing them off and on here for the last few months. I'm beginning to fear the site will be buried before we're able to finish our work."

"Perhaps a bad investment then?" Frederick offered.

"How can all of you behave as if nothing has happened?" Valerie asked. She held her hands tightly together to stop the shaking. "We could have been killed."

"There was no chance of that. It wasn't a terrible one." He looked pointedly at Frederick. "We need the money so we can expedite the digging in case a major quake was to strike."

"I've never felt an earthquake before," Valerie whispered.

Fiorelli laughed quietly. He waved his hand in a wide sweeping motion. "Rest assured. It was nothing like what was experienced by the former inhabitants of this town on that long ago morning in 79 AD when Vesuvius erupted. I can guarantee you that."

Valerie leaned forward, crossing her arms over her knees. She looked off into the shadows cast by the waning fire and fought the urge to pinch herself. She was really here. Really in Pompeii. She took a deep breath and relaxed. "How much of the city do you think you've uncovered so far?" she asked.

"Well," Fiorelli began, "I'd say about one third."

"Only a third?" Valerie echoed.

Smythe chuckled. "You must forgive the girl, Guiseppe. She's most inquisitive. I'm afraid Brooks here lets her study the subject."

"So, that's why she knew so much about the site. And knew Latin as well. Best pronunciation I've ever heard." Fiorelli smiled at Valerie. "I can't say I see anything wrong with that. As far as I'm concerned, a woman with a mind is a pleasant sight to behold. Especially one as lovely as yourself, Signorina."

Valerie's expression became guarded. Thomas had spoken to her so. Of course, Mr. Fiorelli was much older than she and he did know about her foot, she reasoned. Besides, as much as she may feel the need to, she probably couldn't go around suspecting every man for the rest of her life. She relaxed a little bit more. "Thank you, Signore."

Reggie yawned and stretched, setting off a reaction around the fire. Valerie had no sooner than yawned herself when Lucy appeared from the shadows. "Off to bed with the both of ye," she shooed. "The men have yer tents ready. There'll be plenty more nights to sit around and talk."

Valerie stood without arguing. She had to admit she was tired and longed to be out of the stiff corset that seemed to find every opportunity to poke her. She and Reggie followed closely behind Lucy as she led them to their sleeping quarters - small houses constructed of canvas, stones, and stripped logs.

Lucy opened the flap to Reggie's tent. "Please let me stay up a bit longer, Lucy," he begged.

"Don't ye be rollin' yer big brown eyes at me like that. Off with ye." She gave him a gentle push.

After Reggie was settled, Lucy escorted Valerie into her quarters. "Let me help ye with that, miss," she offered. Valerie turned around and the older woman began unbuttoning her dress. Next, she helped her out of the crinoline, then the corset, leaving Valerie in her chemise.

"Oh, Lucy, just think about where we are." Valerie hugged her arms about her, rubbing away the goose bumps.

"I know exactly where we are. In the middle of nowhere," she sniffed. "Not sure I like it, either."

Valerie turned around and smiled, a devilish look in her eye. "You said the same thing about the ship. That is, until you met the steward. I think you're only upset because you had to leave him behind."

Lucy puffed herself up like a pigeon. "I beg yer pardon?"

"I think you heard me quite well." Valerie pulled back the rough blanket and sat down on the edge of the simple cot. "Do you love him, Lucy?"

"I don't think that'd be any of yer business," Lucy replied haughtily. She folded Valerie's dress and placed it into her trunk at the foot of the bed.

Valerie stuck out her bottom lip and rested her chin on the back of her hand. "You're not going to tell me, are you?"

"Like I said -- "

"I know, I know. It's none of my business." She lay back on the cot with a frown, dropping her cane to the floor next to it. Valerie could see she wouldn't get any information out of the servant tonight. "Good night, Lucy," she bade, stretching.

"Sweet dreams," Lucy whispered with a laugh. She carried the lantern out of the tent and into her own next door as Valerie drifted off to sleep.

* * *

"Stop it!" Valerie twisted her body first to the left, then to the right. She was surrounded by people, all clothed in the robes of the ancient Romans. They poked at her with long sharp fingers. The jewels they wore glinted in the sunlight, blinding her.

"No!" she screamed.

"What's the matter, child?" Lucy shook her hard. "Come to yer senses!"

Valerie continued to struggle, shoving Lucy away from her, as heavy iron chains were clamped around her feet. She tripped and felt herself falling, falling. For an eternity she was suspended in the air, never touching the ground.

"Valerie! Wake up!" It was Jacqueline this time. "You're having a nightmare."

"Mama?" Valerie asked, her voice hoarse. She pushed herself up. A fine layer of perspiration covered her body and her chemise clung to her. Jacqueline pushed back the stray locks of hair that had escaped from her daughter's thick braid.

"It's all right, dear. It was just a bad dream."

"But they came for me, Mama." Valerie wiped at her eyes. "They wanted to take me away."

"Who did?"

"The people. They hated me," Valerie's voice broke as she began to sob. "It was the Romans. They were going to kill me."

Jacqueline pulled Valerie to her, resting her daughter's head against her breast. "I understand now. You spent too much time in the ruins this afternoon. Your imagination is acting up." She stroked her daughter's head. "No one is going to take you away from us. You're safe now. It was just a dream."

But the chains had felt so real, so heavy and rough against her skin. Valerie shivered, then began to relax as Jacqueline hummed a lullaby, the same one she used to sing when Valerie was a small child. *It was just a dream*, Valerie repeated to herself. She took a deep breath and closed her eyes. Just a dream.

Chapter Fifteen

Valerie dozed fitfully the rest of the night, the disturbing images hanging in the darkness around her. She rose early the next morning, aching and tired. Did she dare begin exploring the ruins on her own? What if Mama was right? What if the nightmare was a reaction to everything she had seen so far?

She sighed and poured water from a heavy clay pitcher into the small bowl next to her bed. She splashed her face, neck, and arms. You're being a goose, she told herself as she twisted her braid into a tight chignon, fastening it into place with a jet and marcasite comb.

She leaned across the bed and pushed her trunk open. Digging through the contents, Valerie yanked out her corset. She wrinkled her nose and tossed it aside as she retrieved a navy blue blouse and matching skirt folded beneath it. At least the dark color wouldn't show dirt as easily if she were allowed to help with the digging. She stood and dressed, buttoning the high collar shirt and pulling on the long skirt.

Valerie took a step and almost tripped over the length of the garment. Without a crinoline, there was an excess of material hanging around her feet. She thought for a moment; then, remembering the peasant women she'd seen along the road, pulled the skirt up between her legs and tucked it into the waistband. Carefully, she positioned the sides until her stockinged legs were discreetly covered, then left the tent.

Frederick and Jacqueline were already up and enjoying a hot cup of tea near the fire. The smell of sausage frying reached Valerie's nose and her mouth watered. "Good morning," she bade.

Jacqueline glanced up and her expression froze. "What have you done to your skirt?" she asked, aghast.

Valerie shrugged. "It's something I saw the Italian women do. It's so they can walk easier. I thought I'd be able to maneuver around the site better like this."

"Where's yer crinoline?" Lucy ran up behind her, shaking a finger. "Ye'll not be paradin' around here with yer ankles showin'."

"Mama?" Valerie pleaded.

Jacqueline presented her back to her daughter. "Go dress yourself, child. If you hope to spend any time outside of that tent today, you'll come back properly clothed."

Valerie shook her head, tears stinging her eyes. Didn't they understand how difficult it'd be for her to try and manage her skirts over the uneven terrain? Of course, she could use one of Fiorelli's chairs, but that would definitely limit her access to the site. Then, a thought came to her and she hid a smile. "All right. I'll go put the silly thing on." Valerie turned and let Lucy lead her back to the tent. She hoisted the skirt while the other woman fastened the crinoline into place.

"Lucy, I've decided I don't want any breakfast after all. I'm going to begin exploring right away," she said, smoothing her clothes into place.

"Are ye sure ye should be goin' about today? What about them dreams ye had last night?" Lucy asked, worry lining her face.

"Oh, now, I can't be a goose forever. It was just a dream, after all." She tapped her cane on the compacted dirt floor. "Besides, when else will I ever get such a chance to see and touch ruins as old as these? I can't let a nightmare scare me away, can I?"

"Well, I think ye should stay a while. Ye really should eat somethin'." But before Lucy could present any further arguments, Valerie grabbed a hunk of bread left on her nightstand from last night, a canteen of water, and was out the door, her skirt stirring up a cloud of dust as she walked away from the camp.

Valerie picked her way slowly over the raised stepping stones that allowed foot traffic to cross one of the ancient streets and made her way to the other side. Once out of sight, she ducked behind the remains of a wall and removed the crinoline. Tucking her skirt back between her legs, she smiled triumphantly. "Bloody contraption", she swore as she pushed it out of the way with her cane. She turned around and, locating the iron and stone gate she had come through yesterday, she passed through its portal and returned to the City of the Dead.

Valerie stepped into the middle of the road and stopped. In the bright light of day, every detail revealed by the archeologist's fine brushes was visible on the stone and marble tombs. Carved friezes of alternating acanthus leaf patterns, images of the gods and goddesses in their finest raiment, and busts that must represent those laid to rest within, adorned the alcoves built into the sides of the structures. Slowly, she turned in a circle, wondering where to start first.

To her right, pillared mausoleums surrounded her with fountains long dead. She ran a hand gently over the carved braided stone edge of one and scooped up a handful of dust from the basin. Slowly, Valerie let the dirt sift through her open fingers and blow away with the wind. Near another tomb was an outline in the ground of a small garden planted all those centuries ago. Rocks were laid neatly in several rows with statues and seating areas set between them. Here, a visitor could relax and spend time with thoughts and prayers for the deceased.

Valerie took a step forward, then stopped. What was that sound? Was someone walking behind her? She listened for another moment. No, it didn't sound like walking. It sounded more like someone was dragging something. She smirked. The little lizard was always trying to scare her. Expecting to find Reggie sneaking up on her, she turned around. Her heart jumped as she stumbled backward. Not ten feet away was an old woman, shriveled and bent with age, clutching her tattered shawl tightly to her breast. She was shuffling toward Valerie.

"*Buon giorno*," the woman called, her voice low and raspy. She coughed and a cloud of dust flew up around her. "*Puo aiutarmi, per favore*?" She took a few more steps, sidling up closer to Valerie. "*Vorrei bere*."

"Uh, *mi dispiace*. I-I'm sorry. My Italian is not very good. Do you speak Latin?" Valerie asked, not certain what to do. She glanced about her. It was getting hot. The workers must have left to eat or something. There was no one else around.

"Ah, you *Inglese*?"

"*Si, Inglese*." Valerie gripped her cane tighter.

"Will you help me?" The woman pointed to herself. "Water, *per favore*?" She motioned to the canteen Valerie had slung over her shoulder.

Valerie nodded and let her breath out slowly. The poor woman only wanted something to quench her thirst. She handed the container to her. "*Mi chiamo* Valerie. Valerie Brooks."

"Pencia." The old woman wiped her mouth with the back of her hand, leaving a dirty streak across her cheek. Her skin was like tanned leather, lined and tough, and reminded Valerie of the gypsy at Hazel's. "You been nice to me. I tell your fortune."

Valerie shook her head. It was as if the woman had read her mind! She raised a hand in protest. "*Grazie*, but no. I've had enough of fortune tellers to last me two lifetimes."

But before she could argue any further, Pencia grabbed Valerie's raised hand. First, she looked at the back of the younger woman's hand, then the other side. Satisfied, she spit into Valerie's palm and rubbed it around with her thumb. "You never know what fate throw your way."

Valerie grimaced.

"There's magic in saliva, I tell you." Pencia squinted and turned Valerie's palm toward the sun. She pulled it closer to her eyes. "Ah, long life. You will live long time. But, young ladies always want to know amore. You the same?" she asked, a sparkle lighting up her brown eyes.

Valerie couldn't help but smile in return. "Si, amore," she answered quietly. "Tell me of love."

"Love," Pencia repeated. But, as she explored the criss-cross of lines and creases, the smile on her face began to fade. "I see you must travel to find your love." Her eyes met Valerie's. "Travel through the mists."

"The mists?" Valerie asked. She looked at her hand. Not one of the lines made any sense to her, but what had she really expected to see? "What do you mean? Where does it say that?"

Pencia shrugged. She squeezed Valerie's hand, then let it drop. "It not for me to tell. You know soon enough. Good luck on journey. I pray for you." Pencia smiled again. Her teeth were startlingly white against her tanned skin. "I pray to Venus, Goddess of Love."

"Venus?" Valerie shook her head, confused by what Pencia had said and confused even more by the woman's very presence. None of it made any sense at all.

Then, a sudden thought came to her. What if this old woman was one of the ancient ones Fiorelli had spoken of during his tales the night before? She pushed back the panic that was threatening to creep up from her stomach. For heaven's sake, Val, she scolded herself, it was only a ghost story.

Pencia started to shuffle past when Valerie touched the woman's arm. The woman felt light and frail, almost as if she weren't really quite there. "Wait. Can't you tell me more?"

Pencia waved a gnarled hand behind her and kept walking as Valerie let her hand drop. "You know soon enough," she repeated. "Soon enough." Her voice trailed off into a cackle of laughter as she disappeared into the glare of the sunlight.

Chapter Sixteen

Valerie watched Pencia walk away until her form was lost in the distance. She shook her head. What was becoming of her? Had she actually considered for a moment that this woman was from another time? Her imagination was definitely getting too far out of control these days. One of the ancient ones, indeed.

She pulled a small leather-bound notebook out of her skirt pocket and began to sketch the tomb in front of her. Rolling a gum eraser into a small ball, she dabbed at the charcoal until the image of the column had just the right amount of shading to look like the light was reflecting off the marble. Valerie smiled as she put the finishing touches on the drawing.

She was blowing away the excess charcoal dust when, suddenly, a deep rumble shook the ground where she stood. Valerie gripped her cane as the earth shivered around her. She stuffed the book back into her pocket. The ground began to shift and roll, creating brown and green waves. Thick clouds of dust blew up and obstructed her sight.

This quake was so much stronger than the one last night. She glanced frantically around. There, next to one of the tombs, was a small grotto. Moving quickly, she climbed into it, praying it would keep her safe from the quake.

Again, a deep vibration seemed to move from the very bowels of the earth and up toward the surface. The grotto shook violently and remnants of volcanic ash lodged in cracks and crevices fell down, choking her. Valerie put her hands over her head. The ground continued to move and shift violently, listing and rolling like the ocean she had just crossed. Everything solid appeared to become liquid. A column nearby toppled to the ground with a loud thud.

"Stop it!" she screamed as the ash fell more quickly. Then she heard it. Something snapped. She looked toward the noise. The roof of the grotto was cracking. Oh my God. I've got to get out of here, she thought.

Valerie started to move just as a heavy stone came tumbling down from the roof. It looked like it was going to miss her as it bounced off the wall of a nearby tomb. But, before she could react, the stone hit another wall and bounced again, hitting her hard on the head. Knocked unconscious, Valerie fell to the floor in a heap as ash and stone continued to come down in layers around her.

* * *

Christos Campanius Marcellus lay abed, scanning the new frescos that covered the walls of his room. The muted colorations and touches of gold were pleasing to him as his gaze moved from one erotic scene to the next. The deep red background was truly a passionate color and it was a brilliant idea the artist had, painting the progression of the seduction of a young virgin by Zeus. And what better place to paint it than his bedchamber?

He turned over onto his stomach. It was getting late in the day and he should be seeing about his business affairs, but the warmth of the woman next to him was too soft, too alluring to leave behind just yet. Her naked flesh curved around him and he felt his need growing again.

He nuzzled her neck and she laughed. "Christos, it is time I left. You know as well as I that the slaves will talk at the market."

"Damn the slaves," he murmured, taking a full round nipple into his mouth. "Eros has led me down this path," he murmured. "And I will see it fulfilled, Gravia."

The woman arched against him, wrapping her legs about his buttocks as he moved within her. "Oh, Christos," she sighed, "when will you make me an honest woman?"

"You know as well as I that there's no room for honesty in our relationship," he growled against her lips. Would he ever grow tired of her soft and yielding form? He could lose himself too easily in her welcoming embrace, but he knew that was exactly what Gravia had hoped to accomplish.

With one final thrust, she called out his name. "Christos, my love."

With a shudder, he lowered himself until he was laying tightly against her. Gently now, he kissed her lips. Spent from their lovemaking, he rolled over and stretched.

Gravia patted him on the arm, then rose and pulled her creamy white *stola* over her head. The fine wool garment fell into soft folds over her well-rounded figure. She cinched the waist with a belt made of heavy links of gold, a gift fashioned by Christos' own hand. "Will I see you tonight?" she asked as she finger combed her dark blonde hair.

Christos lay back onto the soft feather pillow, resting his head on his arm. "No, I don't think so."

"And why not?" she pouted. "I will miss not having you by my side in the morning."

"I've warned you before, Gravia. Don't get used to having me around." He ran his free hand through the thick tousle of black curls covering his head, his full lips set in a firm line.

Gravia opened her mouth to protest, but was cut short by a loud cry from the street. She hurried to the open window and looked below. "Christos, come see," she called.

"What is it?" he asked, rising wearily. "Another goat loose in the forum?"

"No, I do not think so. Ah, I see the cause." She pointed to the center of the crowd. "There. It is a woman." She leaned over, straining to get a closer look. "What are those ridiculous clothes she is wearing? The top is so tight and the skirt so full. Look how the material drags on the ground behind her. How can she move about? I have never seen one dressed so."

Christos nudged Gravia out of the way. He scanned the crowd until he saw the object of their attention. Just then, the woman in the street looked up and their eyes locked. All her emotion poured out to him in a silent plea for help. He continued to stare, unable to move, as those deep green orbs seared straight through to the depths of his soul. By the gods, it was the woman from his dreams, the ghostly spectre come to life.

He could place no name to this apparition with skin the color of apricots, eyes like emeralds, and brown hair that glinted burnished gold in the sun. But he remembered her just the same. "I am yours," she had said.

"Go home, Gravia," he whispered, his voice strained.

"What?"

"I said 'Go home'," he spoke louder this time, his eyes never leaving the prisoner's. It didn't even surprise him that this woman could hold him there, with only her eyes.

"I will go. But do not expect me to be waiting for you this evening. I believe I will go to Felix's dinner party. You may be interested in knowing he sent me an exclusive invitation." She watched him expectantly, waiting for some sign of jealousy. When he didn't even look at her, she turned and left the room, an angry frown creasing her brow.

Christos' concentration was broken when the crowd grabbed the woman by the shoulders and pushed her on. She stumbled, then got back up. They shouted, "Witch! Witch!"

A witch, eh? Had she enchanted his dreams? Cast a spell in the night while he slept? Is that why he had seen her in spirit before seeing her in the flesh? Christos yelled down to one of the bystanders. "Where are they taking her?"

"To the jail, I think," a man answered.

"Jail?"

"*Ita.* Yes. At least, that's what I heard someone say."

Christos grabbed a short white tunic and tossed it on. He knew he should wear his toga out on the streets, but there was no time to wait for the servants to position the folds just so. He had to get to her.

Quickly lacing on a pair of brown leather sandals, he rushed down the stairs, through the central atrium of the house, and out the front door. Once on the street, he knocked down a small child in his haste. He stopped and helped the girl to her feet, taking a moment to wipe away her tears. Then he continued on, following the crowd to the jail.

* * *

The last thing Valerie could remember was the violent earthquake. She remembered it shaking the grotto where she had gone for safety. She remembered the ceiling caving in around her. She even vaguely remembered she had been hit on the head, but there was no bump or pain.

But that's *all* she could remember. How did it come to be, then, that when she woke up, the ceiling was still intact? It didn't make any sense at all to her. And when she climbed down from the structure, the street around it was neat and tidy, not overgrown with vegetation as it had been when she'd started out this morning. The tombs were well tended, with fresh flowers placed in offering to the gods.

As she left the tomb, she became even more confused. And more than a little frightened. There were a few people standing nearby, dressed in flowing robes and togas of cream-colored linen and cotton. They immediately stopped talking when she had emerged and looked at her strangely, making that odd forked symbol with their fingers Signore Fiorelli had shown Reggie and her last night. The group began walking, cutting a wide path around her. When Valerie tried to speak to them, they hurried away. One of them ran ahead of her, shouting in - no, she couldn't believe what she was hearing – was it Latin? She followed them with her eyes as the people hurried toward the city.

She started to take a step, then froze. She stared straight ahead, eyes wide. The city! There it stood, Pompeii, in all its untouched glory. Every column and building was in perfect condition, the paint and stucco finishes well maintained. Even the iron gate was free of rust and looked to have a fresh coat of black paint over the metal. A fountain situated at the fork of the road in front of her flowed with fresh water and several children stood around it, laughing and splashing.

What had happened to the tumbled down ruins she'd been visiting only hours before? Where had they gone? How did they come to be replaced by this living and breathing town? For heaven's sake, was this another dream or had she died when the grotto collapsed and this was to be her eternal punishment? She placed a hand to her head as she felt the ground begin to spin. She took a deep breath and steadied herself. Well, she couldn't stand here all day. She had to find Papa. He'd know what to do. She reached into the grotto, retrieved her cane, and began to walk.

Valerie re-entered Pompeii through the massive stone columns that flanked the gates as a crowd of people began to gather around her.

"*Venefica*! Witch!" someone shouted. "Look at the strange dark robes she wears."

"We saw her climb out of the tomb. She was trying to raise the dead!" Somewhere in the mob, a small child began to cry.

"No!" Valerie screamed as a man grabbed her. "I don't understand. I'm not a witch! Stop it, please," she pleaded with him. He kicked her legs out from under her. She fell hard to the ground, gasping for air.

"Did not the senate of Rome counsel that we should turn from the menace of witches and sorcerers? Did they not say we should protect the State from their evil influences and magical spells?" He jabbed at Valerie with his toe before turning to face the crowd. "I say we put her in jail."

Valerie planted her cane firmly on the ground and pulled herself up. What had she done to deserve such treatment? Well, he could talk all he wanted about the senate, but there was absolutely no way she would go to jail. She looked around, hoping to find a way through the crowd. She had to get away and hide for a while, until she could figure out what had really happened to her.

The man turned to face her again. With a sneer, he took a step closer. Valerie held her cane out in front of her and swung it in a wide arc. It came down hard on the man's shoulder and he stumbled backward.

"*Obsecro.* Please. Let me go."

The man turned on her, his eyes narrowed, and ripped the cane from her grasp. He slammed it down over his thigh, breaking it in half. "Now let's see you do your magic without this." He threw the pieces down hard on the ground.

"What are you doing?" Valerie screamed. She fell to her knees and retrieved the fragments. Accusations flew around her. Struggling to her feet, she put her hands over her ears and began to shake all over. The same images that had disturbed her dreams just last night were materializing before her.

Another man came at her, brandishing shackles before him. Balancing on her good leg, Valerie kicked at him with her other foot. With little effort, he knocked her to the stone paved street. She cried out as a sharp rock ripped through her blouse and gouged her skin. A woman held her head down while the chains were clamped into place around her ankles. "Why are you doing this?" she cried.

The men yanked Valerie to her feet and gave her a little shove. Without a cane, she stumbled, catching her balance just before she fell. Someone laughed and threw a rotten pomegranate at her back, striking her squarely between the shoulders. Valerie spun around, teetering, and the crowd backed away a little. She scanned the dark eyes that bore into her. Everyone was caught up in the moment. There was no aid to be found here.

She looked past them. There was the statue of Dionysus she'd seen only yesterday, but the building next to it was completely intact. My God, how did I come to be in ancient Pompeii? Her head swam as the crowd closed in around her again.

The people circled Valerie as if she were a wild animal. They started moving and she stumbled again. She clutched her stomach. She couldn't catch her breath. Two men grabbed her by the arms just before she hit the ground, forcing her to move along or be trampled. Frantically, she looked about. Was there no one who could help? Mama? Papa? Signore Fiorelli?

That was when she saw him. The man in the window. Why had he seemed so disturbingly familiar to her in this strange and distant place? It was as if she should know him -- should know his name, where he lived, how he looked when he slept.

Perhaps it was only because his features were like the patrician busts she'd seen at the museum in London. Straight nose, full lips, heavy lidded eyes. She'd studied and sketched them all several times over until she felt as if she knew each and every person.

He looked down at her now and she saw something in those deep ebony eyes. Was it compassion or simply pity? Would he be the one to help stop this madness she knew would soon consume her? She couldn't tell for certain but only prayed it was so as the crowd pushed her again and he disappeared from her sight.

Chapter Seventeen

Valerie fought back the panic that threatened to undo her. The crowd was growing in size, shoving and pressing in upon her, people joining in the march as it made its way along the streets of Pompeii. Someone nearby remarked that they all wanted to see the witch who would bravely cast spells in the full light of day. She searched her memory for references to witches and magicians in this time period, but found none.

She heard another explaining to their companion that ever since the senate had passed its decree condemning the practice of witchcraft, those who partook in the evil rituals had, one by one, been either driven away or sold for a set term of slavery - a just punishment for one who would defy the law.

Two small children, feeling especially daring this day, ran up behind Valerie and hit her with a long stick. The thin reed snapped against her skin like a stinging whip. Valerie cried out. She struggled to break free from those who held her that she might turn and face her attackers, but the men held her firmly in their grip.

Valerie was dragged another step and tripped over the length of her skirt. Without hesitating, the men jerked her back to her feet. She looked into the crowd, anxious for a glimpse of her family or someone she might know. She tried to wipe the sweat and tears from her eyes so she might see more clearly, but they wouldn't even allow her to raise a hand. Valerie flung her head back, tossing her long hair away from her face. The people had become, like the buildings, nothing more than a blur.

Finally, the crowd stopped and Valerie realized they had reached the jail. They paused and she leaned forward, trying to catch her breath. The two men released her for a moment and she could now wipe her eyes. Directly in front of her was the small building that served as a jail. Everywhere, graffiti was scrawled on the heavy stone walls, conveying all manner of messages. It was just like what she had seen when exploring with Signore Fiorelli, but not nearly as suggestive. "Free Honoria" and "Tiberius is innocent" to "I'm voting for Salerno." Suddenly, someone shoved her from behind again. Valerie tripped and fell flat out over the threshold.

"What have you brought me now, Lucius?" the jailer asked as he rose lazily from his couch. "Runaway slave?"

"A witch, Maurus," Lucius whispered.

Maurus rolled his eyes and sighed. "Not another one. I wish the damned senate had left well enough alone. We've always had soothsayers and my guess is we always will, despite the law." He leaned his head out the door and scanned the faces waiting expectantly before him. They wanted blood. He could see it in their eyes. It was time to schedule another gladiator fight in the coliseum. "Go home, all of you. Don't you have anything better to do with your day?" he called to the gathering.

"Kill her!" a man shouted.

"Send her out of our town!" another yelled.

Maurus kicked Valerie out of the way with his foot. He ignored her as she slowly crawled away from him, dragging the heavy chains behind her. He stood in the doorway, his bulky frame filling the space.

"You superstitious old fools. What makes you think she's a witch?" He glanced over his shoulder. The girl had gotten to her feet and was now leaning against the wall. Strange looking thing, that was for certain. She looked half-crazed, with that long hair spilling down to her waist. He returned his attention to the crowd. "I'll see to it she's taken care of. Now, go home before I arrest the lot of you." Once the mob started to disperse, he nodded, satisfied, and went back inside.

Maurus sat down and crossed his arms over his broad chest. "So, tell me Lucius, what makes you think she's a witch?"

"Why, just look at her!" Lucius grabbed Valerie by the shoulder and she swung at him with her arm. She missed and he forced her to her knees. "Look at those clothes she's wearing. Only a witch would wear such a color or something that fits so tightly." He leaned forward and whispered, "she was seen climbing out of a tomb, carrying a staff for casting spells and raising the dead."

"And where is this magical staff of hers?"

"I broke it myself." Lucius patted his chest proudly. "She was going to curse us all with it, I tell you."

Maurus assessed Valerie, his gaze moving up and down her form. "Her clothes are strange, I'll give you that." He stared hard at her. "What were you doing in the Necropolis?"

Valerie slowly raised her eyes to meet his. Did she dare tell him she was hiding from an earthquake in the year 1865? Would he even believe her if she did? She must be a terrible sight with her dress torn and covered with dirt, her hair flying everywhere. As she considered what exactly she might say to convince these men, she lifted a hand to smooth the stray locks. The man called Lucius grabbed her wrist and twisted it behind her back. He pushed her until she was now on her knees.

"See? She was going to send a curse your way." His eyes narrowed. "Listen to how she talks. Go ahead. Say something for him."

Maurus leaned forward and rested his elbows on his knees. "Well?"

Lucius pulled Valerie to her feet and she had to bite her lip to keep from crying as the chains dug into the tender skin of her ankles. She continued to stare straight at the jailer as silent tears streaked her face. No, she decided, it would do no good to explain herself to these two. They had already made up their minds about her. She squared her shoulders. To the devil with all of them.

"Speak to me, or things won't go easy for you at all," he warned.

Valerie raised her chin a notch higher. She'd been beaten and dragged through the streets. What more could they do that they hadn't already done?

Lucius bent down and yanked the chain between her legs. Valerie immediately fell face down on the hard tile floor. Her chest heaved as she tried to catch her wind. She turned over and her stomach lurched as she caught a glimpse of the bloody and bruised mess her legs had become.

In the name of God, what was she doing here? Surely, Papa would be coming in the door at any moment to take her home. Dear Papa. Wasn't he was always there to rescue her when she needed it most?

"A stubborn one, aren't you? Well, if you won't obey me, there's only one thing left for me to do." Maurus' eyes bore into hers. He grabbed the front of Valerie's blouse and pulled her up until she could feel his hot breath on her face. "Lock you up."

"Lock me up?" Valerie repeated, her voice rough and dry from the dust of the streets. No sooner had the words spilled out than she put her hand over her mouth, her eyes wide. So much for her resolve of a few moments ago.

"You *can* speak." He nodded toward Lucius, his eyes never leaving Valerie's. "You're right. Her voice is different. Must be from another province." He continued to watch her. "Not a true Roman citizen, anyhow. Do you have proof of freedwoman status?"

Valerie shook her head, a terrible sense of dread building in her. She knew from her studies how important such a piece of documentation was to anyone traveling in a Roman city.

"Well, that leaves me with just one alternative. Since you carry no papers, I must assume you are an escaped slave." He rubbed the back of his neck. "You'll be sold at the market tomorrow morning." Maurus reached out and roughly handled her breasts. "You're a little too skinny for my tastes, but your curves are all in the right places. I'd say you'll make a fine house slave for some lucky master anyway."

"How dare you touch me?" Valerie swung at Maurus with a fist as she tried to break free of his grasp.

He laughed as his hands crawled over her chest. He gripped her shoulders, digging his nails into the tender flesh.

The pain seared through Valerie, shooting straight up her spine to the back of her head. The loud grating sound of Maurus' laughter bounced off the stone walls and echoed in her head. She put her hands over her ears, trying to wrench herself free as her mind fought against the noise. Her last thoughts were of home as she collapsed to the ground in a heap.

* * *

"You must let me out of here," Valerie pleaded, as the heavy iron door was slammed shut behind her. "I've done nothing wrong."

Maurus chuckled as he turned the key and heard the tumblers latch. "That's exactly what every criminal I've put in here has had to say. You should really consider yourself lucky." He smiled. "You only have to stay one night and then you'll be sold. Some of these poor bastards will stay much longer. And their final destination won't be so pleasant. They'll be executed."

"Executed?" Valerie repeated, her face growing pale.

"Crucified or beaten. That's what happens to runaway slaves." His eyes narrowed. "Best to keep that in mind, in case you have other ideas."

Valerie watched as Maurus walked away with the torch. If it wasn't for the half light of the moon sifting through the small window, she'd be in total darkness. Without her cane, she had to lean against the wall for support as she made her way to the small straw mattress situated in the corner, the iron shackles grinding against the floor.

She let her breath out slowly, forcing her mind to go blank. If she thought too hard right now about everything that had just happened to her, she'd go mad for certain. Next to the pallet were a bowl of water and a round loaf of bread. She touched the bread. It was hard. She knocked on it and it was like knocking on wood. Valerie's stomach growled loudly and she put her hand over it. Why didn't I eat this morning when I had the chance?

Valerie slammed the loaf against the wall and a small piece broke off. She dipped it in the water and took a bite. Chewing carefully, she reached down and pulled up her skirt. She coughed and choked on the bread when she saw her legs. The fine woolen stockings were in blood stained shreds where the shackles were still clamped. Valerie tore off several pieces of her skirt hem and, after wetting them down, tucked them under the bands of iron. She started to take another bite of the bread. Her stomach wretched. Her hands were covered with blood now as well.

To compound her nausea, the sour smell of urine and sweat pervaded the entire jail and assaulted her senses. Her eyes burned and started to water. She tried so hard not to gag but the combination was too much to withstand. Crawling over to the opposite corner of the cramped cell, her stomach heaved harder this time, dispensing itself of the meager fare she had just consumed. She vomited again and again, until nothing remained in her but the bitter taste of bile.

Dear God, please let me go home, she prayed silently as she wiped the beads of sweat from her face. Valerie leaned back on her heels and began to rock back and forth. A wave of panic ran through her. What if I can't ever return? She shuddered. What if I'm to be forever locked into this time? Her heart palpitated. Valerie shook her head. No. There must be a way.

Maybe I'm going mad. She clutched at her head, Maurus' laughter still ringing in her ears. Maybe I never left England. Maybe I'm still at home. Maybe Mama and Papa are right here and I just can't see them. "Mama," she whispered, "I'm here." She listened for a moment. There was no response.

No one could travel through time, could they?

Then, an old woman's cackle echoed off the stone walls of the damp jail and jarred her memory. Pencia. My God. She said I'd have to travel through the mists. Was this what she meant? How could she have known? Why didn't she warn me? Wearily, Valerie crawled to the mattress and lay back against the hard cold wall, too exhausted to think anymore.

From somewhere in the darkness of the jail, a thin reedy voice began to sing. The words were slurred and nonsensical as near as Valerie could tell, but the melody gave her something to focus on outside of herself. After a few moments, she began to hum along with the other prisoner, finally drifting off to sleep just before dawn.

Chapter Eighteen

"Wake up," a voice called.

Valerie stirred slightly. "Go away, Reg," she murmured and turned over.

"I said wake up!" the voice shouted this time.

Valerie jumped and sat up. She opened her eyes, disoriented. As her sight came into focus, she rubbed her forehead. Maurus was standing outside the cell door. Dear Lord. It wasn't a dream. The night had come and gone and still she was in ancient Pompeii.

She struggled to her feet and almost immediately went back down on the mattress. The chains had done their damage. Her legs were stiff and swollen, even her good foot wouldn't support her.

"I - I can't," she whispered.

"For the love of Zeus," Maurus cursed. He threw open the door, grabbed her arm and pulled her up. "Now move."

Valerie stumbled and fell to the wall, scraping her cheek. "Please. I need something to lean on while I walk."

Maurus looked at her suspiciously. "What are you talking about?"

She turned around and pressed her back against the wall. The cool stone penetrated her clothing and helped soothe the mad fever she felt building up inside of her. "Your friend Lucius. He broke my cane. I can't walk without it - or something like it," she explained, her voice breathless.

"Well you won't get one." He laughed. "You think I want my head banged in?"

"Then you'll either have to carry me or drag me out of here." She shook her head. "You don't understand, do you? I need it to walk."

Maurus shifted back and forth. "I'm not about to stand here and argue with you, girl." He gestured with his hand. "Now, get moving before we're late."

Valerie took a deep breath, near tears. She swallowed hard as the now familiar taste of bile worked its way up into the back of her throat. She tried to focus on the jailer's face. You will not give this man the satisfaction of vomiting in front of him, she told herself. She took another deep breath. "I'm crippled."

"Prove it," he ordered.

She sat down and unlaced the black leather shoes and sat them aside. Her stockings were so torn and ripped from the chains, her bare feet nearly hung out the bottoms. Valerie raised her left foot slightly. "See?"

Maurus removed the chains and examined the crooked toes and pulled heel. "All right." He nodded and left the cell as she put her shoe back on. Returning a few moments later, he handed her a waist high, straight stick of red cedar.

Valerie leaned on it and stood. The wood was rough and aromatic as she ran her hand over it. "Thank you."

He yanked her arm and pulled her through the jail cell door. "Don't even act as if you're going to use that as a weapon. One wrong movement out of you and you can crawl the rest of the way to the Forum. Is that understood?"

She nodded, holding her tongue. It would do no good to rile the man any further. She needed the use of a cane if she hoped to escape. Valerie took a step. Her legs felt so light now that they were free of the shackles. She took another and limped ahead of Maurus and out of the jail.

Off to the side of the street, several people had gathered. "She won't bring any money, Maurus," someone observed. "No one wants a witch in their homes."

"Go ahead and put her in a whore house." The woman who spoke followed Valerie's movements. "Looks like she'd do best laying on her back anyway."

Valerie stiffened and squared her shoulders. People were really no different, were they? The *Pompeians* talked about her as if she weren't there the same as the people of her own place and time. Strange, but she had expected justice to prevail here in the Roman democracy. "Why are you doing this to me?"

Maurus sighed. "Look, you come into our city and try to raise the dead."

"But I didn't -- " she interjected.

He threw up his hands. "You were judged by the people. They saw you come out of the tomb. If it had been a month ago, no one would have given it a second thought." He absently gave her arm a tug as she started to fall behind. "But the senate just passed a new law banning the practice of witchcraft. I'm just trying to do my job."

Valerie felt her spirit beginning to tire. She glanced at the fine stuccoed buildings around her with their tall pillars and elaborate entries, but even they had lost their magic. A slave girl carrying a small baby stepped to the side as she and Maurus passed by. Was this to be her fate as well? The girl's and her eyes met and the slave nodded slightly as if she had read Valerie's mind. It would be so.

Maurus snorted, breaking into her thoughts. "Besides, I don't agree with those people back there. I think you'll bring a decent price." He looked at her out of the corner of his eye. "There's been a wealthy citizen asking after you."

Valerie's heart skipped a beat. Could it be Papa? Had he found a way to rescue her? "What did he look like? Did he say he was a relative?"

"No." He stopped walking for a moment and swatted at a gnat. "It was a statesman." He jerked her arm again and pushed her ahead of him. "Quiet now, I've had enough of your questions."

Valerie raised her eyes as they approached the Forum. Here, all manner of people, both free and slave, passed through the tall columned entry and into the open, marble paved center. The massive stone structure occupied several blocks of the city and provided a center for commerce, worship, and meting out judicial decisions.

Passing through the gates, the pair moved slowly through what Valerie guessed to be the market place. The aroma of boiled onions mixed with sweat permeated through the crowd and hung on the still air. All around, vendors hawked their wares.

It really wasn't so different here from the merchant's section of London, except for the clothing of the shoppers and some of the items they bought. Built close to the sea, Pompeii had a vast selection of octopus, dolphin - all manner of fish. She caught a whiff of warm fermented grapes, then spotted a vintner's shop. Tall flasks rested in holes cut into the counter, ready for anyone would want to purchase a taste.

Valerie paused for a moment, watching as a man sitting on the ground tried to coax a snake out of a woven basket with a subtle movement of his hands. She applauded along with the crowd when the creature appeared and seemed to dance in the air.

Maurus spun on his heel and caught Valerie by the hair. He whipped her around in front of him, slammed her hard on the back and sent her sprawling. He stepped over her, hands on his hips. "Don't wander off like that again. Understand?"

She nodded and pulled herself to her feet. "I didn't think I was doing anything wrong."

"You were." Maurus punched her hard on the back again and knocked the wind out of her.

"Please," she began, then stopped, a strangled cry rising up in her throat. There, straight ahead, was the slave market. Wooden stalls, smaller than what horses were kept in back home, lined a long wall. In each, a person stood, scantily clothed, ready for inspection by prospective buyers. All around, people milled, pinching and pulling, looking in mouths and examining teeth. Standing on a wood platform was a man, stripped completely naked. He was being forced to parade back and forth in front of the crowd as bids flew about. She quickly looked away.

To her left, a woman lay in the straw and cried. She wore a sign around her neck saying she was a thief. "Why is she crying?" Valerie asked, her voice strained.

"She knows no one will want a slave that steals. She was a fine lady's servant, but will now end up working in the fields for the rest of her life." Maurus pointed to an empty stall. "There. Take your place."

Well, this would not be her fate, she vowed silently. Valerie turned around and took a step, intent on fleeing, when Maurus caught her by the back of the neck. He yanked her to face him and she cringed as he raised a hand, ready to strike. Slowly, he lowered it. Valerie stared at the fist, wondering if he was merely playing with her and would hit when she wasn't prepared for him.

Maurus leaned down so his face was right next to Valerie's. "I'll tell you something, girl. I know you're not from this town so you best be warned. Should you try and escape before earning your free citizen status, you *will* be put to death. Either by beating or crucifixion."

He gripped her forearm and marched her into the slave stall. He scooped up a length of rough unbleached wool fabric. "Get rid of those clothes you're wearing."

"I beg your pardon?"

"You heard me. Take them off and wrap this around you." He gestured with his hand. "Tie it on like that woman over there."

Valerie craned her neck around the side wall. The woman Maurus was pointing at had looped the material around her body and over a shoulder, letting the excess fall to the ground. Her knees were barely covered, let alone the rest of her legs. She looked at Maurus. "I won't be shown like a piece of cattle."

Maurus cursed. He grabbed the front of her blouse and tugged downward. The small pearl buttons flew in every direction, exposing her corset and bosom beneath. Valerie grabbed frantically at the tattered shreds and tried to pull them together.

"What gives you the right?" She spat the words at him, her face flush with anger and embarrassment.

He cupped her chin and forced her to him until she was standing on her tiptoes. His breath was hot in her face as he spoke. "I have every right. You, who are a slave, have none." He pulled his hand away and she stumbled. "Change your clothes." Maurus turned his back to her.

Valerie eyed him for a moment, fingering the walking stick. Did she dare? No, she would have more of a chance to get away if he thought she was harmless. Moving quickly, she dropped her skirt and what remained of the blouse. She reached first this way, then that, struggling with the corset ties until it was loosened. It too fell to the ground and she could breath once more. Naked except for her stockings and pantalets, she raised the cloth over her head and draped it around her shoulders. Someone clapped and she abruptly looked up. Her heart stopped. It was the man from the window. Had he come to help her? Or was he here only to poke fun like the others?

"A fine show," he commented as he pushed a stray curl of black hair away from his eyes. "I've never seen a woman have so many layers of clothing to remove. Where exactly are you from that they bind you up so?"

Valerie felt her face turn red. "H - how long - ?"

He smiled and winked. "Long enough."

Maurus turned around and tossed a red felt hat at Valerie. "She's not worth your time, Campanius," he muttered.

Campanius raised an eyebrow? "No? You don't believe she's worthy of being a slave?"

"Worthy of being a slave?" Valerie asked, her tone curt. "How exactly is one measured to determine such worthiness?" She waved the hat at Maurus, her eyes narrowed. "What in heaven's name is this ridiculous looking thing for?"

"Put it on. It'll show everyone you're being sold without a guarantee. As is." He looked at the other man. "See what I mean? She has an evil temper. Maybe it would be better to let her go to Livia. She might do best in a brothel."

Brothel? Had she heard right? Were they actually considering forcing her into prostitution? She gripped the walking stick until her knuckles turned white. With a scream, she swung and hit Maurus squarely in the chest. He fell backward as Campanius stepped out of the way.

She raised the stick again and started to swing at this man who stood and grinned at her like a fool. His smile quickly faded as he stopped the weapon in mid air with his hand. Still holding the cane, he used it to pull her to him. He was so close, she could feel the heat of his body. "Don't make that mistake again," he warned, his voice low. He let his hand drop and Valerie fell against the wall.

As Campanius walked away, Maurus scrambled to his feet. He gripped the nape of her neck and backhanded her across the face. Her head flew to one side and he slapped her again. He let go and shoved her against the side of the stall.

Valerie tasted the steely warm wetness of blood as it trickled down the corner of her mouth. Clutching the robe to her breast, she slid down the length of the wall and into the moldy hay that covered the floor of the slave market.

Chapter Nineteen

This isn't happening. It's just a dream, Valerie kept telling herself as she was pulled up the stairs and onto the platform. All around her, people jeered and pointed from where they waited for the sale to begin. The auctioneer stood before her. She looked down at him. He was a small weasel of a man with a whip tucked under one arm and he reminded her of Master Hobbs.

"Greetings. I'm Caias. Let's get in the spirit of the occasion, shall we?" With one sharp tug, he ripped the length of cloth from her shoulder, exposing the soft flesh beneath.

"No!" Valerie gasped. She clutched at the material, trying to wrap it back around her.

The auctioneer raised an arm and backhanded her across the face. The blow reopened the wound inflicted earlier by Maurus and she began to bleed again. The hot summer sun beat down on Valerie's head. She tottered for a moment, not certain if she could stay conscious. Not certain she really wanted to. At least if she passed out they could do whatever it was they planned and she wouldn't even have to know.

"Come on. Off with the rest of it." Caias leaned forward. "Now!" he commanded.

Valerie took a step back, shaking her head. She began to cry, silent tears streaming down her cheeks.

The auctioneer motioned with his hand. Two large men walked up on either side of Valerie, tossed her cane aside, and held her arms out. She struggled against them, but to no avail. Caias grabbed the material and roughly unwound it from her form.

She closed her eyes, squeezing the tears through her lashes, as the last of the fabric fell to the wooden platform.

"What's this?" Caias asked, pointing to the pantalettes. He laughed and several people in the crowd tittered as well. "Only barbarians wear such clothing." With a flip of his wrist, he bade the men holding her, "Get rid of them."

With another tug, the thin cotton undergarments were tore from her as well. Valerie now stood naked before the crowd, wearing only what was left of her stockings, her shoes, and the red felt hat.

She wrenched an arm loose and swung at one of her captors. He dodged and grabbed her again.

Caias approached her. His eyes moved down her body, coming to rest on her full round breasts. He watched as they heaved up and down with each ragged breath the woman took. He glanced up. "Not bad. Not bad at all." He spun around and faced the crowd. "What is my opening bid? Who will take this feisty woman from me?" He scanned the crowd. No one ventured forth with an offer.

Despite the warmth of the midday sun on her body, Valerie shuddered. She turned her head to either side. Her hair tumbled forward and offered a small amount of protection from these eyes. Oh, please dear Lord. This can't be happening. Just let me go to sleep, that I might awaken from this nightmare. She mouthed the prayer silently, swallowing the bitter taste of bile as it rose in her throat once again.

"Look! The witch is casting a spell!" someone in the crowd shouted. With one motion that appeared like a choreographed dream to Valerie, the mob took a step backward.

"We don't want her in our homes. She'll curse us all!" another person called out.

The auctioneer regarded Valerie coldly. "If no one will buy you, I suppose I'll have to turn you over to the whore house." His eyes swept over her again. "Though I can't say that would be all bad. Perhaps I could come and visit with you?"

"I -I don't understand. Can't you just let me go?" She was desperate to be rid of the place. To think, she had even wondered what it would be like to live here, in this time prior to the eruption. Now, she wanted nothing more than to forget she ever heard the name Pompeii. How in the world could she have held such a fascination for this ancient city?

He laughed. "And how will the jailer be repaid for the lodging and food he offered so generously?"

A murmur went up from the crowd. The auctioneer turned around to see what was the matter. As the people parted slightly, a dark haired man stepped forward. Valerie caught her breath. It was Campanius. The man she had spoken to earlier. Remembering the threatening scowl on his face as he left her in the stall, she wondered how her earlier intuition could have been so wrong about him. She hadn't seen compassion in those black eyes when she'd been dragged through the streets like a common criminal. And he obviously wasn't here to help her now. He was only here to further humiliate her.

"I'll take the girl," he stated flatly.

"No, Christos. She'll destroy your house with her black arts," Lucius urged from behind him.

Christos looked at the people nearby. They all seemed to be holding their breath, waiting for his decision. "Don't be ridiculous, Lucius. She's just a girl."

"Well, then, what will you pay me for her, Campanius? She's a fine looking thing, certain to decorate your household quite nicely." Caias waved his arm and the men holding Valerie forced her forward. They pushed her to her knees and made her lean over so her face was near Christos'. "What do you think? Is she not pleasant to look at?"

Valerie closed her eyes again. Her face burned as this man studied her countenance. She jerked her head away when he ran a finger lightly down her cheek. She opened her eyes only to find him staring intently at her. His eyes never left hers.

"I'll pay you the going rate, Caias, and not a *sesterces* more."

The auctioneer opened his mouth to speak. Christos interrupted him. "Don't even think of trying to get any more from me. She's been cuffed, beaten and appears to be crippled." He continued to watch the woman as the two men pulled her to her feet.

She stood with her eyes downcast, no longer fighting, no longer seeing the two men who were busy deciding her fate. The shock of the last two days was unbearable, and she had reached her limit. Steadily, Valerie began to retreat within herself, looking for a place of safety. In her mind, she found a small measure of peace as she pictured herself in a field of amethyst heather. Nearby, Reggie ran and laughed as he chased a yellow butterfly. She smiled.

"Come on down from there, girl." Christos motioned with his hand.

Valerie continued to stand perfectly still, not hearing, an odd smile on her face.

"I said come here," Christos commanded more loudly this time.

She ventured a quizzical look in his direction. Who was this man who would interrupt her while she was busy studying the many shades of spring flowers? Had Reggie heard him?

Christos climbed the platform steps and picked up the length of fabric Caias had removed from the slave. Gently, he wrapped it around her, then handed her the walking stick. The girl never moved or looked in his direction. He took Valerie by the hand. Where was her fire now? he wondered. Only a short while ago, she was coming at him with that stick, ready to bash his skull in. Where had the impassioned woman he'd dreamt of so many nights before gone? Now, she appeared to him to be half-dead, her spirit nearly broken. He gave her what he hoped was a reassuring smile. "Everything will be fine. We're going home now."

Silently, she watched the heather fade from her mind as it was replaced with the image of the man before her. He smiled again and directed her off the platform. Without speaking, Valerie descended the same steps she had climbed only a few moments before. Everything in her life that was comforting and familiar was gone, lost to her. Even the heather.

In the span of two days, she had been transformed from a free woman of England to a slave of Pompeii. She blinked hard, fighting the tears that hung just below the surface. The sound of her heart pounded out a heavy rhythm in her head and threatened to drive her to madness. A slave, she repeated to herself. Here only to serve. Here only to be abused as her master may see fit.

With a deep breath, Valerie forced her concentration to keeping up with this man who now owned her. Christos' stride was too fast, too long and it was a difficult struggle to not fall behind. Valerie stared hard at his back as he walked. His bearing was arrogant and spoke of privilege. The taut play of muscles beneath his tunic spoke of one who was conditioned for battle, ready to spring at a moment's notice. No wonder he had countered her earlier attack so easily.

Valerie clenched her free hand and, for a brief instant, imagined sinking a blade between those strong shoulders that she might make her escape. She sighed, wondering if she had the mettle to kill. There was something so disturbingly familiar about this Christos. And she felt instinctively it wasn't just because he resembled the museum pieces she'd seen. No, to her chagrin she found he was more like a dream one has night after night. Blurry and faded around the edges, but comforting in its presence.

Just then, a young boy and girl ran by and threw several rocks at Valerie's back. She cried out in surprise and pain as they began to chant, "Witch. Witch. Witch."

Christos spun on his heel. Behind him was a handful of people, all seemingly intent on following him home. His expression grew dark as he studied their faces. There was more than just idle curiosity at play. They hoped to see the witch cast her spells, giving them reason to harm her even further. "What's the matter with all of you?" He looked at Valerie where she stood on the fringes of the gathering. Someone shoved her forward and she stumbled. Christos caught her by the arms and steadied her. "Are you hurt?" he asked.

Valerie half smirked and shook her head. After everything she had been subjected to, why would someone suddenly be concerned? She felt her defenses beginning to crumble, her strength slipping away from her. "Please," she whispered. "Can't you just make them go away?" She was so tired of having to defend herself. Even the smallest of children seemed to be after her.

"By the gods," he swore loudly. "This woman is not a witch. She is to be a slave in my house and I'll not have her abused by any of you." He looked at each and every person standing near them. "If anyone else raises a hand against my property, I'll levy charges against you in the Basilica." Christos turned around and continued walking. "Well, come along," he called to her over his shoulder.

Valerie stared after him as she followed. She was his property, which was the only reason for his defending her. Pain twisted in her breast like a knife and took her breath away. She clutched at her chest, trying to force the ache aside.

Enough of pity, Valerie told herself. Enough! As if by speaking the words in her mind, she could make them true. She pushed away the confusion and hurt, burying these emotions deep in her soul. If she was going to survive in this place and time, she needed to learn everything she could about these people and their culture. To learn as much as she could about this man who called himself her master. To find his weakness, then use it against him to escape. To use whatever she could learn to return to her own world.

The pair walked without speaking past a low-roofed building that served as a bakery. One side of the structure was entirely open, exposing several large cone-shaped stone ovens. Sitting nearby on a section of wood shelves were many round loaves, their steam mixing with the hot summer air. The aroma of yeast reached Valerie and her stomach growled in response. She stopped for a moment, tempted to relieve the baker of a small roll, when someone grabbed her roughly.

"Slaves don't stop unless the master does. And, in case you were wondering, they don't talk unless they're spoken to," a large burly man breathed in Valerie's ear. "They keep their mouths shut." With a shove, he let her go.

For heaven's sake, how was she supposed to know every nuance and aspect regarding slaves and slavery? She couldn't very well play the game if they didn't tell her the rules. She eyed the man. Was he another citizen, intent on doing her harm? Valerie glanced at Christos. He was busy haggling with a seller over a bag of legumes. "Don't touch me," she warned, gripping her cane tightly in front of her.

Christos stopped talking and turned around. "You know, I can't quite place that accent if yours. Say something else."

Valerie looked at him. "I beg your pardon?"

The other man thumped her hard on the arm. "Are you deaf? He said to say something for him."

Valerie rubbed the spot where he hit her. It was already beginning to turn red and swell. Did this Christos save her from the crowd only to let this man beat on her? Was this how he was entertained?

She drew herself up, her temper flaring. "Damn you to bloody hell! I've had enough abuse from all of you. Is this how the visitors to your fine city are always treated?" She slammed the heavy cedar cane into the man's side. The force she hit him with sent her flying backward. Christos caught Valerie just before she struck the stone pavement and steadied her.

The large man took a step forward, hand raised. Christos grabbed him by the forearm before he could strike. His eyes bore into the other's. His voice was low as he spoke. "No, Julius. She's been through enough for one day. Besides, violence only begets further violence."

"She deserves a good beating, Christos. Let me teach her a lesson or two." He grinned and ran his hand across her chest. "I'll break her in real good for you. Make her a slave to be proud of. Trust me."

Christos ignored the man and turned to Valerie. "Julius is my personal guard. He looks out for me." His eyes glinted like jet, void of all emotion. He stared hard at her. "I may not let the townspeople harm you, but I would have to let Julius here offer some discipline if you made the mistake of striking him again. Do you understand?"

Valerie jerked away from Julius' touch and took a step backward. Her eyes narrowed as she shook her head. "I'll not let any of you touch me again." She squared her shoulders. "Do *you* understand *me*?"

Christos laughed out loud. The woman's eyes glowed like a caged cat. Her spirit was returning to her. "Sorceress or not, you do have a witch's fire, girl. If you were a free woman, I'd wager Athena, Goddess of War, would be your patron. Or perhaps Diana, Goddess of the Moon and its cycles." He tapped a long finger against his chin as he considered his purchase.

"More like Kronos, God of Time," Valerie replied with a terse smile as she made circles in the dirt with her cane. She thought of the knife again.

"So, you know of our gods. But your accent is not Roman." He cupped Valerie's chin, forcing her to look into his eyes. She was tall for a woman, but this man stood a good head taller than she. The intensity of his stare took her breath away. "Where are you from?" he asked, his voice low.

"Brittania." The ancient Roman word rolled off her tongue like a lover's name and she pushed back thoughts of home. She would only be able to indulge her memories when she was alone now.

"Impossible!" Christos laughed and dropped his hand. "I was there with the army of Rome and saw nothing but savages; people who wear skins and live in stick and stone hovels."

Valerie forced herself to stare back at Christos, sensing she needed to hold her own with this man if she hoped for even a small measure of his respect. "I am from the town of Londinium. We are different there."

"Londinium, you say? I was busy fighting in other areas. I never ventured to that particular place." He took a step closer and she could feel the heat of his body radiate out and touch hers. "Tell me. Are the people correct in what they say? Are you really a witch?"

Valerie shook her head. She was so tired. The weariness sank into her bones and ate at her soul. Would she ever be allowed to rest? "No, not a witch. Just a woman."

"Ah, not just a woman." He leaned forward and his breath caressed her cheek. "You are now the property of Christos Campanius Marcellus." With his thumb, he smeared away some of the dirt that covered her face. "Your skin is soft and unblemished under the filth. I imagine you might be quite lovely after you're cleaned up."

Valerie's head pounded with a dull ache. She tugged at the material wrapped around her. It seemed impossible to keep any modicum of decency with the garment. Of course, after what had happened earlier, why should she care? She swallowed hard. "What are you going to do with me?"

Christos turned and started walking. "Can you get around without that stick?" he asked over his shoulder.

"No."

"Then I suppose you'll have to work in the kitchen since it would require the least amount of movement. Besides, Stella's always grumbling she could use some help." He glanced back at her. "And, of course, there's always the need to see to your master's pleasure. Of course, we'll have plenty of time to explore that aspect of your duties after you've had a bath."

Chapter Twenty

Falling into step between Christos and Julius, Valerie ventured a cautious look about. She was careful not to slow down or appear too interested in any one item, all the while trying to memorize the path they were traveling through the Forum. If she were lucky enough to be allowed to visit here again, she needed to have an escape route planned and ready for use.

"What do we have here, Christos, my love?" asked a petite woman as she approached Christos. Her dark blonde hair was arranged in intricate curls on top of her hair and she smelled of expensive perfume. She looked back over her shoulder, wrinkling her nose in distaste. "My, but she looks like one of those wretched children who live in the caves by the sea. When was the last time you visited the baths?" she asked Valerie.

Valerie drew herself up. Perhaps this woman would like to hear about the less than sanitary conditions in the prison and the deplorable way visitors are treated. She opened her mouth to speak but was cut short by Christos.

"She's been in jail, Gravia," Christos answered for her. "I just bought her at the auction, so we haven't quite had the time to get her cleaned up yet."

Recognition lit Gravia's face. "She is the one we saw being dragged through the streets, is she not?"

"She is."

"But, Christos, everyone says she is a witch." Gravia's eyes grew wide. "How could you bring her into our house?" She looked at Valerie, a slight smile on her red lips. "She'll bring the heavens - and the senate - down on our heads. You can't afford to garner the counsel's disfavor."

Our house? Valerie wondered. Strange, she wouldn't have pictured a man like Christos married to a woman like Gravia. She was close to thirty - not much older than he was but, with her ostentatious jewelry and painted beauty, she resembled a woman who desperately wanted to reclaim the first blush of youth.

"*Our* house, Gravia?" Christos stopped walking and turned to the woman. He rubbed his chin as he spoke, "Just what have you been telling people?"

"Why nothing, Christos. Except that I care for you a great deal." Gravia weaved her arm through his and smiled sweetly up at him. "Can I come over this evening?" she purred into his ear. "You look so tense. I would love to help you relax."

"Mmmm, perhaps."

"Do not tease me," Gravia pouted.

He laughed. "I suppose we could have dinner in my room if you like."

Gravia released his arm and clapped her hands together. "I would like that very much." As she hurried off, she called behind her, "Later, my love."

So, they weren't married after all. "Is she your betrothed?" Valerie asked as she watched Gravia leave.

"What did I tell you about talking, girl?" Julius asked roughly. He jabbed her in the back with his finger.

Valerie shot him a look over her shoulder, her eyes narrowed.

"It's all right, Julius. I don't mind a few questions, as long as they don't become too troublesome."

Christos looked at her, his eyebrows raised. "Well? Was there something you wished to say to me?"

Valerie shrugged as she adjusted the cloth around her shoulders. "It's nothing, really. I had thought she, Gravia that is, was your wife. I guess I was mistaken."

He began walking again. "Gravia and I know too many dark secrets about each other to be married. Actually, she's my mistress."

"I -- I see," Valerie murmured. In her own time, no gentleman would have admitted so freely to keeping a woman for pleasure only. But, she had to remind herself, these people had an entirely different set of moral standards that they lived by.

"I don't see why you let her stay around, Christos," Julius said. "She's bad, that one is."

Christos laughed. "Julius here doesn't think I should see Gravia, if you couldn't tell." He looked at the man. "If I didn't know any better, I'd think my friend was jealous."

Julius snorted. "I don't hardly think so. Personally, I wouldn't give her a second look."

"Now I know you're lying. I've seen the way you watch her when she comes to visit." Christos clapped him on the back and sighed. "Like a dog in lust!"

The two men laughed as the trio turned a corner. Leaving the Forum, they entered into a residential district. The houses in this *insula* were built tightly together, each structurally dependent on the other. Valerie wondered for a brief moment if she would ever fit into this society as neatly.

"I don't understand something. If Julius is a slave, why is he allowed to speak so freely?" Valerie asked.

"He isn't a slave at all. Julius was my second in command in the army. When our commissions were completed, he came to work for me. It'll take some time, but you'll eventually figure all of this out." He glanced at her. "At least, if you're as intelligent as I believe you to be, you will."

Valerie stopped and stared hard at Christos' back. 'As smart as I believe you to be'? Indeed. He had no idea at all about the type of person she was. Nor did she care for him to find out. She would be long gone from this evil city before he had a chance to really know her. Julius interrupted her thoughts with a push. She hurried to catch up with Christos as he turned another corner.

Stopping in front of an elaborately painted and stuccoed house, Christos reached inside of his tunic and pulled out a key from where it hung on a gold chain around his neck. He unlocked the heavy wooden door and walked in, leaving it open behind him.

Valerie followed Christos into a narrow hallway that was flanked by mosaic scenes intricately set into the walls. The ocean at night, with several different types of fish leaping out of the water, were depicted here, and reminded Valerie of the mural aboard the *Fast Alice*. She ran her hand along the artwork as she walked, feeling the cool uneven texture of the small *tessarae* tiles. She came to an abrupt stop as she walked into the open atrium of the house.

Turning slowly around in a circle, Valerie looked up through the middle opening and into the clear azure blue sky above. Beneath the roof, and circling the atrium, was the second level of the home. Tall fluted columns with elaborate Corinthian capitals supported the red clay tile roof, creating a colonnaded corridor in front of several doors. She smiled, delighted, when she spotted the various styles of downspouts attached to the roof's drainage system - dogs, demons, and gods. From there, she followed the path of the gutters to where they emptied into the central pool built into the floor.

Christos watched in mild amusement as she made her assessment. "Quite different from a house made of sticks and stones, don't you think?"

"It's beautiful. I've never seen anything like it. Did you have an architect, or did you design it yourself?"

"I designed it, for the most part. This front entry and atrium were original to the house. My father had it built when he settled in Pompeii over forty years ago. Later, after he died, I added on the back portion," Christos explained as he pointed down another long corridor.

Valerie walked to a simple wood frame couch off to the side of the space and ran her hand over the heavy linen upholstery. The afternoon sun hit the wisps of gold weaved into the fabric just right and it sparkled and winked at her. "Beautiful," she breathed.

"*Gratias.*" He gestured to Julius who pulled a small bundle out from the folds of his tunic. The other man handed the package to Valerie. "I thought you might like to have these," Christos explained.

She accepted the offering with a mixture of wonder and trepidation. What could he possibly be giving her? But her fear turned to joy when she discovered her navy blouse and skirt within the package. She hugged the garments to her breast. "Thank you," she whispered as tears welled in her eyes. "You don't know how much I appreciate this."

Christos inclined his head. "Julius, why don't you take her to Stella. She'll have plenty of time to explore her new home later. Tell her to see to it that the girl's cleaned up." He turned and disappeared down another corridor.

Julius grabbed Valerie by the arm and pulled her toward the back of the house. She yanked her arm free from his grip, crossed it tightly in front of her, then walked on in silence next to him.

"Who is there?" A woman's voice called from the back of the kitchen and the sound echoed against the bare stone walls.

Valerie peered around the corner. This room was so plain compared to what she had just seen. The floor was laid of simple red clay tile, the walls left unadorned. At the back of the kitchen and standing before a heavy stove built of stone was one of the roundest people she had ever seen.

The woman finished stirring the bronze pot before her, put down the wooden spoon, then turned around. With the back of her hand, she pushed away the wisps of graying hair that clung to her brow. The heat of the room was stifling and she moved slowly, each motion deliberate. "Well? I asked you a question, girl."

Julius gave Valerie another shove. "This is your new help, Stella."

Stella's eyes narrowed as she looked Valerie over from head to toe. She gestured toward the cane. "What's the matter with her?"

"Don't know." He shrugged. "I think she's a cripple."

Stella threw up her hands. "Well, I've seen everything now, I have. Leave it to the master to bring me half a servant." She shook her head. "He's always bringing in strays off the street. Problem is, they can't hardly do anything. Then who has to do all of the work?" She jabbed a chubby finger at the center of her chest. "Stella, that's who!"

"I don't know what to tell you other than your master says you're to get her cleaned up."

She nodded and winked. She smiled knowingly and her mouth disappeared into the folds of her chin. "Ah, I see. She's to be his entertainment, then, is she?"

"Entertainment?" Valerie took a step forward. "What are you talking about?"

Julius didn't even look her way as he continued talking to the other woman. "I don't think so, Stella. Gravia is coming over tonight. I think it's like you said. He just felt sorry for her." He turned and left the room.

Valerie swallowed hard and wiped the sweat from her brow. So, he just felt sorry for her. That explained why he made her a gift of her clothes. And also why he was allowing her to ask questions. She shook her head. What was she thinking of? Had she really expected to be treated so differently by a man who had just bought her? After all, she was a slave in some distant time and place.

Well, it didn't matter, she told herself. She wouldn't be here long enough to worry over it. Carefully, she composed her expression into one she hoped would convey calm acceptance and servitude.

"If you would show me to the bath, I would like to get myself washed. Then, if you like, I'll help you prepare the evening meal." Valerie's mind raced, wishing she could retract that last statement. Why had she said it? There must have been something else she could have offered to do. For heaven's sake, she hadn't the faintest idea how to cook anything. Mae always took care of that.

"What exactly do you know how to cook?" Stella asked. It was as if she had read Valerie's thoughts.

Valerie took a deep breath. Better to be honest than to be proven a liar, Papa always told her. "Well, you see, I've never actually assembled a dinner. But I'm a fast learner," she added quickly.

Stella sighed and, with a plump hand, fanned herself. "I can't say I'm surprised. What's your name, girl?"

"Valerie. Valerie Sherwood Brooks."

"Never heard a name like that before. Of course, I never heard a voice like yours either." She looked at her. "Where you from?"

"England. I mean, Brittania," she corrected herself.

"Brittania? Never heard of it." Stella lumbered over to the sink and pumped some water into a glazed terra cotta basin painted with wildflowers, the only adornment in the room. She washed her hands and dried them on her white apron. She turned her attention back to Valerie. "All right. I'll give you a chance. But, I'm warning you. Let me down just once and I'll see to it you're sent to the vineyards. As far as I'm concerned, it makes no difference to me if you rot in here or out there, in the dirt."

Valerie thought of the woman she had seen lying in the slave stall, crying because she was going to be sent out to farm. She straightened her back. "I assure you, you will have no need to be concerned."

Stella shook her head. "We'll see. We will see."

Chapter Twenty-One

"Clarus!" Stella called out through the back window. "Come here, girl!"

A thin, tow-headed child of about eleven peeked into the room from the kitchen courtyard. She clutched a bunch of lettuce leaves to her breast, squeezing them tightly. "Yes?" she asked, her voice barely a whisper.

"Take this new slave to the bath and make her presentable." Stella glanced at Valerie and wrinkled her nose. "And find her something more appropriate to wear. She'll distract everybody trying to keep covered up with that length of cloth."

Clarus dropped the lettuce and fell to her knees, wringing her hands in front of her. "Oh, please, isn't there someone else who can do this?" She raised her eyes to Valerie, then quickly looked away. "She's a witch!"

Valerie sighed and shook her head. "I am not a witch."

Stella stared hard at her. "Keep quiet, you. It makes no difference to me what you are. The master brought you into this house and that's all we need to be concerned with." She drew herself up and shook a finger at Valerie. "But don't even think about practicing your black arts in my kitchen. I find one toadstool and I won't be held responsible for my actions. I run a good kitchen and I won't have you spoiling it."

"I assure you I haven't the faintest idea what it is you're talking about." Valerie crossed an arm in front of her and stared back at Stella. This was beyond belief. But then, what wasn't beyond belief these days?

Having spoken her piece, Stella turned her attention back to Clarus. She raised an arm and, before the girl could react, cuffed her hard on the ear. The child fell to her side, whimpering.

"How could you?" Valerie took a step forward, but Stella stepped in front of her, keeping her eyes on Clarus.

"Now, girl, you will do as you are told with no argument. Is that understood?"

Clarus nodded as tears ran down her cheeks. "I - I'm sorry." She unfolded her gangly legs and stood, unsteady as a newborn colt. Walking past Valerie, she hesitated for only a moment before speaking. "Follow me."

As the pair left the kitchen, Clarus had to fight the urge to turn and stare at the strange woman everyone called a witch. She wished for a moment she had eyes in the back of her head so she could watch the witch more closely. She shrugged. Nature had not deemed it necessary to her survival. Perhaps if she were more like Athena's wise old owl, she could turn her head all the way around. Yes, she decided, that would work very well.

Oh, why did *she* have to be the one to tend to the woman? The other servants had warned her about witches and their evil spells. Dear Juno, but Clarus shook at the very thought of getting close to her. Why couldn't Stella have listened to her for once? Of course, why should today have been any different? *No one* paid much attention to anything she said.

Clarus, deep in her thoughts, quietly led this person called Valerie down the long corridor to the back atrium where the house's private bathing area was located.

"Where exactly are you taking me?" Valerie asked, breaking into the girl's thoughts. "Will we be going to the Forum?" If only she could get back to where they had found her, she might find an opportunity to escape.

"Of course not. You heard Stella. She says you're to be cleaned up." She cast a quick glance over her shoulder. The walking stick was doing just that - helping the witch to walk. At least she wasn't trying to cast a spell. She let her breath out slowly. "Master Christos likes his slaves to keep themselves presentable. Where else would I be taking you but to the bath?"

"But we aren't going outside." Valerie looked past the girl and toward the back of the house. "I thought the Roman bath houses were all located in the central part of the city."

Clarus turned around and continued to walk backward. She sighed and threw her hands up, much the same as she had seen Stella do on many an occasion. Didn't this woman know anything? "Master Christos is very wealthy. He doesn't need to go to the public baths. He has one right here, in the house."

"I see," Valerie answered as Clarus spun on her heel and faced forward again. Valerie felt a warm breeze brush against her cheek as they approached the bath. She finally found it at the end of the passageway, enclosed in a peristyle garden. Here, the construction of the atrium was similar to the front one. Decorative downspouts were located to spew forth rainwater for collection in a well.

"See that small tub in the corner over there?" Clarus asked, pointing. "That one's for the servants. We're only allowed to bathe early in the morning and we can never enter if the Master is in here. Master and his guests use the large tub over there."

"And his guests?" The image of a small blonde woman crept into Valerie's mind. "Male and - and female?"

"Of course." Clarus turned around. "There is nothing wrong with washing together. Besides," she shrugged, "it saves water during the dry months."

Valerie shook her head. This concept was not new to her and she really shouldn't be in the least bit shocked. In her studies, she had learned that the ancient Romans often shared their bathing rituals with friends and family.

Clarus shifted nervously.

"What is it?" Valerie asked, noticing the movement.

"Is it true? Are you really a witch? Will you cast a spell and turn me into a snake if you don't like me?" the girl asked, the words all tumbling out together.

Valerie didn't answer for a moment. A snake? Had she heard right? The poor child looked like a frightened rabbit. "Of course it isn't true. I'm not a witch, nor do I know how to turn young girls into snakes."

"You don't?"

She laughed, and the soft throaty sound bounced off the columns and carried through the house. Valerie put her hands on the girl's shoulders. She wasn't much taller than dear Reggie. "I promise."

Clarus smiled, soothed by Valerie's words. "Please sit here and I'll help you." She motioned for the woman to sit down on a marble bench. The girl then knelt and removed the leather shoes. "I've never seen foot coverings like these before. We'll have to get you some sandals."

"Sandals do sound more practical, but I'm not certain they'll work well with my foot." Valerie crossed her left leg over the right. "See. I don't think I'd be able to keep them on."

"Maybe not," Clarus said as she helped Valerie out of her stockings. She made a face as the thin fabric pulled away from where it was stuck to the sores. "I'll ask Stella for some ointment for your legs. They don't look too good where the chains were rubbing against them. Maybe she'll know of someone who can help your foot, also."

"It was damaged when I was very young. There's really nothing that can be done for it. But thank you anyway." Valerie winced as the stockings were removed. "You're quite smart for your age." She watched the tow-headed girl for a moment. "How old are you?"

"I'll soon be eleven." She leaned toward Valerie. "And someday I'm going to marry Master Christos." She sighed. "He is so handsome and kind."

"Does he know of your plans?" Valerie asked, suppressing a smile. The girl was so serious, she didn't want her to think she was making fun of her.

"Well, no. It would not do for a master to marry his slave. But someday, I will buy my freedom. Then I will surprise him with a wedding."

"I see." Valerie patted the girl on the shoulder. "Has the master ever been married?"

Clarus nodded. "Yes, but his wife died while trying to birth their son. I will be very strong and will bear him many sons without dying. You won't tell, will you?"

Valerie felt a pang of sadness. How terrible to have lost both a wife and a child, all within the same moment. "You don't need to worry, I'll keep your marriage plans secret."

Clarus smiled, then began humming a simple tune as she helped Valerie out of the piece of fabric she had been holding so tightly around her.

Damn the slave trader! Valerie thought as the cloth fell to the ground in a pile. She pushed it away with the tip of the cane.

"You get in the bath and I'll go after the ointment and some clean clothes," Clarus bade.

Valerie watched as the child left, and then lowered herself into the water. She was surprised to find it was very warm. She leaned over the side and saw where lead pipes were plumbed into the tub itself. Running heated water? In ancient Rome? Most English houses didn't even have such a luxury. Valerie shook her head and eased back with a sigh, allowing the stiffness to soak out of her muscles.

* * *

The sound of a woman's sweet laughter rose and found Christos' ears. Following the song, he leaned over the balcony and peered into the atrium below. Just off to one side, he could see the woman he had bought today. He smiled as dear little Clarus helped her out of her clothing. But his smile quickly faded as the dusky light of evening brushed the woman's form. It touched the round peaks of her full breasts and caressed her buttocks when she turned. He felt a stirring as he watched her settle into the water, her shimmery brown-gold hair spread out around her. Maybe she really was a witch after all.

"Gravia has arrived, Christos."

"Hmmm? Did you say something, Julius?" Christos asked absently, his eyes never leaving Valerie.

Julius looked below and found where his friend's attention was drawn. "Looks like she's cleaning up quite well," he commented.

"Quite well, indeed." He shook himself free from his thoughts. "I'll meet Gravia in my room. Have the girl bring up our dinner."

"Do you think that's wise? You know how jealous Gravia can be."

Christos smiled crookedly and winked. "I know."

* * *

"Now, see if you can balance this tray with one hand." Stella placed the bronze servery piece on Valerie's outstretched hand.

Next, she piled on some bread, honey, and two golden goblets of warm wine. "Can you manage this?"

Valerie took first one tentative step, then another. "I think so."

"All right, then. Go out this doorway and into the atrium. You'll see the stairs. The master's bedroom is upstairs and at the far end of the corridor, near the bath."

Valerie made her way to the stair, then paused, trying to decide exactly how she was going to manage to climb it with cane and tray in hand. Just then, Clarus ran up beside her. "Can I help?"

"Thank you, Clarus," Valerie said as she handed over the tray. She followed the girl as she made her way to the second story. Once they reached the floor, Clarus handed the tray back to Valerie.

"Don't tell anyone I helped you. I'm not supposed to."

"Why not?"

Clarus shrugged. "We're only to tend to our own tasks, not the tasks of the other servants as well. But I've decided I like you. If you need me, just let me know and I'll see what I can do."

Valerie smiled warmly. "I really appreciate everything you've done for me," she said, remembering how the girl had tended her cuts and bruises after the bath. And how, so gently, she had worked the tangles out of her long hair with a wide toothed comb, then braided it for her. "If ever there's anything I can help you with, please ask as well."

Clarus nodded, then quietly disappeared back down the stairs.

Carefully, Valerie walked the remaining distance to the end of the corridor. Glimpsing over the handrail, she could see quite clearly where she had bathed. She'd had the strangest feeling earlier she was being watched.

Was it possible Christos had seen her bathe? Did he like what he saw? Oh, for heaven's sake, Valerie! she scolded herself. Put a rein on those wicked ideas! Besides, you're a cripple. How attractive could he find you? Still, she allowed herself a small smile as a strange sense of anticipation fluttered through her. But anticipation of what? A woman's laughter broke into her thoughts. She knocked on the door before her.

"Enter," the woman called out.

Valerie pushed the door open with her cane. She walked into the room, careful to keep her eyes lowered as Stella had instructed. She might not like being a slave, but it would be foolish to not play along with these people. Her body could ill afford any more beatings. If hurt badly enough, she may never be able to escape. "Where would you like me to put the tray?"

"Look at me," Christos bade.

Valerie raised her deep green eyes to meet his ebony ones. The desire she saw in the dark depths of his completely disarmed her. Never had a man looked at her so. Not even Thomas when he still believed she was only injured and not permanently crippled. The thoughts of Thomas sobered her. He had called her undesirable. She wasn't appealing to a modern man, so why had the foolish idea so suddenly entered her mind that this ancient man might find her so?

"I'm pleased to see I was right about you. You look much better, now that the layer of grime has been removed," Christos commented quietly.

Valerie felt her cheeks grow hot under his perusal as his eyes moved over her body. With cane in hand, she awkwardly tugged at the side of her tunic.

"Put the tray down next to the bed." Gravia gestured imperially with one hand from where she lay on a couch near Christos.

Christos rose and took the tray from Valerie. She pulled her eyes away from his and ventured a look around the room. Up a few steps and near the center of the expanse was a large bed, carved of wood, and covered with striped bedding. Sheer silk drapes hung around it, partially concealing the flicker of the oil lamps positioned near the headboard. She felt her cheeks grow even hotter as she scanned the painted images on the walls of nude men and women engaged in all manner of private activities.

"What is that you're wearing?" Christos asked quietly, his eyes caressing her small nose, well-defined cheekbones, and full lips.

"Is there something wrong with it? It's the clothing I was given."

"Slaves aren't supposed to wear long *stolas*, just short ones. Someone may mistake you for a free woman. Clarus didn't forget to tell you, did she?"

Valerie frowned, remembering how she had been shown to dress by Clarus. She was supposed to wrap a short *stola* around her so that her everything below her thighs would remain bare. The girl wasn't the least bit happy when Valerie had asked for additional pieces of fabric, insisting on covering herself completely. She hoped she hadn't gotten the child in trouble.

"I'm sorry. It's my fault. I insisted on dressing like this. In my ti -- I mean country, women don't walk around bared for the world to see."

"Have them both beaten," Gravia offered with a sneer. "I will tell you, Christos, these slaves of yours are much too impertinent. You must starve them for a while, then take the whip to their backs. They will be much more obedient."

"Oh?" he asked, an eyebrow raised. "Is that how I should treat you then, my dear? Will you mind better if I have a whip in hand?"

"Perhaps," Gravia answered as she rose slowly. She moved to where Christos stood and rubbed her body against his. She shimmied up and down, spreading her legs and running one hand along her inner thigh. "We shall have to try it sometime." She grabbed Christos head and roughly forced his lips to hers.

Valerie took a step back as Gravia's tongue flitted in and out, licking Christos' mouth. Christos glanced in her direction, his eyelids heavy. He sighed. "You've never told me your name. What are you called?"

She cleared her throat. "V-Valerie."

"Valerie," he whispered as his hands cupped Gravia's buttocks, forcing her against him.

Gravia moved away from Christos' embrace and unfastened her gown. Letting it drop to the ground, she revealed her nakedness. Valerie's head swam. She shifted nervously. My God, didn't these people care that she was standing right here? "Please, may I leave now?" she whispered.

Gravia returned to Christos. "Send her away. I want you to myself tonight."

Christos walked away from Gravia and toward Valerie. He grabbed her long braid and pulled her to him. "Please, let me go," Valerie pleaded. Was he going to rape her, here and now, in front of this woman?

He ignored her plea. "You do know you're mine, don't you, Valerie?" Christos lowered his mouth near to hers and she was filled with the same feeling of anticipation she had felt earlier. "I own you."

She put a hand on his chest, knowing she should fight him. But, for one fleeting instant, she wondered what it would be like to be kissed as she had seen him kiss Gravia. Would his touch be gentle? Would he think of only her as they kissed?

Christos took advantage of her hesitation and his lips met hers. Slowly, he caressed her mouth with his warm, moist kisses. Valerie tingled where his hands moved over her arms, brushing them softly with his finger tips. His kiss grew more urgent and he forced her lips apart. Just as Valerie had seen Gravia do, Christos now licked her, pushing his tongue into her mouth. The warmth of it filled her and she leaned against him, wantonly answering his need with her own. What was this passion he was bringing to life within her? How could she feel so strongly about someone she had only just met? Why, it was positively decadent.

She opened her eyes slightly and found Christos staring into hers, his half closed with passion.

"Christos!" Gravia called from where she stood. "I'm growing cold, if you follow my meaning."

Christos raised his head and sighed. "I'm coming." He looked down at Valerie and caressed her cheek with the back of his hand. "Would you like to join us, little Valerie."

Valerie's eyes flew wide open. "J-join you?" she repeated. "Wh-what do you mean? I'm afraid I don't understand."

Gravia laughed bitterly. "She's a stupid crippled child and I don't want her ugly form in my bed. Send her away."

Christos tensed. "Perhaps I should send *you* away, dear Gravia," he growled. "Your evil tongue wears on my nerves."

"Now, Christos, my love -- " Gravia began as Valerie wrenched herself free from Christos' embrace. She shoved him away from her, an angry flush covering her face. Stupid child, indeed. Valerie limped out into the hallway and slammed the door behind her, not wanting to hear anything else the woman may have to say.

For heaven's sake, what was becoming of her? She was in this city for only a short time, and already she had forgotten her morals. She paused at the atrium railing for a brief moment. Heaven help her, but part of her wanted this Christos to chase her down, to stop her from leaving him. It wanted him to take her into his arms, send Gravia away, and finish what he had begun.

She wiped roughly at her tears with the back of her hand. She should be angry and disgusted, not desirous of a man she had only just met. She had to try to avoid him, if at all possible. Yes. That was the only way to keep safe.

Quietly, she made her way back to the kitchen, followed only by the sound of Gravia's laughter as it echoed through the atrium.

Chapter Twenty-Two

Valerie lay on her side in the loft above the kitchen, on the hard straw mattress that served as her bed. She tossed and turned, trying to find some measure of comfort where there was none. She wrapped her arms around her shoulders, fearful she might disappear into the darkness if she didn't hold on tightly.

Mama, Papa, I miss you all so. Silent tears ran down her cheeks. Somehow, I will find my way back to you. A weighted sigh escaped her lips as she rolled over onto her back. Somehow.

Through a small crack in the tile roof, the bright white light of the moon shone. How many days had she been here? Seven already? Only a week, but it seemed like a lifetime.

How much longer would she be able make excuses to stay in the kitchen? If it hadn't been for Clarus' help, she would have had to face Christos long ago. As she drifted off to sleep, ebony eyes emerged from the shadows of the night, heavy lidded with passion. Valerie shifted uncomfortably. Her skin remembered his touch and tingled. Then, directly behind the dark eyes appeared cat-like blue ones, laughing and mocking. She rolled back over and punched at the blanket she used for a pillow. It would be another long night.

* * *

Valerie rose earlier than usual this morning, before the other servants. She quietly made her way to the bath, her bare feet lightly padding against the tile floor. Here, she hoped to have a moment to collect her thoughts before the day began. A week's time had passed and still there was no clue as to how she could return home. If only she knew what the key to her passing in time had been, she may be able to figure something out. Valerie shook her head as she walked. Even if she did find out the secret, she still needed to escape this house, but Stella and Julius rarely let her out of their sight, let alone outside.

Reaching the bath, Valerie placed her tunic for the day on a stone bench next to the tub. She had conceded to wearing the shorter garment in order to avoid a further confrontation with

Christos. And she was amazed at the newfound freedom the clothing afforded. With no corset or crinoline to bind her, she could move with a grace and ease she had never known.

Valerie shrugged off her robe and let it drop to the floor. She lowered herself into the tepid water and, with a sigh, leaned back and closed her eyes.

In her mind's eye, she saw Mama and Papa having their morning tea and biscuits with strawberry jam. Every morning, it was the same. She smiled to herself, remembering the day Reggie had discovered her romance novel. Mama was so cross at first. Into the picture drifted Thomas Smythe with his sweet talk and declarations of love. "Damn his bloody hide," she swore softly under her breath.

All of it seemed like a lifetime ago, and she knew that it was. But she was determined to return to that lifetime again, despite the difficulties she'd encountered.

She dozed in the warmth that surrounded her and, unbidden, her thoughts now filled with dark eyes and heavy caresses. Christos Campanius. "Do not forget that I own you now," he had told her almost everyday since her arrival to his house. She had been so right about him that first day in the slave market. He was arrogant, but she couldn't deny there was something in his arrogance that spoke of self-assuredness rather than conceit.

She squirmed. Thank heaven he hadn't touched her after that first night with Gravia. The man was totally unnerving, always lurking in the shadows, quietly watching. What did he hope to discover? That she could still do her job despite the fact she was crippled? No, it was more like he wanted her to be kept off guard, wanted her to remain tense in his presence.

Absently, Valerie touched her lips. His kiss had sent fire racing through her veins with their intensity - a feeling she had never experienced - even with Thomas. She felt an empty ache growing deep inside her belly. Would she ever know what it would be like to have these flames quenched?

"*Salve*, Valerie," a deep masculine voice called out softly.

Valerie's eyes flew open. She instinctively crossed her arms over her breasts. Christos stood at the foot of her bath. "How can

you still be modest?" he chided. "Put your arms down. I would see again that which you guard so mightily."

She shook her head. "It isn't right."

"Ah, now, what isn't right about the human body? What evil lies there that we should hide it away in the darkness and behind our hands and arms?" Without making a sound, he stepped closer to the tub and sat down behind her. Lazily, he let a hand drop, lightly fanning the water with his fingers. "You've been avoiding me, haven't you?"

"I'm afraid you overestimate yourself, sir." She shifted nervously. "You see, I've been busy in the kitchen with Stella, learning my duties." But even as she spoke, she sensed he knew she was lying. He was handsome, this master of hers, with his thick curly hair and flashing blue eyes. She feared greatly the emotions he had awakened in her. She feared even more what her response to him would be if he took her in his arms again.

"Julius tells me you don't like to be ordered about. That you act almost aristocratically when he tells you to do something," Christos commented, his voice casual.

"Please know that I'm trying very hard to do as I'm asked. But some of the things he orders me to do are beyond reason."

"I seek no explanation. I can see you're not used to this work or station in life." He reached across her shoulder and lifted her hand, examining the palm and fingers. "See? There are no calluses or scars to show you have labored."

"I won't deny what you say." Valerie pulled her hand away and slowly dragged her knees to her chest.

"You were gently bred for finer things, weren't you? Like love, perhaps? I could order you to come to me, you know. But I am a man who prefers his women to come willingly with their arms open wide." He raised his hand and let warm drops slide down Valerie's spine. She shivered despite the heat of the water. "Tell me, Valerie, were you married in your native land?"

"No, I wasn't," she answered. In what direction was he now taking the conversation? "Why do you ask?"

"I didn't think you were, especially since no one claimed you from the jail." He lightly touched the back of Valerie's neck. Long tendrils of her hair fell from where they were piled on top of her head, and he twisted them around his finger.

"Would it make a difference? Would I still be a slave?" Valerie held her breath, waiting for his answer. If she could somehow recant her story, maybe he would let her go.

"Of course you would. I bought you in an honest deal. I only sought to make certain there would be no jealous husband coming to hunt you - or me - down."

Valerie's spirit fell. It didn't matter to him whether or not she was married. Christos let his hand drop back into the water again. She glanced at him out of the corner of her eye as he took a bottle of scented oil from the side of the tub and poured it into his hands.

"I understand from the other servants that you were married once," she said. She knew it was none of her business, but she could think of nothing else to say. Christos' presence was maddening. Why didn't he go away?

He raised an eyebrow. "Do you now? What else have they been gossiping about?"

"Nothing, really. I -- I'm very sorry about what happened to her and your child."

"Well, it may have been my wife who died, but it wasn't my child." Christos snorted.

Valerie looked over her shoulder. " I didn't know."

"Well, you must have been the only one in all of the empire who didn't. Five years ago, I was away on campaign -- in your Brittania. Segis took a lover, became pregnant, and died in childbirth before I returned." He slipped the glass stopper on the oil bottle and put it down. "The gods are ironic in their justice."

She felt her stomach catch at the bitterness in his words. "And you've never remarried?"

"I need no more pain in my life."

Christos answered far too quickly, Valerie thought. After all those years, his voice still carried the hurt he must have experienced at his wife's betrayal. Some instinct deep inside her stirred, and she wrestled with the urge to reach out to him.

As she did so, he changed the subject of their conversation once again. "So tell me, Valerie, how do you like being here so far? Is it as bad as you would have imagined?"

She cleared her throat, acutely aware of how his hands were now massaging her shoulders and working the scented oil into her skin. "You've a pleasant house and, from what I've seen, you treat your servants well. But I'd still prefer to be home."

"Home? *This* is your home."

"No, this is *yours.* As I told you before, mine is far away from here." She looked up into the brightening sky. "As far away as the moon and stars."

"I would not have guessed a poet's heart beat in your breast." Christos leaned forward and his lips brushed against her ear. "You are like a flower, dear Valerie. Open up to me. Let me sample your sweet nectar."

Without even realizing it, Valerie leaned into his kiss as his mouth moved over her jaw and down her neck. Slowly, his hands slid past her shoulders and forced her arms away. He cupped her breasts, lifting and kneading them. His touch sent pleasurable waves through her body as he teased the light brown nipples into hardness.

"You cannot deny me, Valerie. Remember, I own you."

Christos' words reached out and slapped her. Valerie jerked free from his embrace. "How could I forget? After all, you see fit to remind me so at every turn." She grabbed her robe and, standing, yanked it on.

Christos' expression grew dark and forbidding. He rose and laughed harshly. "You like this little game we play, don't you? You pretend to be the virgin and me, the satyr. Tell me something. When you sacrifice yourself to me, will you enjoy it as much as I will?"

Valerie rubbed her head, the aggravating tension of their encounter growing within her. What did he mean 'pretend'? "What are you talking about? Didn't you just say you wouldn't force yourself on me?"

"I won't have to. You were made for the pleasures of the flesh. Can you deny this?" He shook his head. "The way you give yourself so freely when I touch you - why, your body is crying out. It senses the enjoyment I can give to it." He ran a wet finger down the side of her cheek and whispered, "Perhaps you should listen."

"Never!" Valerie hit her cane down hard on the floor, accenting the word. In that instant, a low tremor shook the room. Another earthquake! her mind screamed. Frantically, she glanced about. A heavy clay vase tumbled from its pedestal and went crashing to the floor.

"Come with me." Christos scooped her into his arms and rushed out into the open garden, away from the structure of the house. He held her tightly against his chest. Then, just as quickly as it had began, the rumble subsided. He let her slide out of his arms and took a step backward, his eyes never leaving her form. "How did you do that?"

"I didn't do anything," Valerie answered as she straightened her robe with shaky hands.

He reached out and shook her hard, sending her hair tumbling down her back. "This walking stick of yours. You banged it against the floor, then the earthquake came. What magic is this?"

"It's not magic, I tell you." Valerie pulled away from him. Then, a sudden far-reaching thought filled her mind. My God. No. It couldn't be true. Could it? Had she actually been transported to ancient Pompeii only to meet her death? "Tell me, please, what day and month is it?"

"Augustus. I believe it's around the third day." Christos looked at her closely.

Valerie's eyes grew wide like a child's who has just awakened from a nightmare. "What year?"

Christos didn't answer.

"I mean, who is the emperor and how far are you into his reign?"

"Titus is emperor. His rule has only just begun." He ran a hand through his hair and his eyes narrowed. "What are you about, woman? Tell me what you know."

In her mind, Valerie quickly calculated what year she was in. Oh no, she thought. She swallowed hard, choking out the words as she spoke. "In three weeks time, Vesuvius will destroy Pompeii."

Christos looked hard at Valerie. "How can you make this claim? Do you have the gift of sight?"

"No." Valerie shook her head. She turned around and studied the hunt scene painted on the wall in front of her. Several tall cypress trees were planted on either side of it and a vine of ivy was beginning to creep up and over the artwork. Could she convince him of the coming eruption without giving herself away? What would he do with her if he knew her secret? She ran a hand alongside her neck and leaned wearily against her cane.

"I'm a student of history." She took a deep breath. "Particularly Roman and Greek history."

"But what you're saying about Vesuvius, if it's true, is part of the future. It hasn't happened yet." Christos turned Valerie around and forced her to look at him.

"I know this sounds ridiculous but you must believe me." Her eyes met his. "If you want to live, that is."

Christos rubbed his forehead and smiled slightly. "You know, it was those green eyes of yours that caught my attention when the people dragged you through the streets. It was those same emerald jewels that haunted my dreams before you ever appeared before me in the flesh. Their image scorched my brain and drove me to the auction, beckoning me." He leaned forward and she was burned by the intensity of his gaze. "If you say you can predict the future, then you must truly be a witch."

Valerie pulled away from him, her head swimming. Christos obviously didn't believe her so why did he insist on perpetuating this idea when she had so resolutely denied it? She had to laugh. A witch? Well, why not. She bowed before him. "Yes, great Campanius, you've guessed my innermost secret. I am a witch and I can control the elements." Her eyes narrowed. "I can control you, if I so choose."

It was Christos' turn to laugh. "Show me."

Valerie hesitated for a moment as she thought. Did she dare? She took a step forward and dropped her cane. Lacing her arms around his neck, she pulled his face close to hers. She brushed against him as she had seen Gravia do. Her nipples grew taut against the filmy wet fabric of her robe. "Kiss me," she bade, her voice low and seductive.

Christos gathered her into his arms and pulled her tightly to his body. With a groan, his mouth melded with her's. "Ah, sweet,

sweet, Valerie." His hands moved in a heavy caress down her sides and over her buttocks. He pushed against her and she could feel his hardness through the toga he wore.

Unbidden, Pencia's prophecy ran through Valerie's mind. You must travel to find your love. Travel through the mists. Could Christos be the man of whom she had spoken? She was being ridiculous. To him she was only a slave, personal property. Her mind raced and, suddenly fearful, Valerie pulled away from Christos.

He looked at her, askance.

"Did I not say I could control you?" she whispered, her voice shaky.

Christos smiled crookedly. He ran a hand along her bare arm. She shivered in response to his touch. "Tell me truthfully, witch. Who controls who?"

Chapter Twenty-Three

"Take the master his midday meal and be quick about it," Stella ordered. She slowly moved her bulk to a small stool and Valerie was amazed it didn't give way under the load.

"When you get back, we'll need to go to the market." She stopped talking for a moment, catching her breath. "We must finalize the selections for tomorrow night's banquet."

Valerie nodded, biting her tongue to keep from crying out in joy. They were going to the market! Finally, she was going to be let out of this house. If she were lucky, she might find a chance to escape.

Her heart tugged at the thought of leaving Christos. No, she told herself. She had to get home. She couldn't stay in the past, especially with a man who only saw her as property and not as a woman. Especially in a past set on a course with destruction.

Quietly, Valerie arranged a hunk of fresh bread, goat cheese, and a carafe of warm wine on a bronze tray. She looked closer, then realized it was the same tray she had carried to Christos' room her first night there. She smiled an evil looking smile as she pictured the same tray bent over the head of a certain blonde-haired woman.

"What are you grinning about over there?" Stella asked, her voice sending Valerie's mental image scattering.

"Oh, nothing really." Valerie hoisted the tray up to rest on her shoulder. "I was just thinking, that's all."

"Well, stop it!" Stella stared hard at her. "You don't fool me, you know. You think you're too good for this work. I've seen your hands. They've never done a hard day's labor."

Valerie carefully placed the tray down on the table. With deliberate movements, she pulled a stool up opposite Stella. Their eyes locked. "I've never lied to you, Stella. I came from a wealthy family where we had our own servants. I told you my first day here I didn't know how to prepare a meal, but I am trying."

"Trying to make your way right into the master's bed, as near as I can tell." Stella laughed and her whole body shook. The stool creaked in protest to the motion.

"Please understand, Stella, that I have no argument with you and I'd prefer to keep it that way." Valerie stood and placed the tray on her shoulder once again.

Stella grabbed her by the wrist just as she was picking up her cane. Valerie stared down at the woman's hand, then wrenched her arm free from her grip. Her voice was low as she spoke. "Don't touch me again, Stella." Valerie grabbed her cane, then turned to leave the kitchen.

"I've seen it before," Stella called after her. "He buys a pretty young thing like yourself, uses her for his pleasure, then sells her off." She shook her head as Valerie disappeared from her sight. "She's just like the others. Just like them."

Valerie followed the sound of clanking metal out into the back atrium. She was surprised to find a pair of heavy wooden doors had been pushed aside, revealing a small workshop. As she approached, the hammering stopped. She found Christos bent over a hot fire built in a heavy stone container. Beads of sweat ran down the sides of his face as he held a sheet of gold in the flames. She put the tray down on a nearby marble bench, then went near him. "What are you doing?" she asked, fascinated.

"Working," he answered as the metal turned a glowing molten red. At the exact moment it threatened to turn to liquid, he dropped the hot sheet over a wooden mold. Valerie watched in fascination as the gold formed itself around the carving, creating a woman's image.

Christos put down the heavy iron tongs he had been holding and sat down next to the tray of food. "Simple fare for a working man," he commented as his gaze swept over the bread and cheese.

Valerie shrugged. "Stella said you weren't to fill yourself up today. She said you needed to save your stomach for tomorrow night's feast." She leaned over the jeweler's bench and explored its contents with her eyes. Vials of colored powder, faceted and cabochon stones, gold, silver, and copper covered the surface. She paused when she found a pair of pink tourmalines carved with delicate intaglios resting near the edge.

"Did you do these yourself?" she asked, running a finger gently over the concave surface.

"Yes, I did," he answered as he broke off a hunk of bread. "I thought a setting of granulated gold would display them nicely."

Next to the tourmalines Valerie found a golden serpent armband, its eyes glowing red with rubies.

"Go ahead. Try it on," Christos urged.

Without hesitating, Valerie slipped it over her hand, pushing it into place above her elbow. She held her arm out and admired the handiwork. He hadn't missed a detail in designing the piece, right down to the scales along the creature's back.

"It's beautiful. I saw one like it once at the museum in London."

Christos glanced up from his food. "I beg your pardon? Did you say museum?"

"Did I say museum? What I meant was, my father once told me of one like it he had seen in dealing with traders." She quickly took off the armband and placed it back on the workbench. Desperate to change the subject, she asked, "Is this how you support yourself? By creating jewelry?"

"Not hardly." Christos laughed. "My family has been in Pompeii for generations and I inherited my wealth from those ancestors. The jeweler's art is more of a pastime than anything, something I learned to do from an uncle when I was very young." He patted the bench where he sat. "Come, sit by me."

She didn't move, recalling their game of one-upmanship after the earthquake a few days ago. Who controls who? Well, she would not be ordered about so easily by this man. "I'm quite comfortable standing, thank you."

"You're an obstinate one, aren't you?" he observed. "What ever am I to do with you, dear Valerie? I've tried to be patient with you. As I've said before, I know you're not used to this kind of life." He picked up the simple clay goblet and took a drink. "But you are still a slave in my house. And I am still the master. The sooner you accept this simple fact, the happier you'll be."

"I won't be happy until you set me free," she murmured.

Christos snorted. "And where would you go? You've forgotten too soon the good citizens' reactions to your presence." He leaned forward and rested his elbows on his knees. "Why else do you think you haven't been allowed outside of the house these past weeks?"

Valerie considered Christos for a moment. "You mean to say you've been protecting me?"

Christos smiled warmly. "I wish you no harm. Surely you know that by now."

"No harm?" Valerie slowly walked over to him, a tight smile playing about her lips. She ran a finger over his arm as she spoke. "The same as you would wish no harm to come to, say - your house or furnishings?"

"Mmmm, I suppose you could put it that way," Christos answered, the hint of a question hanging in his tone.

Valerie leaned over and pointed that same finger in Christos' surprised face. "To the bloody devil with you, Master. While you may consider my body to be one of your personal possessions, you'll never own my soul!" She straightened and looked to the heavens. The sun was high in the sky and beat down on her face, heating it to the point where she felt consumed by a great fever. Valerie shook her head, and returned her gaze to his. She remembered what Stella had said. "I actually feel sorry for you and your need to purchase women. You'll never know love."

Christos rose slowly, his eyes were dark and threatening and never left Valerie's. "You don't know what you're talking about."

"Oh, I know only too well. I've known men like you. Your mind is set to seek only pleasure and the woman be damned." Thomas' shocked expression at finding out she was crippled ran through her mind. You're undesirable. The words taunted her. "No wonder your wife took a lover." But even as the words tumbled out of her mouth, Valerie realized she had gone too far.

Christos grabbed her shoulders, digging his fingers into the tender flesh. "You need to learn to curb your tongue, woman." He spun Valerie around and ripped the back of her short tunic down the middle, exposing her bare skin. Christos then untied the leather belt he wore and folded it in half. With a quick snap of his wrist, he cracked the belt loudly in the air.

Valerie cried out in surprise and struggled to get away from him. Christos grabbed her by the hair. "You will stay and receive your punishment!"

She turned and faced him. No matter what, she would not give him the satisfaction of hearing her beg. When the leather sung through the air for a second time, she raised her hand and tried to wrestle the belt from Christos' hand.

He shoved her away from him and she tripped and fell hard to the ground. She lay there for a moment, dazed, expecting to feel the sting of leather against her skin at any moment. But when the attack didn't come, Valerie slowly stood and turned around. Seated on the ground in a crumpled pile was Christos, his body shaking and wracked with silent sobs.

He looked up through his tears and raised a hand to Valerie. She placed hers in his and let herself be pulled to her knees. "Please forgive me," he whispered. "I wouldn't hurt you. I'm sorry. I'm so sorry."

Valerie looked into his eyes, her own tears clouding her vision. Could it be that his arrogant facade was finally cracking? What manner of man would she find beneath it? She let her breath out slowly as the momentum of their encounter withered away.

Her first instinct was to pull him to her and offer comfort. But she knew she couldn't. She would help him, but he had to ask for that help if there were to be peace between them.

By God, Christos desperately needed to be taught a lesson. He couldn't buy and sell human flesh without emotion. Nor could he take women at his pleasure and then cast them aside with no thought for their feelings. Silently, she vowed she would not be used so by this man.

Valerie leaned forward, resting her hands on her cane to steady herself. They looked at each other in silence for a moment.

"I'm sorry," he repeated, his voice a ragged whisper.

Very softly, Valerie replied, "Go to Hades." She stood and went back inside.

Chapter Twenty-Four

"Hand me that bowl over there," Stella instructed.

Valerie absently picked up the clay bowl and passed it to Stella, the image of Christos and his tears still etched in her memory. The pain of his wife's betrayal had shone brightly in his eyes and she understood now it was Segis he had wanted to beat, not her. It was obvious he had demons to wrestle and make peace with. It was obvious, too, that he had come to know the great hurt that other people could inflict, even those who professed their love. She wondered for a brief moment if the ache in her own heart would ever be put to rest.

Valerie started to let go of the bowl before the other woman had hold of it. She grabbed it just in time before it crashed to the ground.

"Pay attention to what you're about, girl, or I'll have Julius beat you! Would you like that?" Stella shouted.

Valerie gave her a sullen look.

"I thought not. Now, put some wood in the fire before it goes out."

Stooping down, Valerie picked up a sizeable log and placed it inside the stone stove. She poked at the glowing embers with a long stick, sending flames up through the gravel covered top. A large pot of water sitting on an iron grate began to boil.

"Is there anything else you'd like me to do, Ma'am?" Valerie stressed the last word, heaping it with sarcasm. If she didn't escape this house soon, she could simply not be held accountable for her actions where Stella was concerned. The woman seemed to live only for the chance to make Valerie's life a hell on earth. Drained emotionally after her encounter with Christos earlier, she just didn't have the patience to deal with the woman.

Stella eyed her. "Hand me that box over there. And this time, try not to fumble." She shook her head. "You'll never make a kitchen maid, as clumsy as you are."

"Well, I am truly distressed over that matter." Valerie ventured a glance in Stella's direction as she passed the box, then smiled sweetly. "So tell me, when are we leaving for the Forum?"

"Not for a while yet. We need to prepare a few items first," Stella explained.

How long? Valerie wondered, but didn't dare ask. If she risked angering the cook anymore, or even acted as if she were anxious to leave, she may not get to go. "What are we going to cook first?"

"These." Stella dipped her hand into the small wooden box and extracted a brown mouse. Its nose twitched in fear as it wriggled in her fingers, trying to get away.

"Mice? You're going to cook mice?" Valerie gasped. "You can't be serious!" She reached for the creature, recalling all the dear little mice Reggie had collected. He had given each and every one of them a name and paperboard nest.

Stella pulled her hand away and, with one quick motion, broke its neck between her thumb and forefinger. She dropped it into the boiling water and grabbed another one.

"For heaven's sake, how could you do that?" Valerie held a hand to her mouth.

"What's the matter with you? Never had mice to eat?"

"Of course not!" Valerie was beside herself. "Who ever heard of eating mice, unless of course you happen to be a cat. Besides, I can't imagine there's even enough meat on them to bother with."

"Mice are a delicacy. We always serve them at dinner parties. It's a tradition with the Romans," Stella explained, her voice growing more and more impatient. "But I don't suppose you'd know that, would you?" She dropped another into the water.

Valerie knew she'd have to continue to adapt to her new environment until she could escape, but eat mice? She shuddered. Not likely. "What do you do with the poor things after they're boiled? Surely you don't eat the fur as well?" She raised her eyebrows in question.

"Of course you don't eat the fur." Stella tossed the last of the mice into the hot water and wiped her hands on her apron. "They only cook for a moment, then you scoop them out. The fur will slip off nice and easy." She handed Valerie a small wood strainer with a handle attached. "Here, you try it."

Valerie shook her head, her stomach roiling. "I couldn't."

"I think you can just fine, or will I have to call Julius to come and make you mind?" Stella hoisted herself onto her favorite stool and crossed her arms, her eyes never leaving Valerie. "I can't imagine you'd want a beating, but maybe you're one of those girls who like to be abused. I'm sure Julius will be quite accommodating."

Quietly, Valerie considered the woman, weighing her options. She didn't doubt for a minute Stella would bellow for help. If she had a run in with Julius, he could decide to forbid her from going to the market as well. And there may not be another opportunity to get outside and plan an escape route before the eruption. With a grimace, Valerie dipped the spoon into the pot and extracted one of the mice.

"I thought you might change your mind. Now, grab the fur back by the tail and give it a good tug." Stella smiled, obviously pleased.

Valerie closed her eyes for a moment, composing herself. When she opened them, she took a deep breath and lifted the mouse out of the spoon by its tail. She held it at arms length away and pulled the fur. She was surprised to find that it did indeed slip off easily, just as Stella had said it would. "Now can we go to the market?" Valerie asked, her stomach churning as she dropped the small pelt to the floor.

Stella laughed, obviously enjoying Valerie's discomfort. "Not until you finish." She handed Valerie a bowl of honey. "Now, dip it in here."

Still holding the creature by its tail, Valerie let it sink into the sticky amber liquid. As soon as it was completely covered, she pulled it out, letting the excess drip back into the bowl.

"Over here," Stella waved her hand.

Valerie took a step forward and stumbled, a wave of dizziness washing over her. She leaned on her cane. It was so unearthly hot in this kitchen. It felt like the room was closing in around her. Was there never a slight breeze to cool the day? "Haven't we tortured this poor creature enough? Surely there isn't anything else that can be done to it."

"Shows how much you know," Stella sniffed. "Here, roll it in these poppy seeds, then lay it out straight to dry."

Valerie swallowed hard, then rolled the honey-covered animal in the small seeds until it was barely discernible as a mouse. Next, she laid it out straight as an arrow on a tray.

"Good." Stella smiled and it disappeared into her heavy jowls. "I'll be in the atrium preparing the benches. Come and get me when you're done, then we'll go to the market place."

Valerie watched as Stella left the room, her dress caught between the folds of sweaty flesh. A sudden impulse came over Valerie and she stuck her tongue out as far as she could in the direction the woman had just gone. She giggled. Poor Lucy would have surely been beside herself if she had witnessed Valerie pulling such a stunt.

She wiped the sweat from her brow and peered into the kettle of boiling mice. The smell was hideous, like the pair of Reggie's moldy stockings Aunt Mabel had once found stuffed under the kitchen counter.

Valerie closed her eyes again and took a deep breath, steadying her nerves. She made another face, then went to work, praying the food she had eaten earlier would remain in place for a while longer.

Chapter Twenty-Five

For a full hour, Valerie skinned, coated, and rolled mice until, at last, she was done. To her amazement, her stomach had withstood the task and Stella now inspected her handiwork, carefully scrutinizing each and every morsel.

"Not bad," she finally conceded. "Now, let's get going to the Forum. It's getting late and we're going to miss the best deals." She called for Clarus and the girl scurried in from the kitchen garden.

Valerie followed the pair through the house and outside. As she ventured into the street, she looked first one way, then the other. The whitewashed buildings glowed brightly in the midday sun and the accent colors of red, blue, and gold used on the doorways and trim seemed to vibrate against the starkness. The area surrounding Christos' house was fairly deserted and she relaxed a little. Perhaps no one would bother her today. Or, maybe they had all forgotten about her.

The trio stepped across the rocky street and a wave of heat, carried on a slight breeze, ran over them. The stifling air entered Valerie's lungs and she shuddered. It was much too hot here, even for August. The ground beneath her feet even felt heated through the leather soles of her shoes.

"What's that smell?" Clarus asked. She raised her nose in the air and sniffed.

"I don't smell anything," Stella answered, her reply curt. She waved a pudgy hand. "Keep walking. I want to finish up as fast as we can. We have a lot of work to do for tomorrow night."

"I think it smells like rotten eggs." Clarus sniffed again. "Yes, that's exactly what it smells like."

Valerie inhaled deeply. Clarus was right. There was the faintest odor in the air. Only she recognized it from Master Hobbs' science experiments to be sulfur, not rotten eggs. Valerie looked off into the distance. There, silhouetted against the azure blue sky, sat Vesuvius in all its glory. It wasn't flat and misshapen, like she had seen it to be in her own time. Here, in this period before the eruption, the cone was fully developed into a full mountain peak. She squinted and could see a thin trickle of gray steam escaping through the top. Valerie raised her hand to wipe the sweat from her brow and it was shaking. Quickly, she pulled it back down to her side.

"What's the matter?" Clarus asked as they walked. "You look as if you've seen the dead come back to life."

"And so I have," Valerie murmured. She realized she had less than two weeks before the volcano would release its fury on the unsuspecting city. Less than two weeks to find her way home.

"I beg your pardon?" Stella eyed Valerie. "What in Zeus' name are you talking about?"

Valerie shook herself out of her thoughts. "You wouldn't believe me if I told you." She looked down into Clarus' face and saw a flicker of fear behind the large brown eyes. There was no need to alarm the child. She patted her on the head. "At least it smells better than boiling rodents. Don't you agree?"

Clarus smiled, nodding. "Most anything smells better than that!" With a hop and a skip, she ran off toward Stella.

Valerie hurried along to catch up with the pair, her cane making a hollow thumping sound against the stone pathway. "I was wondering, Stella," she called, "what will we prepare next? Earthworm stew?"

Stella drew herself up as they continued down the street. "I've heard enough complaining from the two of you. Behave yourselves or I'll have a talk with Julius. He'll straighten you both out."

The woman was so intent on letting Julius mete out punishment, Valerie wondered if Stella herself were really as great a threat as she had believed earlier. A small child ran past, giggling. Without even thinking, Valerie braced herself for an attack. The girl kept going, though, oblivious to her presence. She let down her guard a little and continued to watch the child for a moment. The girl's long black hair flew behind her, so wild and carefree.

Valerie sighed, reminded of all the summers spent with her family at her Grandmother's country home when she was young and still able to run. Before the accident, she had felt as free as a flying bird when she raced through the bright yellow and green meadows of the hills and through the purple beds of heather. She shook her head. She was being ridiculous again. None of that mattered now.

Lost in her thoughts, she didn't notice the dark shadow the sunlight cast on the wall behind her. It approached steadily, then lunged, jarring her with a sharp jab to her back. Valerie stumbled, grinding the tip of her cane into the dirt. Ready to defend herself, she turned around, expecting to find a threatening crowd. Instead, she found Julius.

"Just wanted to let you know you're not alone. In case you thought you'd be able to get away with anything."

"And, pray tell, what do you suppose I'd be trying to get away with?"

He studied his fingernails. "Mmmm, maybe escaping."

"And where did you get the idea I would even want to escape?" Valerie asked, feigning innocence. "Especially considering how well the Pompeians have treated me." She turned to follow after Stella and Clarus. Julius grabbed her arm.

"Stella's right. You do think you're too good. I'm thinking you need to be taught a lesson." He raised a hand and Valerie kept her eyes on it, ready to dodge, but he simply rubbed his chin.

She let her breath out slowly. She didn't like what was becoming of her. Every time a person came near, she expected some sort of attack. She drew herself up. "What gives you, or anyone else for that matter, the right to judge what I need? I've had enough of you men and your little lessons." Valerie stared hard into Julius' eyes, exasperation filling her. "I'm not a school girl who needs a nanny to make her behave." She waved her hand and started walking after Stella and Clarus. "Please. Why can't you just leave me alone?"

Julius stood rooted to the spot he occupied on the street, his face growing red. "Because I don't like you." He shook a meaty fist in the air. "You'll pray to the gods for mercy before I'm finished with you. I promise you that!" Just then, a wagon came speeding down the street. With a yell, Julius jumped back and landed in the drainage ditch on the side of the road. He stood, sneering, and wiped the mule manure from his backside.

Clarus glanced over her shoulder at the commotion. Her eyes grew wide as Valerie caught up with her. "You're in trouble for sure. Look what happened to Julius."

Valerie turned around. She was certain Julius considered himself to be a great and noble warrior, but the sight of him covered in mule droppings was just too much. She laughed out loud. "Perhaps Sir Julius should be more careful where he sits."

"That's enough, you two," Stella interrupted. "Julius is a fine man and I won't listen to you making fun of him."

Clarus and Valerie glanced at each other and the child rolled her eyes. "I think Stella has feelings for Julius," Clarus whispered. "I've seen him climb the stairs to her loft many a night."

"You can't be serious!" Valerie exclaimed. The image of the tall burly guard and the wide sweaty woman just didn't fit in Valerie's mind. She shrugged. Perhaps some things were beyond understanding. Like time travel, for instance.

The trio turned a corner, leaving the tightly set houses of Christos' insula, and entered the wide expanse of the Forum market. On both sides, booths with brightly colored awnings were situated, proudly displaying each of the vendor's wares.

"How about a nice scarf for your mistress?" one of the merchants shouted.

"They don't want your trash," another man yelled. "Come over here. I sell only the finest garments."

Valerie ignored the men, intent on keeping up with Stella and Clarus. She tried to hurry, but they moved much more easily than she over the rock-paved streets and had already gone on ahead to the food stalls.

"How about a fortune? I could tell your fortune, you know."

Valerie froze. That voice! Where had she heard it before? Slowly, she turned around. An old woman approached her from the depths of an alley. It couldn't be, could it? "Pencia? Is it really you?"

"Who might you expect?" Pencia laughed and her cloudy brown eyes sparkled. "Some ghost?"

"How did you get here?" Valerie's head swam and she leaned against a stuccoed stone wall for support. "Were you trapped in the earthquake, too?"

"Course not." Pencia waved a gnarled hand. "I knew it was coming."

"But how?"

"Let us say I have my ways." She looked closely at Valerie, studying the younger woman. "I see something in your eyes I don't see the last time. You meet someone?"

Valerie blushed.

"Ah, I knew it would be so. This is good. Maybe young lady never go back to her world. Maybe she want to stay in Pompeii forever?"

"I can't stay forever. You know what's getting ready to happen next week. The city will be destroyed, thousands of people killed." Valerie grabbed Pencia's hand. "Tell me, how do I get back to my own time? How do I find eighteen sixty five again?"

Pencia pursed her lips, the motion serving to accentuate the heavy wrinkles lining her tanned face. "I cannot tell."

"You can't or you won't?" Valerie watched Pencia closely, her eyes narrowed. "You must travel back and forth all the time. How do you do it?"

"I think I don't like your tone." Despite the heat, the old woman pulled her tattered shawl close around her shoulders. "As I say, I have my ways. Problem is, they can't be yours. The traveling is different for everyone. You must find your own path."

"My own path?" Valerie ran her free hand over the roughhewn cedar of her cane. "How do I do that when I haven't the faintest idea how I got here?"

"Ah, now, it's like I say before, too. You grown up now. It's been good for you to be on your own. Have faith. You'll figure it out." She tapped her chest and raised a finger to the heavens. "The heart'll lead the way for you, but you got to pay attention to what it says."

"The heart? My heart?"

"*Si*. The path of the heart." Pencia touched Valerie's cheek, then turned to leave. "I go now. Just so you know, your family is good."

"Pencia, please. Don't leave me!" Valerie tried to hurry after her, but stumbled and fell to the hard stone pavement. She pushed herself back to her feet and reached for the woman, clutching at the air, but she had already disappeared back into the shadows of the alley.

"Follow your heart," Pencia called behind her from the darkness. "It get you home."

Valerie leaned back against the wall. Tears welled in her eyes and tumbled down her cheeks. At least her family was well. Oh, but she missed them so. "Please Lord," she whispered, a heavy ache filling her soul. "I want to go home. Please show me this path." Still leaning against the wall for support, she drew herself up and, spotting Clarus in the distance, headed toward the girl.

Behind Valerie, another figure emerged, unseen, from the shade of a covered entryway. Gravia's eyes were wide as she stared after Valerie. The heat must have gotten to the poor stupid girl. What was it she had said? The city would be destroyed next week? And where exactly was this 1865 place? She had never heard of it before.

"What do you make of it?" she asked the man standing next to her.

Julius walked out onto the street, straightening his tunic and tying his belt. "Who knows? Something isn't right about any of this. Did you see where the old woman went?"

Gravia craned her neck around the corner, but there was no one to be seen. "She must have turned into one of those buildings." She tapped a short finger against her chin. "The girl wants to escape."

"Of course she does. Every slave dreams of the day they'll be free." Julius laughed and made a grab for Gravia's breast.

She pulled away and slapped his hand. "Stop it! Someone might see you and tell Christos!" She crossed her arms. "I think perhaps we should help her get away."

"What? Have you gone mad?"

"Of course not, but I want her out of Christos' house. Maybe you could let her think you wanted to help her." She smiled prettily at Julius and caressed his arm. "After she is away from the city, you can do with her whatever you like."

"What makes you think she'd actually believe I'd want to do something like that? She knows I don't like her."

"You underestimate yourself. You can be quite convincing when you try."

"I think you're jealous, Gravia. You've seen how Christos looks at the girl, haven't you?" Julius shook his head. "Tell me, would you kill for him?"

"I would stop anyone who would take him, and his wealth, away from me. Besides," she continued, "I think you might enjoy taking care of the slave." She raised her eyebrows. "Am I wrong?"

Julius laughed. "Not much goes by you, does it Gravia? I'll tell you what. I'll see if I can 'help' the slave tomorrow night. With the dinner going on, Christos will be too busy to notice she's missing."

Gravia clapped her hands together. "Perfect. I knew I could count on you, dear Julius." She smiled again. "Come by in a few days and I will give you your reward."

Chapter Twenty-Six

"Hurry, everyone! The guests will be here soon!" Stella bellowed to the kitchen staff. Six slaves scurried in circles around Valerie while she struggled to fill several heavy clay pitchers with hot spiced wine. She started out of the kitchen, carrying a container to place on one of the small portable iron and stone stoves in the garden, when Stella stopped her.

"I don't think I'll let you serve tonight. I'm certain you'd spill something or knock a platter over onto a guest." Stella eyed her leg, shaking her head. "I want you positioned near the entry to the dining area. You'll be washing the visitor's feet as they arrive. Maybe later I'll let you near the garden."

Valerie slammed the pitcher down on the table. Had she heard correctly? The other slaves stopped dead, watching in silence. "I'm not certain I understood you. Did you say I was to . . . wash feet?"

Stella drew herself up. "That's exactly what I said. That way you'll be on your knees and won't cause any embarrassment to Master Christos."

"Oh? And was this the master's idea?" Valerie asked. *You're undesirable.* She closed her eyes for a moment, trying to compose herself.

"No, it was mine." Stella tapped her chest proudly. "I won't have you bringing disgrace upon the House of Campanius with your pitiful display of limping."

Valerie took a step backward. She felt as if she had been slapped. *You're undesirable.*

Clarus walked up and slipped her small, rough hand into Valerie's. "She'll call Julius, Val. It's not worth the punishment to argue," she whispered as tears welled in her eyes. "Please, just agree with her."

Val. Clarus had called her Val. Her vision clouded as, in her mind's eye, she was transported to her bedroom in England. Reggie was standing in the doorway and, as tears ran down his freckled cheeks, he reached for her. Valerie bent down and embraced the child, hugging her close. Her eyes locked with

Stella's. "I trust someone will demonstrate exactly what it is I'm to do?"

"I didn't think you'd give in so easily. Hmph. Maybe you're smarter than I thought," Stella conceded. "Clarus here will show you what to do." She stuck her chin out and stared hard at the child. "Don't think you're going to do the work for her, either. She'll do it herself."

Valerie squeezed the girl tighter. It was one thing to take Stella on herself, but Clarus didn't need to be in the middle of their disagreement. "May we leave now, Stella? Or do you need to call dear Julius and ask him his approval first?"

Stella sputtered, but before she could form a single word, Valerie and Clarus were out of the kitchen, giggling as they rushed out of harm's way.

* * *

"Welcome, my friends. So good to see you again." Christos stood just inside the front entry, his stark white toga almost glowing in the lamplight, and bid his guests enter. Friends and acquaintances came wearing their brightest clothing, the ladies intent on showing off the finest of their jewels.

After Christos' greeting, Clarus led the visitors to a spot just outside the garden dining area. Everyone marveled at the extent of decoration as they walked down the long corridor. Laurel wreaths hung over each doorway, scented petals were strewn on the floor and the finest of linens were draped over the marble dining couches.

"I see he's added another mural," one lady commented as she adjusted her gold armband. "The 'Dance of Dionysus' is an old classic and suits this house well. Christos has the most refined taste I've ever seen in a man."

"Ah, yes. Quite exquisite. I believe it to be the work of Marcus Apollos. He does create such handsome art," the other replied.

"Here we are." Clarus directed the ladies to where Valerie waited on her knees, near a large column by the garden. She was surrounded by the array of items she had assembled - a stack of linen cloths, soft leather slippers, and a bowl of warm scented water.

"Please, have a seat," Valerie bid, directing one of the ladies to a stool positioned in front of her. She was careful to keep her eyes lowered as she had been instructed, lest they think her insolent. Insolent, indeed. They should all have the pleasure of meeting Lucy then they could see what insolence in a servant really meant.

Valerie desperately tried to hide her distaste as she removed first one sandal, then the other. The Romans bathed regularly, but the dust of the streets seemed to cake itself between their toes. Well, that was just too much, she thought, her eyes running over the woman's foot as she rinsed it. She simply would not clean their toenails. Stella could call Julius and he could beat her all he wanted, but here she had to draw the line.

Quickly, Valerie slid a pair of comfortable leather house slippers onto the woman's feet, hoping she wouldn't notice the missed spots. As the lady stood, Valerie bade her to enter the dining room, "Right foot forward." Clarus had said something about it being bad luck to walk into a room with the left foot in the lead. She shrugged. A superstitious lot, these Romans were. Not unlike a few Englishmen she knew.

Valerie was in the midst of washing the other woman's feet, when she felt eyes on her. She had to fight not to look up. It was no use. She would never make a good servant. The sensation of being watched over took her and she glanced up from under her long lashes. Standing off to the side was Christos. He was having a conversation with an older man, but his eyes were fixed on her.

Valerie pushed back a stray strand of hair, feeling extremely self-conscious. Did the man always have to be so close? Did he always have to watch her so intently? What did he care of her? After all, she was only a slave, and not a very worthy one at that, what with her crippled foot and all. At least, that was the way Stella put it.

In her frustration, she splashed the water too high and spotted the green silk *stola* of the auburn-haired woman sitting before her. The woman jumped to her feet, kicking the bowl over. Valerie grabbed a handful of linens and began frantically wiping up the water.

"What in the name of the gods are you doing, girl?" The woman raised her arm and cuffed Valerie on the ear, sending her reeling to the right. In the next moment, Christos appeared at her side and knelt down. "Are you all right?" he asked, his voice a rough whisper.

Valerie nodded as she rubbed the side of her head, still dizzy from the blow. Didn't this woman know an accident when she saw one?

"Come now, Petronia. You can see it wasn't done on purpose." Christos bent over and placed the slippers on her feet himself.

The anger left the woman's eyes and she seemed appeased for the moment. It was a great honor for the head of the household to adorn a visitor's feet.

"There now, go on ahead to the dining room. And remember, right foot forward."

Petronia gave what Valerie assumed to be a smile, but the woman's lips were so tight they threatened to split open. "You're much too solicitous of your slaves. I'd beat her if I were you," she offered before leaving.

"But you're not me, are you?" Christos replied. His voice barely hid the anger Valerie detected in his eyes. He turned his attention to her. "Are you certain you're all right?" he asked quietly.

"You needn't worry after me," Valerie replied, her voice shakier than she would have liked it to be. It was the first time he had spoken to her since their encounter in the garden. Did he honestly believe he could just run to her rescue and she would immediately forget he had almost beaten her? She glanced up. Everyone was standing around, watching them. Now was not the time or place to talk to him, but talk she would later on. "I'll finish now, if you like."

Christos smiled as his eyes swept over her figure. "I like very much. But *we* can finish later."

He waved his arm. "Everyone, come. Let's offer a prayer to the *lares* and request a fine and entertaining evening."

The guests clapped their hands together and murmured their approval as Christos approached the shrine of the household gods.

Carefully, he opened the heavily carved and gilded doors of the tall wooden cabinet, exposing the small altar contained therein. A servant appeared and offered a tray containing bits of grain, cinnamon, and salt. Christos lit the sacramental oil lamp and adjusted the flame until it glowed with a yellow heart. He took the toga the servant carried as well and positioned it over his head, covering the curly black locks. His lips began to move in a silent prayer as he sprinkled bits of the offerings into the flames. The pungent aroma of cinnamon filled the room and wafted out into the night air.

Valerie imagined she was that scent, and followed its path over the roof, past the rows of houses, and into the dark August night. She hugged her arms around her, watching in fascination as Christos concluded the ceremony.

As he finished, another servant led the guests to their assigned seats. She knew Stella had taken great care in making certain the most influential and important people were at Christos' table. The least important ones were scattered in less conspicuous places about the garden. Valerie watched with amusement as the *Pompeians* reclined on the couches, shoulder to breast against the person next to them. How in the world they could maintain any level of comfort eating this way was beyond her. Of course, they'd probably think the same of her dining habits.

"I would make a toast to our host." One of the guests, a patrician-looking, fair-haired man, raised a goblet of wine that had just been poured. "May this evening be free of lustful glances, coarse conversation, and foul language."

"Felix, you take all the fun out of having a party." Everyone turned in the direction of the voice. Making her entrance into the garden was Gravia, her bright red *stola* floating behind her in a billow. Her blonde hair was piled high on her head with gold threads and jewels strung through the curls.

Valerie started to step away, but Gravia saw her before she could escape. "Will you not wash my feet before dinner?" she asked, her eyebrows raised.

Valerie came forward and considered the woman. Gravia was much too smug to suit her. "You mean to say you haven't bathed properly today?" Valerie asked, her expression a mixture of concern and disgust. Those nearby gasped and leaned forward, eagerly awaiting Gravia's reaction to the insult.

"Of course I have bathed!" Gravia stomped her foot on the mosaic tile floor. She plopped herself down on the stool. "You will do me this courtesy," her eyes narrowed. "Or else."

"Valerie."

She turned slightly. Christos was standing near the entry. "You will please honor my guest." He looked directly into her eyes and she saw how very tired he was.

"You plead with a servant? What has become of you, Christos?" Gravia asked, her voice high. "Are you growing soft in the head?"

"Perhaps." He laughed and it broke the tension in the room as everyone joined in.

Valerie couldn't help but smile herself. What did it matter? She would be gone from this place soon enough. Carefully, she lowered herself to her knees and washed Gravia's feet. When she was finished, Christos took Gravia by the hand and led her to his table. She pushed another blonde haired woman out of the way so she could be the one to lie next to Christos. Valerie rolled her eyes. The woman was so obvious, it positively turned one's stomach.

As she was watching quietly, a drum began to beat behind her. Moving as if in slow motion, several slaves marched past, playing instruments the likes of which Valerie had never seen before. The musicians situated themselves behind a sheer pink curtain at the opposite end of the garden and began to play songs, their mood low and ethereal.

"What do you think you're about?"

Startled, Valerie jumped at the voice. "You told me to stay out of the way, Stella, and that's exactly what I'm doing." She turned around and smiled at the woman. "Is that all right with you?"

"Of course it's not all right." Stella puffed herself up and thrust her great chest out even further. "One of the slaves has turned up ill and I'll need you to clean away the dirty plates and goblets. Drop even one and I'll ship you to the fields for the rest of your life. Is that understood?"

"How could I help but understand, dear Stella, when you ask so nicely?" Valerie offered a stiff curtsy, then turned and walked through the peristyle and into the garden, her cane tapping out a steady beat against the tiled floor.

Chapter Twenty-Seven

Clarus motioned to Valerie as she entered the garden. The young woman stepped carefully over a row of low growing shrubs that divided the sitting area from the rest of the house and took her place at the girl's side.

"Now what?" Valerie asked, her voice a low whisper.

"We wait until they have finished each course, then we will remove the soiled dishes to the kitchen," Clarus explained quietly. As she finished, the music grew louder. "Look." She motioned with a nod of her head. "The first course is arriving."

Valerie watched as several slaves carried in large bronze and silver platters piled high with appetizers. Sardines, sea urchins, and lobster claws adorned one tray, while another held nightingale tongues and the mice rolled in honey and poppy seeds. She covered her mouth and looked the other way as a guest downed one of the poor creatures in a single bite.

She grimaced. "I still can't believe people actually eat those things."

"Did you try one?"

"Of course not." Valerie pulled at her skirt, straightening it.

"Then I do not think you should be criticizing." Clarus' eyes met hers. "If we are lucky, there will be food left over and we will dine as well as the guests."

Valerie glanced down, her cheeks growing red. "You speak with a wisdom that goes beyond your years, Clarus. I'm sorry. I've never been very good at keeping my opinions to myself."

"So I have noticed. It is hard for me to believe slaves in your country are allowed to speak so freely."

"We don't have slaves in my country, only paid servants," Valerie explained.

"You mean you were given money for your services?"

Valerie shook her head. The past few weeks had taken their toll and, as she thought of home, she suddenly felt so tired. "Dear Clarus, I wasn't a servant. I'm the daughter of a knight of the realm. A banker by profession who employs his own servants."

Clarus silently considered her companion for a moment. "I do not understand what it is you say. You speak so strangely."

"I know." She looked over at the girl. "Tell me, can you keep a secret?"

Clarus squeezed her hands together. "I am the best! Please tell me one!" She leaned forward, eager to listen.

"Well, I know of someone who lives in Pompeii. She's not certain how she came to be in this place. She misses her family very much. But, somehow, she traveled here from the future and doesn't know how to return. She just wants to go home." Home. The word tugged at Valerie's heart and she swallowed hard.

"You are telling me a story, not a secret!" Clarus exclaimed, stomping her foot on the ground. She stuck her bottom lip out. "I thought you trusted me."

"I do trust you. This *is* a secret and it happens to be very true. She honestly doesn't know how she got here."

Clarus looked at Valerie closely, as if judging her and the content of the secret. "You are this person, are you not?"

Valerie nodded slightly. "I am."

Just then, the music grew to a frenzied pitch and she could feel the drum beat in her body. Two slaves arrived in the midst of the sound, carrying a roasted wild boar. The animal was adorned complete with a shield and helmet of some foreign army. Another slave ran after them, brandishing a Roman sword. As the tray was placed in the center of Christos' table, everyone clapped. The servant with the sword attacked the meat, slicing it into huge chunks for the guests to enjoy.

Gravia passed her plate to Christos, nudging him gently with her shoulder. Her lips brushed against his jaw as she requested a piece of the thigh. "Just a small one, dearest Christos. I cannot risk too much as I fear I would grow too fat and lazy here on your couch."

Felix laughed from his position across the table from the pair. "Since when, Gravia, do you worry about such matters? Why, at my party, you consumed more food and drink than any man there."

Gravia drew herself up. Her eyes spat venom at the man. "That is not true at all. I cannot believe you would say such a thing about a lady."

"I wouldn't say it about a lady, but I would certainly say it about you."

Valerie giggled from where she stood near the table and a few nearby guests turned to look at her. Quickly, she covered her mouth and dissolved into a coughing fit. Once composed, she went to Felix's side. She felt an immediate kinship with this fair-haired man and his honesty where Gravia was concerned. "May I remove this plate for you, sir?"

Felix smiled and nodded. His blue eyes swept over her figure as she leaned across the table. "Where did you find her, Christos?"

"At auction." Christos answered easily enough, but the cold stare of his eyes betrayed a deeper emotion.

"Of course. I remember now. She's the one the townsfolk were calling a witch. I would guess she could cast a spell on any man, with those green eyes of hers."

"I do not see where the attraction lies," Gravia began, her lips formed into a pout. "She *is* a cripple, after all. How attractive can that be to a man?"

Valerie stepped forward, her eyes blazing. For heaven's sake, how could they talk about her as if she had no ears to hear what they were saying? It was as if she had never left England. She opened her mouth to speak, but stopped short when Christos' eyes locked with hers.

"It makes no difference what form the body may take, Gravia," he stated quietly, his eyes never leaving Valerie's. "What is important is the heart that beats within. If it be a strong and true heart, one of courage and unwielding love, then it is attractive no matter the container." He smiled crookedly and Valerie felt her resolve to be angry with him quickly slipping away. "Of course, a pleasant face and well-rounded shape doesn't hurt."

"A toast to that, dear friend!" Felix raised his goblet high and tipped it slightly to Valerie. "To the witch in our midst. Though a slave in body, may her soul travel to the heights of ecstasy and freedom in a man's embrace." He leaned toward her and whispered, "I could be that man."

Valerie felt her cheeks grow hot and retreated into the shadows cast by the peristyle. So many flowery words she had never heard before, even from Thomas whom she knew considered himself an expert in the art of seduction. She would do well to keep her distance from this Felix.

"Careful, Felix," Christos admonished, his voice low. "I would remind you she is mine."

"And you would not allow her to offer comfort to your oldest and dearest friend?" He motioned with his hand toward Gravia. "Why, even Gravia here has deemed me worthy of such compassion as you would not allow a slave to give."

Christos' eyes met Felix's. He regarded the man coolly. "Gravia is a free woman and can do as she pleases. There are no words between us that would bind her fidelity to me."

Gravia pushed her plate away and rested her breasts on the table. She ran a finger over Christos' cheek. "You do not really believe Felix, do you, my love? You know how he likes to carry on."

"Do you think me the fool, Gravia?" He shook his head and chuckled. "I know you too well."

"But I *love* only you," Gravia retorted.

As Gravia spoke, a bright flash of lightning streaked against the moonless sky. On its heels was another, followed by the low rumble of thunder.

"It seems the gods would argue with you." Christos picked up his goblet to take a sip, but stopped when the mixture began to shake of its own volition. On the table, the plates jumped and rattled as the ground moved. Several platters slipped and crashed to the ground. One of the small wine warmers toppled over. The clay *amphora* split in half as it hit the hard tile. The blood red wine soaked into the crevices between the stones, staining the mortar.

From the other side of the garden, a woman screamed. Her cry was followed by another. The guests clutched the edges of their couch, their faces dark with terror. Then, just as quickly as it had begun, the quake subsided.

"This does not bode well," one of the diners commented. "The gods are angry."

"We have done nothing to anger them," another reasoned.

"I would guess it is just a tantrum," Felix observed. "You saw the lightning. Perhaps Zeus himself is having a fight with his lady love." He looked pointedly at Christos. "The same as our dear host."

Christos signaled the musicians and they began to play again. Slowly, the tension in the room began to ease as the debris from the earthquake was cleared away. He smiled as another course was brought into the room. Dear Stella, she wouldn't let anyone, even the gods, interfere with her dinner.

* * *

Valerie glanced desperately about as the earthquake shook the tiled floor beneath her feet. Clarus ran by along with the other servants, all of them on their way toward the kitchen. She followed as quickly as she could, stumbling and tripping while the ground heaved and rolled. From the darkness of the corridor, someone grabbed her by the arm and pulled her aside.

"Come with me," the voice ordered.

As her eyes grew accustomed to the dark, she saw who it was. "No, Julius. I'll go with the others." She pulled her arm free and started back in the direction she had been heading.

"They are foolish! The house will collapse on all of their heads." He looked at the front entry door. "Come, or you will die with these people."

Valerie hesitated. Were her calculations wrong? Could this be the day Vesuvius would destroy Pompeii? "I need to find Christos."

He grabbed her arm again. "He sent me after you. He said he'd meet us outside."

The ground shook once more. "All right, Julius," Valerie relented. "I'll come with you."

He shoved her ahead of him and glanced over his shoulder. "To the door!" he shouted over the rumble. "I'll take you to safety!"

As Valerie and Julius stumbled out the front entry and into the street, another figure stepped forward and ran after them.

"Valerie! Wait!" Clarus yelled. "Don't go with him!" But when she reached the doorway, they were nowhere to be found. The pair had already disappeared into the milling crowd outside.

Chapter Twenty-Eight

Julius pushed his way through the thick throng of people in the streets, pulling Valerie behind him. Everywhere, people were standing outside their homes, waiting as if they weren't certain if they should flee or not. Babies and children cried. Men shouted to each other over the din. Another rumble and an old woman fell to her knees, praying.

As Julius and Valerie hurried around a corner and left Christos' *insula*, the quake subsided. The crowd in the street hovered for only a moment before rushing back to their homes, anxious to see how much damage had occurred.

"Where's Christos? You said he was meeting us, didn't you?"

Julius glanced around, a smirk on his face. "It looks like he changed his mind."

Valerie took a step backward. Fear started to grow in her stomach, tickling her insides. "Perhaps we should return to the house again. It seems the earthquake is over."

Julius didn't answer, but grabbed her arm and began to dodge through the crowd.

What was he doing? They were still going in the opposite direction of Christos' home. "Julius?" She ground her heels and cane into the dirt, pulling herself and the man to a halt. "Did you hear me? I said we should go home."

"Of course I heard you." He yanked on her arm and she tripped over a raised stone in the walkway. He pulled her upright, as one would a child who has fallen, and continued on. "It won't be necessary."

"Why is that?" she asked. Apprehension twisted in her brain. She glanced over her shoulder. The area behind her was deserted now. There was no one who might help.

He patted the center of his chest. "Because I've decided to give you your freedom."

"I - I thought only Christos could do that." Valerie looked around again, trying to memorize the path they were taking. She wasn't too far yet from the house. She could get back on her own if she had to.

"Christos is a fool." He stopped and shoved her against a doorway. "He doesn't understand your spirit, like I do. You should be free." Julius ran a callused hand across her throat. His fingertips were icy cold. "I offer you that freedom. Will you turn it down?" With a quick motion, he gripped her neck and squeezed ever so gently. "Will you?"

Valerie struggled. She dropped her cane as she tried to shove him away from her. "Stop it!" She choked out the words.

He leaned forward and she could see clearly every pore and scar that covered his face. His tepid breath reeked of wine. "You aren't going about this the right way at all." He rubbed his chin with his free hand. "Say you want me to set you free."

"Julius," she pleaded, her voice a raspy whisper.

He squeezed her throat a little tighter. "Say it!"

"I - I want you to set me free."

"Say please."

"Please. Please." Valerie watched as the crazed glow in his eyes mellowed into a smile. What demon had possessed the man? How was she going to get away from him?

"Good." He released his grip on her. "Let's go." Julius bent down and easily scooped Valerie up into his arms.

"I can walk." She pushed against him, but he held her firmly. "Just let me get my cane."

"You won't need it where I'm taking you." Julius stepped from the shadows and into the street again. As he hurried down the road, a deep chuckle rose in his throat and burst forth, disrupting the quiet that had only just returned to the night.

* * *

Unable to find Valerie and Julius, Clarus walked back into the house. She should have told Valerie what she'd heard Julius tell Stella. She should have warned her so that her friend wouldn't have gone with him tonight. She just hadn't had the chance to, what with all the preparations for the banquet.

"Soon, I'll have her out of your way, my love." That's what she'd heard him say, late last night when she couldn't sleep. It was so hot. How could Julius and Stella stand to lie so close together in that small bed of hers? "She's been a problem since the day she arrived. I'll enjoy getting rid of the woman. And I'm doing it all for you."

But who would believe her? Who could she tell? After all, she was only a child. No one listened to Clarus the serving girl -- ever. She considered her options for a moment longer. But *he* might listen to me, she thought. She squared her shoulders and headed toward the garden.

* * *

"Where is that lovely slave of yours, Christos?" Felix asked. "I have a pile of dirty plates I'd like her to take away." He gestured toward the center of the table. "I haven't any room left for a dish of dessert and I was so looking forward to Stella's pomegranate cake."

"I think I saw her going out the front door during the disturbance." Gravia flicked a crumb of bread from her arm. She raised her eyes to Christos. "She probably took advantage of the diversion to escape. What do you think, my love?"

Christos eyed his companions. They might be his oldest friends, but that definitely didn't mean he had to trust them. He stood and walked about the garden, pretending to be checking on his guests, but inspecting every corner and niche as he did so. Unsatisfied, he called to Stella, who came lumbering out of the kitchen at his command.

"What is it, Master?" she asked, her breath coming in short gasps.

"Where is Valerie?"

"I thought she was out here, sir, where I told her to be." She looked nervously about. "I fear my cake is going to burn, Master. May I please return to the kitchen?"

"Have Julius go looking for her."

Stella bowed her head. "Yes, sir."

With a wave of his hand, Christos dismissed the woman. He walked back to his dining couch. Turning his attention to Gravia, he asked, "If you saw her leaving, why didn't you say something?"

"Why, Christos, I was so terrified by the earthquake, it took all of my strength to hold on to you." She glanced at him again through her lashes and smiled. "She is just one slave. Someone will probably return her in the morning. After all, how far can she get, considering she is crippled?" Gravia patted the empty space next to her. "Come, finish dining with us."

"Please do, friend," Felix bade. "If the girl doesn't show up by morning, I'll go with you myself to fetch her home."

A frown creased Christos' brow as he lowered himself to his seat. Gravia wasn't *that* scared by the quake. She'd been through plenty of them before. And Felix was being too damned accommodating. They knew something and there was no way to find out at the moment without creating a scene. He could hardly leave his guests to run off in search of a slave, especially after just telling Stella to send Julius out after her. Valerie was foolish in thinking she could be rid of him so easily. She was his, after all.

He looked off across the garden, not focusing on any thing in particular, when the lamplight glinted against a woman's necklace. An emerald, it brought to mind another woman's eyes, pleading for mercy as she was dragged through the streets. A woman's eyes, smoldering, as she played the game of seductress. A woman's eyes, pained by betrayal as he raised his hand against her. He closed his eyes, pushing the images out of his mind. He had given her every excuse to run away, and none to stay.

"Christos, I asked if you would like a piece of cake." Gravia licked her dark red lips as she offered him a bite with her own hand.

Absently, he opened his mouth and accepted the offer. Everyone at the table smiled and applauded. He shook his head as if to clear it, then realized what he had done. "Forget it, Gravia. It won't work."

"But you just accepted my proposal of marriage, did you not?" She waved her arm in a wide sweeping motion. "And I have all of these witnesses."

"Perhaps his feet are already growing cold," Felix offered.

Gravia smiled, triumphant. "Do not worry, my love. I will warm them for you, for the rest of our days."

Chapter Twenty-Nine

Clarus scurried down the hallway and into the garden. She tripped over the shrubs and fell, face first, at Gravia's feet. She raised herself to her knees, panting.

"Why are you in such a rush?" Christos asked, an amused smile playing about his lips. "Are there demons chasing you?" He looked over her shoulder, a mock frown creasing his brow.

"It's Valerie," she gasped.

"We know all about how Valerie has run away," Felix said. "Now, why don't you clear these plates away for me. When you're through, you can fetch me some cake."

Clarus opened her mouth to speak, but Gravia interrupted her. "Will you be so impertinent as to question your master's guest? Do what you're told, girl, and be quick about it!"

Clarus looked at Christos, tears welling in her eyes. "Let the child speak, Gravia," he said. "Felix's belly will wait a moment longer." Christos leaned forward, smiling again. "Now, what is so important that you must interrupt this dinner?"

"I-I'm sorry, master. It's just that I know Valerie did not run away."

Christos' smile faded. "And how can you be so certain?"

"She is an escaped slave," Gravia stated flatly. "She deserves no further attention from us." She studied her long fingernails. "Julius is going to take care of her."

"I know! That's the problem." Clarus took a step closer to Gravia.

Gravia spun her head around. "You dare to talk back to me?" With one swift motion, she backhanded the girl across the mouth. Clarus fell and slammed her head with a sickening thud against one of the portable stoves.

Christos jumped to his feet and rushed to the child's side. He lifted her and cradled her limp form in his arms. When he pulled his hand away, it was stained bright red with blood. "You are truly a cold woman, Gravia, to attack a small child so viciously." He ground out the words as his eyes bore through her.

"She is not a child. She is just a slave, for the love of Zeus." She shook her head. "Really, Christos, I think you grow too attached to these servants of yours." She stood and straightened her gown. "One would think you exhibit, shall we say, an unnatural affection for the girl?"

Christos' eyes narrowed. "Your games grow tedious, Gravia. You may leave now." He stood, lifting Clarus up in his arms. The remaining guests milled about, as if they weren't certain what to do next. Christos sighed. "Perhaps everyone should go home. It would seem as if the gods were playing a hand against our having a good time tonight."

As his friends left, Christos climbed the stairs to the loft above the kitchen. Gently, he laid Clarus' still body on her bed. He put an ear to her chest. Thank the gods. She was still alive. He poured some water into a clay bowl and began to bathe her wound. "Please, little one, you must awaken. I need to know what has happened to our Valerie."

* * *

"Julius! You can't leave me here!" Valerie screamed as she clutched at him. He kicked her hand away as he climbed up the steep incline of the damp, dark cave, taking the torch, the only source of light, with him.

"Don't fret. I'll return soon enough." He turned and the firelight distorted his face. He grinned at her, looking like a demon of hell. "Now, tell me you'll miss me."

"What?" Valerie reached for him again. He *had* to listen! "Please, Julius, you must take me with you."

He stuck the torch into the cave opening, sending a thin shaft of light into interior. Valerie crawled toward him. "I – I will miss you very much. I don't want us to be apart." She raised a hand again as she began to slip. "Please, take me with you."

Julius grinned again and ducked back out of the cave. In the darkness, Valerie could make out his shape as he began to roll a heavy stone in front of the opening.

"What are you doing?" she screamed. Again, she tried to crawl toward him, but the steep floor of the cave was wet and slimy. She slid back to the bottom and landed in a heap. "No!"

she screamed again as the last bit of light from the torch disappeared from sight.

Her chest heaved and her body convulsed with sobs. Oh, dear God, how am I going to get out of here? Her thoughts raced as she forced herself to calm down. Valerie, you won't find your way out if all you do is cry, she admonished herself. But still, the tears ran freely down her cheeks. Why was Julius doing this to her? Did Christos know? Had he ordered her to be punished because of her behavior at the party?

Valerie sneezed as the soggy moistness of the cave worked its way into her bones. She took a deep breath and the smell of salty sea air filled her. She reached down and felt the ground, scooping up a handful of the substance that covered the rocky floor. It was sand. The cave must be located somewhere near the water, if not right on the shore.

Something scurried by, and she pulled her legs up as best she could, tucking them beneath her. She shifted as she tried to find a halfway comfortable position where she sat in the rocks and sand. Valerie took another deep breath. She reached out to the sides, feeling the rocky walls of her dungeon. They weren't more than an arm's length away, all around. Valerie swallowed hard. She must be at the bottom of some sort of natural well. Considering she was so close to Vesuvius, it might even be a lava tube.

"Help!" she shouted. "Is anyone out there?" The sound bounced off the close walls and echoed in her ears. Valerie put her hands over them and shuddered. There was no way out, except up.

She raised herself and tried to find the footholds Julius had used to climb down the steep sides and back up again. Good. There was the first one. Valerie gripped it tightly and pulled, slipping her good foot into another under it. She found the next one and grabbed hold. Raising her damaged foot, she forced it into one of the openings. She put her weight on it slightly, testing it for support. A scream escaped her as she tumbled down to the floor.

"Damn," she cursed and sat upright.

She tried again and again to no avail, her crippled foot keeping her back. Finally, exhausted, she slid over to a rock and climbed up on it. She ran a hand through her hair and nestled back into a small niche in the side of the cave. Valerie hugged her arms around her chest and closed her eyes, forcing herself to remain calm. There would be no way out of her prison, at least not until Julius returned.

* * *

"Julius, my love," Gravia purred. "Tell me again how you got rid of her." She rubbed a hand along his thigh and he moved closer.

"It was quite easy, really. The earthquake was the perfect diversion. I simply told her she would be safe with me." He shrugged his shoulders. "Can I help it if I'm so convincing?"

Gravia laughed and clapped her hands together. "I love it! But for now, you must return to Christos' house. They think Stella sent you in search of the girl." She cast a sidelong glance at her companion. "Will the woman lie for you?"

"Stella? Of course she will." He nuzzled her neck. "She thinks I got rid of Valerie for her, the silly woman." Julius lowered himself between Gravia's legs. "If she only knew."

* * *

Clarus shifted and Christos jumped to his feet. He groaned, stiff from spending the night on the hard floor. He saw where the bright light of morning had worked its way through a crack in the roof and touched the girl's eyelids. She swiped at it, as if she could make the disturbance go away.

"Clarus?" he whispered her name. "Are you awake?"

"I'm thirsty," she murmured, the words slurring together.

Christos face broke into a smile. "I'm so happy to hear that, little one." He raised her head slightly so she could drink from the goblet of water he offered. He frowned as he felt the large bump on her head. Gently, he lowered her back to the pillow. "How are you feeling today?"

"My head feels as if it is on fire." She slowly opened her eyes. "What happened? Why are you here in my room?"

"I was too worried about you to let you sleep alone. So, I thought I'd stay here with you." He smiled again. "I hope you don't mind."

Clarus started to nod, then stopped as the pain became unbearable. "I remember. Mistress Gravia. She hit me." Tears rolled down her pale cheeks. "Why, master? Why?"

"I can't answer your question. Everyone is ruled by their own conscience and, apparently, Gravia's allows such acts." He wiped her brow with a cool cloth. "Last night, you started to tell me something about Valerie. Do you remember?"

Clarus scrunched up her face as if deep in thought. Suddenly, she tried to get to her feet. Christos carefully pushed her back down. "Please, you must let me go. I have to find her."

"I wish to find her as well. Do you know where she has gone?"

"I only know what I heard yesterday, before the party. Julius told Stella he was going to get rid of her." She took a deep breath. "During the earthquake, I saw him push Valerie out the front door."

"But when Gravia said she saw Valerie leave, she didn't mention Julius." He eyed her intently. "Are you certain of what you heard?"

"Valerie would not run away," Clarus whispered, her voice growing more and more tired.

"How can you be so certain?"

"Because she can't get home from here."

"I know, dear Clarus. Valerie used to live across a great sea and would need a boat to travel home."

"No, that is not why. She is from another time. She told me her story. She came from the future and does not know ... why ... or ... how ... to ... get ... home." Clarus' voice trailed off as she drifted back to sleep.

Christos leaned back on his heels and wiped the damp cloth over his own eyes. The future? Impossible! But then, he remembered their conversation in the garden from a few weeks ago. What was is she had said? She was a student of history. And she knew of the earthquakes. Slowly, he stood. She had also said Vesuvius was going to destroy Pompeii.

Quickly, he exited the room. As he made his way down the stairs and into the atrium, the front door pushed open. Julius entered. Christos approached him warily. "You look terrible, my friend. Where have you spent the night?"

"That's just it. I haven't slept at all."

Christos rubbed his chin, considering the man. "Really? I thought you would have found time to rest. Or, at the very least, a pair of willing arms to offer some comfort."

Julius grinned. "Well, under usual circumstances, perhaps. But when Stella said you wanted me to find the runaway slave, I was so intent on my duty that I didn't rest." He stomped his feet, knocking off the sand that still clung to the inside of his sandals.

Christos nodded toward the floor. "It would seem your travels took you quite a ways from here. I wouldn't have thought the girl could have traveled fast enough to reach the sea last night."

"Yes, I wished to inspect every possibility. She might have had an accomplice." He looked away, fidgeting. "That *is* why you keep me around here, isn't it?"

"Ah, Julius, you are truly a friend." Christos clapped the larger man on the back. "And I want you to know your loyalty will not go unrewarded."

Julius coughed and pulled away slightly. He looked into the other man's eyes then quickly glanced away. "You know, I'm very hungry. Do you mind if I go to the kitchen now?"

"In a moment." He dropped his hand and walked behind him, as if sizing him up. "So, where's the girl?"

"Oh, didn't I tell you?" Julius coughed again. "I, uh, I haven't found her yet." He turned around and looked at Christos. "I'll head back out as soon as I have something to eat. That is, if you'd like me to."

Christos smiled. "I would like that very much, friend. Very much indeed."

Chapter Thirty

Christos leaned casually on the railing of the atrium, his hands dangling over the edge. He spotted Julius as he was leaving the kitchen, then stretched and yawned.

Julius stopped halfway to the front door. "Did you not sleep well last night?"

"No, I didn't. I was too worried about Clarus. Gravia hurt the child badly." He yawned again. "I do believe a nap may be in order." Christos motioned with his head toward the door. "Are you going out now to look for the slave?"

"Uh, yes. That's exactly what I thought I'd do, unless you've changed your mind."

Christos rubbed his eyes. "Of course not. The girl's much too arrogant in thinking she can get away. She thought too highly of herself all along, didn't she? Do me a favor and bring her back in one piece so I can give her a sound lashing."

"She *was* much too arrogant for a slave," Julius agreed, gritting his teeth together. He bowed low. "I'll do as you wish." He reached the door and stepped outside, slamming it shut behind him.

As he left the house, Julius glanced over his shoulder. Good. The sun was just barely over the tops of the houses. It was still too early for anyone to be about, except for a few slaves.

Carefully retracing his steps through the city, he made his way past the marketplace where the vendors were just now raising their awnings, past the bakery, the tavern, and out beyond the stone and iron front gates. Walking steadily, Julius moved through the Necropolis and headed east for the sea. He checked the sun again. The tide would soon be in and he definitely didn't want to miss it.

* * *

A heavy sigh escaped Christos' lips as he ventured into the streets. He caught sight of Julius' large form, just ahead of him. He hurried to catch up, careful to keep out of sight. What evil had driven this man to betray his trust? He shook his head slightly as he walked. How could the man he called friend, the man whose very life he had saved innumerable times on the battlefield, steal from him?

By the gods, he swore, Valerie had better be unharmed when I find her. He rested his hand on the hilt of his sword as he trotted through the city of the dead. Julius stopped and Christos quickly ducked behind a column. He wiped the sweat from his brow. It was much too hot for this early in the day.

His eyes followed the direction of the other man's, but Julius appeared to be only looking at the sun. What could it possibly be telling him, other than the time of day?

* * *

Julius laughed to himself as he approached the sea. The water was growing higher. The tide rolled in with a rush onto the sand and he jumped back from the stinging cold spray. Carefully, he picked his way over the black volcanic rocks that lined the shore. He stopped and rubbed his chin. Now, where did I leave the girl?

He heard a faint call for help and turned his head to listen. Ah, there she was. The water was just beginning to reach the opening to the cave. Some of it may even be trickling in by now. He spit on his hands and grabbed the heavy stone. Rolling it to the side, the well was bathed in sunlight.

Valerie stepped away from the beam of light and shaded her eyes. "Julius?"

"*Saluto*, my pretty witch," he called down the steep incline.

"Help me out of here." She reached for him. "Please."

"I couldn't do that." He leaned over the edge of the opening and rested his chin on his hands.

A rush of cold water spilled into the cave, splashing Valerie across the face and soaking her dress. She stumbled back and ran into the wall. The jolt sent her to the ground. "What's happening?" she shouted. "For heaven's sake, why are you throwing water on me?"

Julius laughed. "I'm not. Nature is. If you are truly a witch, you should be able to fly out of there, now that the opening is clear." He motioned for her with one hand. "Come on. Fly toward me."

"I'm not a witch nor can I fly!" She slipped a hand into one of the holds and started to pull herself up again, when another rush of water came. A steady stream followed it and the cave began to fill at an alarming rate. Valerie glanced down. The water was up to her knees. "Julius! Why are you doing this to me?" she screamed. "Get me out of here! Now!"

Julius looked down at her, a benign expression on his face. "I would cleanse Christos' house of your witchery," he replied. No sooner had the words left his lips than his expression changed to anger. She saw him stand and could hear voices. He was arguing with someone. A loud clanging rang out over the sound of the sea. Why was he fighting the other person? "Help me!" she yelled, hoping whoever else was out there would hear her over the water. It was up to her waist. She grabbed another handhold and pulled. The swirling wet mass tugged at her clothing, yanking her down.

Suddenly, she heard a gurgling scream. The bright flash of sunlight against steel burned her eyes and she looked away for an instant. In that moment, the tide washed a heavy object down toward her. Valerie looked up just soon enough to see Julius' head roll past her. It bobbed up and down, taunting her with its sightless eyes and gaping mouth. She screamed and almost lost her hold as her stomach turned and roiled.

"Valerie?"

She quickly looked up. "Christos! Hurry!" she yelled. "The water's up to my shoulders."

Slowly, Christos began a steady descent into the blackness of the cave. Valerie caught her breath and held it when he slipped. She breathed again when he regained his foothold. He reached down toward her and clasped his strong hand around her wrist.

"I'm going to pull you up, but you've got to help if you can."

Valerie nodded. "Please, just get me out of here."

Christos smiled through the dark tangle of wet curls that hung over his eyes. "As you wish."

Steadily, they climbed together, Christos supporting Valerie when her foot wouldn't until, at last, they reached the top. Christos leaned over, fell to the sand, and pulled Valerie up behind him.

Exhausted, she crawled near him and collapsed.

* * *

"Oh, Mama, this is the book I've been wanting. How did you know?" Valerie stepped back and smiled, holding the novel up over her head with one hand.

"And how could I not know, when you remind me at every turn?" Jacqueline patted her daughter on the shoulder. "Just be certain your studies don't falter."

Valerie hugged the book to her breast. "I promise they won't." She kissed her mother on the cheek. "I love you, Mama."

"Valerie?"

Someone else's voice entered her dreams. A man's voice, deep and strong. What was he doing in her bedroom? She looked at her mother who seemed to not even hear him. Jacqueline caressed her cheek. "*Pulcher*. Beautiful."

"Mama? I didn't know you spoke Latin."

"To what ghosts are you speaking your strange language? Awake, that I might help you keep them at bay."

Slowly, Valerie opened her eyes. The room was as black as pitch, with only a small crescent sliver of a moon offering comfort in the night. She rose up, rested on an elbow and looked around, trying to make out the unfamiliar shapes in the darkness. "Where am I?"

"In my room."

Valerie turned her head in the direction the man's voice had come from. "Christos?" she whispered.

"*Ita*." He ran his warm smooth hand over her brow.

Valerie lay back down. "I was dreaming. I thought I was home." She raised an arm over her eyes. "My mother was there." A tear ran down her cheek and glistened as a small ray of moonlight touched it. "I'll never see my family again, will I?"

"For now, you need to rest." He continued to caress her face. "We can talk of your home later."

She hugged her arms around her and pulled her legs up. The soft cotton coverlet fell away, revealing her bare arm. Christos leaned forward and kissed her shoulder, leaving a trail of warm moist kisses down to her elbow.

Valerie continued to cry, sobbing silently.

"Shall I stay with you tonight?" Christos asked, his voice as soft as his kiss. Her eyes met his. "It's your choice."

Her heart ignored her admonishing conscience and spoke for her. "P-please hold me. I'm so frightened."

Christos smiled. "Ah, now, there's no need to fear. I've slain the demon who would do you harm." He stood and removed his clothing and sandals. Carefully, he slipped into bed beside Valerie and scooped her into his arms. He held her close, with her smooth back against his strong furred chest, his arms locked tightly about her. They lay together, each seeking comfort from the closeness of the other, for the remainder of the night.

Chapter Thirty-One

Christos awoke in the early hours between night and morning, when the first glowing rays could be seen at the edge of the horizon. He smiled and nuzzled the neck of the woman at his side, not knowing when last he had slept so well. The comfort and peace he'd found in the soft form beside him was one he hadn't known for years, if ever. He pulled Valerie closer and she sighed, her breath a soft caress against his arm.

How had it come to pass that he could feel so strongly for a slave? But he knew in his heart that she would never be slave to any man. The words she had spoken were true. *You may own my body, but you will never own my soul.* He couldn't buy her, but perhaps she would someday give herself freely. After all, though she obviously didn't remember, she had told him in his dreams she was his.

Christos smiled to himself again. "I will be your slave," he murmured in Valerie's ear. "A slave of love."

He nuzzled her neck once more and ran his tongue along its base, then licked the lobe of her ear.

Lost in a dream, Valerie shivered and turned her head, opening her neck to him that he might explore more. Gently, Christos ran his hand down her back, massaging lightly. Her skin was as soft as down. He took a deep breath. May the gods help me. I have been bewitched by this woman.

Christos let his lips trail the same path his fingers had just taken. Kisses as light as the touch of a butterfly's wings were gently scattered on Valerie's back.

Still sleeping, she sighed and pushed against him. The full roundness of her buttocks fit snuggly into the curve of his lap. Valerie turned slightly, allowing Christos a partial view of her bare bosom.

He had to remind himself he'd had her undressed and put to bed only because he was worried about her. He rested here now only because of her plea to be held. Would you take advantage of her when she sleeps so peacefully in your care? he asked himself. In his mind, Christos' conscience argued, but his hands moved of

their own volition. Soft and slow, he tugged and teased her nipples into hardness.

Valerie stirred and half-opened her eyes. "I was dreaming again," she whispered.

"What was it about?"

"I dreamed someone was touching me." She looked at him through thick lashes, a faint blush covering her cheeks. "Everywhere."

Christos smiled. "Not everywhere," he whispered into her ear. Gently, he rolled her onto her stomach and massaged her buttocks. His hand swept over her hip and down her thigh, forcing her legs apart.

She started to pull away from him. "Christos. I don't know . . ."

"There's nothing to fear, no need to doubt," he said as his hands continued to move up and over the back of her thighs.

Valerie's skin burned, the heat of Christos' touch moving through her. In a few more moments, she knew all would be lost. She turned her head, sighing.

"Ah, my sweet Valerie, would you deny me your love?" Very slowly, his eyes never leaving hers, he slipped his middle finger into his mouth and pulled it out. His movements were slow and seductive and Valerie felt a delicious ripple of excitement run through her loins.

She laid her head on the pillow, her breath growing ragged as his hand moved back down to her thighs. She knew she should run and hide from the feverish glow in Christos' eyes, but they held her there, mesmerized. He was the witch, not she.

Christos squeezed her buttock, then ran the damp finger between her legs. He stopped halfway and allowed it to touch and slightly penetrate her growing wetness. Gently, he moved in and out, caressing her from within.

Valerie gasped. "What magic are you working?" Her body pushed toward him, encouraging him to continue his explorations.

"The magic of love," he whispered as he began to kiss her neck once again. He rolled onto his back, pulling her with him. "Please, let me love you." Christos ran his hands under her hips and urged her forward until she was kneeling over him on her hands and knees. He slid down and caught one breast in his mouth. He licked the nipple, then gently blew on it until it grew hard. He licked again.

Valerie groaned and felt the dampness between her legs begin to spread. As he kissed her, Christos slipped a hand between her thighs and massaged her softness. Again, he slipped a finger into her and circled it around, his thumb resting on her most sensitive spot. Valerie lowered her head, then raised it, arching her back. She was overcome by one wave after another of aching desire.

Christos continued to probe and she pushed against him. "It's not time yet, my love."

"Time for what?" she murmured. Valerie sensed there had to be something else, something that would take this sweet pain from her, but what?

"Ah, my sweet innocent." He felt deeper inside of her and pushed gently against the barrier which lay there. "There is much to learn."

"Teach me," Valerie whispered, her voice husky with passion. She lowered herself so she lay flat against his chest, the dark hair tickling her skin.

"Come." He gently urged her forward until she was straddling his face. With both hands, he spread apart the soft wet flesh, revealing the tender heart that lay hidden within. He flicked his tongue gently up and down and she began to pulse against him. Christos' tongue circled and explored. Valerie gasped. Cupping her buttocks, he slid his thumbs into her and moved them in and out as he continued to lick.

The tantalizing movement of his tongue was too much to bear. She would disintegrate into the half-darkness that surrounded her if there were no release from the magic he was working on her body. She pushed against him again, harder this time, then began to move wildly as the endless, delicious tension Christos had built within her came to a peak and released itself.

As Valerie's movements began to slow, Christos gently pushed her onto her back and slid on top of her. His mouth came down firmly on hers, his tongue forcing her lips apart. Valerie groaned and ran her fingers over his sides. He took her hand and placed it on him, directing her movements up and down. He raised himself and looked into her smoldering eyes. His eyes never leaving hers, he lowered his hips until they rested between her thighs.

"Open yourself to me."

With a delicious shiver, Valerie spread her legs apart and rested her heels on his back. Probing gently at first, he entered her. Then, with one swift movement, his lips met hers as he pushed forward. Valerie cried out with the sudden rush of pain. Christos kissed her face and neck, waiting until she caught her breath.

The pain gone, she found the tension he had created within her was still unsatisfied. "We aren't finished, are we?" she asked, uncertain.

Christos chuckled. "No, my love. This is just the beginning." He started to move within her again, gently pulsing.

With a warm smile, she urged him deeper and deeper. She ran a finger down his cheek and he took it into his mouth and sucked on it.

Christos leaned back slightly and pushed her legs up, resting them on his shoulders. He moved faster now, one hand on her stomach, the other supporting him.

"Christos," she murmured, her lips swollen, her eyes glowing.

Every time she moved against him, a jolt went through her. Grinding her hips, the pleasure of his touch created a luscious ecstasy. She arched her back in a feverish release as he continued to massage and thrust. In a sudden rush of tension, Christos released himself within her.

After a moment, he slowly eased out of her, and lay down at Valerie's side. Gently, he scooped her into his arms and pulled her close. With his free hand, he pushed the damp strands of hair out of her eyes.

Christos smiled and kissed Valerie's forehead. She looked at him, her eyes still dark with passion. "If only I had known," she whispered.

Chapter Thirty-Two

"My, my. This is quite an interesting scene."

Valerie's eyes flew open. She clutched the coverlet to her breast and sat up.

Clarus ran into the room on Gravia's heels. "I am sorry, master. I told the mistress you were not to be disturbed."

Christos stretched, then stood, heedless of his nudity. "What are you doing here?"

Gravia looked pointedly at the blood on Christos' upper leg. "I see the slave has left her mark on you. I would not have thought her to be a virgin, though, considering her status." She shifted her gaze to Valerie. "I hope you know I will not tolerate you in his bed after we are married."

Valerie's eyes met Christos'. "Married?" She repeated the word in a whisper, stunned.

Christos slipped a white tunic over his head. "Gravia has grand designs for me *and* my wealth, but that's all they are."

Gravia walked to where Christos stood. She laced her arms about his neck and pulled his face close to hers. "Did you not eat the cake from my hand?"

"It doesn't matter."

"See, he does not deny the action." She dropped her arms and smiled. "We have wedding plans to make, my love. Get rid of the slave."

Valerie tugged at the cover and wrapped it around her. "That won't be necessary." She stood, then stumbled. Tears stung her eyes. She grabbed the headboard and steadied herself. Why did she have to be without a cane at a time like this? "Clarus, would you please help me?" she asked, mustering up every last vestige of dignity she possessed.

Clarus hurried to her side. Valerie placed a hand on her shoulder, allowing the child to help her toward the door.

"Valerie, wait." Christos shoved Gravia out of his way.

Valerie stiffened. "There is nothing for you to say." She glanced over her shoulder. Her eyes met his and they were full of warmth and tenderness. Her stomach turned over. How could he look at her like that, after what he'd done? "I do trust the good master has enjoyed the use of his slave?"

"Our night together wasn't about slave and master. We pleasured each other. You know it and so do I." He ran a hand through his dark curls and whispered, his voice hoarse, "I almost lost you once, I will *not* lose you again."

Gravia approached Christos from behind. With a quick movement, she released the fastener at her shoulder and dropped her *stola* to the floor, exposing her nakedness beneath. She smiled at the other woman.

A sharp pain ran through Valerie's heart and she began to cry. "Do you honestly believe you can keep both of us?" she asked. She covered her mouth, stifling a sob, as Clarus led her from the bedroom.

Christos took a step toward the door. Gravia grabbed his arm. He spun around, his face dark and forbidding. "Tell me, Gravia, was Julius as good in bed as Felix? Or how about me? Was he *that* good?"

Gravia's eyes grew wide for a quick moment, then she composed herself again. "I do not know what it is you are talking about." She turned and walked toward the couch. Sitting, she patted the spot next to her. "Come, sit by me."

Christos remained where he stood. "Julius is dead." He continued to stare at her, waiting for her reaction to the news.

Her face paled. "I -- I did not know that. Wh - when did this happen?"

"Yesterday." Christos moved until he was standing directly in front of her, his hands on his hips. "I killed him myself."

Gravia jumped to her feet and shoved him out of the way. "You did not! I do not believe it! Julius was your friend!"

"*Was*, Gravia. He lied to me. He stole my property and sought to do it harm." He grabbed her by the arm and swung her around. Christos leaned down until his face was next to hers. "Why did you help him?" He shook her. "Tell me now or I'll see you dead as well."

Gravia yanked her arm free. "I do not know you anymore. This slave has tainted your brain with her strange ways."

Christos shook his head. "I knew I couldn't trust you, but it didn't matter when I was the only one you were betraying. How many men have you treated so? Julius, Felix, and countless others I would venture to guess."

"What I do with my body is my business. If you cannot appreciate me, then perhaps we should not marry." She studied her fingernails. "I have received countless letters of despair since our engagement was announced last night. You should see the graffiti that covers a wall by my house." Her eyes met his. "There are other men who would have me, Christos. Does that not make you a little jealous?"

"No, Gravia. It makes me a little sick." He grabbed her *stola* from the floor and threw it at her. "If I find out you've been near anyone in this house, I swear I'll kill you myself." He shoved her out the door.

"You and the cripple deserve each other," she spat as she pulled the garment over her head. "May the gods bring down the heavens on both of you!" Gravia ran down the stairs and slammed the front door shut behind her.

Christos went to the washstand in the corner of his room and splashed cold water on his face. "Venus Fisica, forgive me," he sighed. "By the gods, I've made a mess of things." He finished washing, and then left the room in search of Valerie.

* * *

The sun had long ago reached its apex in the sky and was now beginning its gradual descent. The last rays shone down through the atrium and into the garden. Valerie sat on a marble bench near Christos' workshop, staring at the rendered scene on the wall before her. Diana, goddess of the hunt, appeared to be giving bow and arrow instructions to Athena. Off to the side of the pastoral, Jupiter aimed a thunderbolt at one of the women's hearts.

"Strike me instead, dear Jupiter," she murmured. "Take this pain from my breast."

"I would not wish it to be so." Christos approached her from the confines of the house. "I would that he take me, for I deserve the punishment."

Valerie stayed with her back to him, afraid to look in his eyes, lest she see the closed, bitter man that used to be there. Lest she see his love for Gravia.

"Please, turn around and face me," he bade quietly.

From the sound of his voice, Valerie knew he was standing directly behind her. Sadness and pain and anger - all of them filled her being. Why had she been fool enough to believe she would be treated differently from any other slave? She was his property, after all. In this world, he had every right to use her as he deemed. She rested her forehead in her hands, not replying.

Valerie felt the warmth his body generated as Christos sat down next to her. He placed a hand on her shoulder. She pulled away.

"I have a gift for you. Won't you accept it?"

She turned slightly and he held up a new cane for her to see. It was crafted of fine ebony - ebony as dark as Christos' eyes. The handle was the same woman's head she had seen him casting a few weeks ago, in the garden.

"It's beautiful. Thank you," she murmured as he placed the object in her hand. She rolled it between her fingers, and the wood was warm and smooth to the touch.

Christos let his hand fall to his lap. "I've been wrestling my demons for weeks now. That day out here, you stirred up a past I thought was long ago forgotten, long ago healed." He sighed. "Little did I know it would take a woman such as yourself, a woman from another time, to make me see the truth."

Valerie turned again, her eyes wide. "What did you say?"

"I know the secret you keep close to your heart. I'm not certain I believe it, but stranger things are said to occur in this world." He took her hand in his and dropped to his knee. "I lost my soul and you have restored it to me. For that I am ever grateful." He drew her into his arms and held her close. She felt her anger begin to abate. "For that, I give you your freedom."

She pulled away and looked at him. "Do you know what you're saying?"

He nodded. "I would let you go with the hope you would choose to remain with me."

She studied his face. "What of Gravia?" she asked, not sure she wanted to know, but unable to leave the question unspoken.

"I've sent her from this house. She won't disturb us again."

Valerie reached out and caressed his cheek. There was a certain sadness around his eyes that tugged at her heart. She ran her thumb over his brow, smoothing the deep furrows. He kissed her palm. She sighed as he took her into his arms once again. His lips met hers and she felt the uncertainty in his touch.

"If it be God's will, I'll stay with you for always, my love," she whispered against his mouth. "But I swear to you, Vesuvius *will* erupt. You must promise me we'll leave the city."

Christos stood and scooped her into his arms. Gently, he placed her on a thick cushion behind the curtain where the musicians had played during the banquet. "Soon," he repeated, running his hand over her bare arm. Carefully, he unwound the coverlet from her body and lowered himself to her open embrace. "Soon."

Chapter Thirty-Three

A low rumble followed by an ear-shattering blast tore through the tranquility of the new day. Jolted awake, Valerie and Christos weren't even to their feet when another roar shredded the air.

Christos yanked back the curtain. Though it was now morning, the sky was as dark as the sea at midnight. Another burst of sound and the earth rolled beneath their feet. Valerie was tossed against the garden wall. Dust and dirt sifted down over her head as she struggled to maintain her footing. Beyond the curtain, ash and pumice began to rain down on the city at an alarming rate.

"My God." Valerie choked back a cry. "How could I have miscalculated? I swear I thought we still had a few days." She turned to Christos. "It's Vesuvius."

Christos took her by the hand. "Come. I've been through an eruption before, when I was young. If we can reach the sea, we should be safe."

Valerie shook her head. The ash was already almost a foot deep and still falling. Visions of plaster cast bodies and excavated buildings ran through her mind. "I'm so sorry. It's too late. If we were to survive, we needed to leave days ago."

Christos picked up Valerie's cane and robe and handed them to her. "Take these. I won't sit here and wait to die. Come on."

He held Valerie close to his side as they dodged the falling debris and hurried into the house. While they rushed down the long corridor past the kitchen, several of the slaves appeared and ran to Christos.

"Come. We need to head for the sea," he called out as he and Valerie approached the front door.

"It is only another mild eruption," Stella observed as she walked into the vestibule. "It will do us no good to panic."

Clarus tugged at Christos' toga. "Take me with you. Please."

Christos smiled at the child as he patted her head. "Of course, little one. Anyone else who wants can follow us."

The staff looked to Stella. She crossed her arms over her full bosom. "I'm staying," she stated flatly.

"How about the rest of you?" Christos asked. "We have to leave now if we're to have any chance of escaping the volcano."

A few hedged toward Christos, but many more chose to stay with the cook. After all, she was the one whose direction they trusted above all others, even their master. "We will stay and prepare dinner for your return."

"You'll die here. All of you," Valerie warned.

Stella looked at each and every slave. "You're being ridiculous. All of you."

Christos released the latch on the front door and tried to push it open, but the door stuck. He shoved his body against it and the force opened it just enough for them to pass. Looking out into the street, he saw where hot ash had fused to the wood. A thick layer of the cooling material, now at least knee deep, had fallen over the city and into the street. And still it continued to come down. He motioned for Valerie and Clarus to follow.

Once outside, Valerie looked off in the distance, in the direction of Vesuvius. A bright red-orange glow illuminated the black sky as sparks flew through the air. Half of the volcano had blown away. A heavy cloud the shape of an umbrella pine suspended upside down hung in the air. Fiery lava ran along the mountain's side and off in the direction opposite of Pompeii. Heavy wet pumice still fell through the air and, coupled with noxious sulfur fumes, filled their lungs. People all around tried to run through the debris. Others sat, huddled together, in doorways and under eaves. Valerie scanned their faces as Christos dragged her along. So many were already dead as the ash piled up around them, preserving their forms for future generations to discover.

"Christos!" Valerie screamed over the din as she tripped and fell to her knees in the muck.

He picked her up and, with Clarus still firmly gripping his toga, headed for the gates. Trudging slowly, his foot hit an object in the ash and he stumbled. He let go of Valerie when he saw a woman's hand. Bending over, he pulled the lifeless form to the surface. It was Gravia, still clutching a purse full of gold tokens and jewels.

"It would seem Zeus has brought the heavens down on your head as well," he whispered as he let her slide out of his arms.

Valerie swallowed back the bile that rose in her throat. Gravia's mouth, nose, and eyes were caked with the wet ash. "I'm so sorry."

Christos looked at her through the downpour with a sad smile. "So am I."

Just then, another violent quake shook the ground. Looking up through the falling ash, he caught sight of a fragment of building facade tumbling toward them. He jumped forward, shoving Valerie and Clarus out of the way. They landed in the hard debris that covered the street.

"Christos, are you all right?" Valerie called over the thunderous din of the volcano.

He raised his head and shook the ash from his hair. "Don't worry about me." He yanked off his belt and tied it tightly above his knee. A deep gash beneath it continued to bleed profusely.

"You're hurt!"

"It'll be fine. Let's go."

The trio crawled forward, pushing themselves to their feet. Moving as fast as they could, they dodged the hundreds of other inhabitants who sought safety. Those still able to move seemed to be heading in the same direction, to the sea.

Lightning lit the sky and Valerie saw the gate where she had first entered the city. They ventured past the tall columns that lined the passage and hastened into the Necropolis. Again, the ground shifted and rolled beneath their feet. Unable to see clearly now as the ash continued to pelt them, they walked close to the tombs, feeling their way along.

"Christos! Look out!" Valerie called as a tomb collapsed, sending a column out into their path.

Again, he shoved Valerie and Clarus out of the way. Only this time, he didn't move fast enough through the disarray of stone and volcanic rock that littered the graveyard. The monument came crashing down, knocking him to the ground.

"No!" Valerie screamed. She stumbled as if in slow motion through the now almost thigh deep mess and to his side. Damn this foot, she cursed silently. It took what seemed like an eternity to reach him.

Christos opened his eyes when she touched his arm. "Seek shelter, my love."

Valerie shook her head as Clarus stood, whimpering, behind her. "I won't leave you."

"You have to," he gasped. The fumes were so dense here. "Clarus, take care of her for me. Remember, Valerie, in you I will continue to live." With a shudder, he closed his eyes.

Valerie grabbed his shoulders. "Christos!" she screamed. She started to sob when he didn't respond. "Please! I love you! You can't leave me!" Valerie cried out loud and clutched her arms about her. She began to rock back and forth, stopping to brush the ash away as it began to pile up and cover Christos' body.

"Valerie." Clarus touched her shoulder. "We can't help the master now. You have to come with me so I can take care of you, just like he said."

She looked up through her tears. Nearby, she spotted the tomb she had hidden in so long ago. She began to cough. The overpowering smell of rotten eggs hung thickly in the air. "Over there," she motioned with a nod. "It has a roof. We can be close to Christos."

Clarus helped her and together they made their way to the tomb. A sense of *deja vu* came over Valerie as she brushed the ash and pumice from the opening with her cane, clearing it for them to enter. Crawling on her hands and knees, Valerie climbed through the opening first. She turned and reached for Clarus but the child had succumbed to the fumes as well.

"Clarus!" Valerie screamed. The child didn't stir, she just lay there as the ash continued to fall.

Valerie's eyes burned as her lungs filled with the gases unleashed from the volcano. She couldn't stop coughing and retreated into the recesses of the niche. She continued to stare off into the distance, toward where Christos had fallen. Was there someone standing over him? She squinted, but his still form became lost to her in the downpour.

"Soon I'll be with you, my love," she whispered.

Closing her eyes, Valerie gave herself over to the fumes. Even her foreknowledge couldn't save them. Vesuvius had won.

Chapter Thirty-Four

"Valerie? Are you in there?"

Valerie raised her arm, shielding her eyes from the straight thin ray of bright sunlight.

"Papa?" she whispered. Was she really hearing his voice?

"Val?"

"Papa!" She shouted the word this time. "I'm in here!" But no sooner had Valerie spoken the words than panic gripped her. If he stayed, he would die! "Get away from here, Papa! You'll die if you stay!"

A deep laugh echoed inside the tomb. "She's safe," Valerie heard him call. "I'm not going to die today, daughter. And neither are you."

"But the volcano! It's erupting!" she cried out.

"I don't know what you're talking about. There's nothing dangerous out here, except of course for Lucy's temper." He laughed again, then moved away from the opening.

One by one, the heavy stones covering the entry fell away as the men continued to dig. Dirt and dust sifted in and Valerie shut her eyes. A breeze blew in through the opening the workmen were creating. She took a deep breath of air. *Of fresh sea air*! Where was the sulfur odor? Was she - no, she didn't dare think it - home?

Finally, an opening large enough for her to slip through was made. Frederick's strong hands reached in and pulled her out. Gently, he placed her on the ground. He squatted down and retrieved a handkerchief from his pocket. He lightly dabbed at the moisture gathering in his eyes.

"You had us terrified, young lady," he admonished through his smile. "Goodness, it's good to see you."

Valerie reached out and hugged her father. "It's good to see you, too," she whispered through her own tears.

When she released him, he stood and looked down at his daughter, taking in her appearance. He whistled through his teeth as he removed his jacket. Placing it around her shoulders, he said, "Out and about without your undergarments again, eh? I'm sure your mother will have conniption fits when she sees you dressed like this." He winked. "That is, if she's not busy being too excited to see you safely home."

Valerie looked down at her clothing. Disappointment filled her. She was dressed in her long dark blue skirt and blouse, exactly as she was when she left her own time. Had any of it happened? Was it all a dream stirred up by her overactive imagination? She glanced quickly around her. The Necropolis was just as she left it in her own time.

"We'd better get back to camp so you can clean up," Frederick offered.

"Yes, Papa," Valerie replied, her head bowed. It had all seemed so real. She touched a finger to her lips. Christos had seemed so real.

"Excuse me, sir." One of the workmen motioned for Frederick. "Here. Your daughter forgot this." He pulled his hand out of the opening and handed Valerie's cane to her father.

Frederick raised his eyebrows as he handed the ebony walking stick to his daughter. "Say now, where did you come by this?"

Valerie stumbled as she grabbed the cane out of his hand. Catching her balance, she turned it over and over in her hands. It was the one Christos had made for her! That meant she hadn't dreamt him! Dear God in heaven he was real!

And if the cane was in there, maybe Clarus was too! "Please," she called to the workmen. "Is there anything else in the tomb?"

After a few moments of searching, they returned to her empty handed. "Sorry. Nothing else."

Valerie let out her breath. Clarus didn't survive either. But she had been real. Christos had been real too and she had the cane to prove it. She thought of the last time that she saw either one of them, both lying fallen in the ashes of Vesuvius, suffocating to death. She began to cry.

"What is it, child?" Frederick asked.

"Oh, Papa." Valerie wiped at her eyes. "I wish there was a way I could tell you." She took a breath to compose herself and forced a smile. "I guess I'm just happy to be home."

Frederick smiled and nodded as he took Valerie by the elbow and led her from the Necropolis. "Be certain and fill in that hole so no one else gets trapped in there!" he shouted over his shoulder.

Valerie stared hard at the beautifully wrought handle on her cane and began to cry again. She had traveled through the mists and found her love only to lose him. What was she going to do?

* * *

"You should have seen her, Mama!" Reggie exclaimed as he tossed a stick into the fire. "When she walked into camp, she wasn't wearing that birdcage under her dress and was as filthy as a gutter dog."

"You will watch your language, Reggie," Jacqueline scolded. "It isn't polite to call your sister a gutter dog." She put her arm around Valerie's shoulders and pulled her daughter close. "I was so worried about you when you didn't come home yesterday. We were all frightened for your safety. I only wish I hadn't been off looking in the other direction when they found you today."

Valerie pulled away from her mother and nervously tugged at the strings of her dressing gown. No sooner had she returned to the campsite, than Lucy had seen to it that she had a hot bath and change of clothes. She wrinkled her forehead. "Yesterday? What are you talking about, Mama? I've been gone for almost two months."

Jacqueline exchanged a worried look with her husband. "I promise, dear. It's been only a day." She caressed her daughter's head. "You must have taken a worst bump than we imagined, though, for the life of me, I can't find where you were hit."

Lucy appeared from out of the shadows. "Here's a nice poultice fer ye." She tied the heavy cheesecloth around Valerie's forehead, despite the younger woman's protests. It reeked of mud and soured herbs.

"I'm all right, Lucy. I don't need this smelly thing, really I don't."

"Nonsense. I been carin' fer ye since ye was little and I think I know what's best." She patted Valerie's shoulder.

Valerie shook her head and couldn't help but smile. What a contrast her life here was to the one she had just experienced in the past. Where she had to do the pampering for everyone, now she was the one pampered. Amazing.

She watched her father for a moment as he moved about absently in his seat near the fire. He leaned forward and twisted and turned, trying to face his book just so in order to read by the firelight. He must have felt her looking at him because he glanced up and smiled. All was right in his world once again.

Valerie smiled back at him. "I love you, Papa. And I love you too, Mama." She hugged her mother tightly.

"My goodness." Jacqueline laughed. "Whatever brought that on?"

"I missed you both so much. If you only knew how badly." Ever watchful, Lucy handed her a cup of tea. She sipped the warm, honey-sweetened liquid and stared into the campfire. In her mind's eye, she saw Christos once more, knocked to the ground, ash quickly covering his body. Would her family believe her story? Dare she tell them? At the very least, they'd probably believe her to be mad. Maybe she'd talk about it another time, when the memory didn't hurt so much – if there ever was such a time. "I think I'd like to go to bed now, if you don't mind."

"Of course not." Jacqueline stood and offered her arm to her daughter. "You never did tell us where you found that beautiful new cane."

Tears welled in Valerie's eyes. "You wouldn't believe me in a thousand years." Overcome with sadness, she looked off in the distance as she spoke. "Nay, nearly two thousand."

* * *

Lucy clucked and fussed the next morning as she packed the trunk at the end of Valerie's cot. "Things never seem to fit back in as well once they're taken out," she muttered under her breath.

Valerie rubbed her eyes and sat up. "What are you doing?" she asked, following the woman's movements.

"We'll be leavin' this day." She sniffed. "And none too soon, I don't mind tellin' ye."

"Leaving? But haven't we only just arrived?" Valerie swung her legs to the floor and stood. Gripping her cane tightly, she walked to the opening of the tent. She pushed back the flap and peered out into the campsite. She watched quietly for a moment as the workmen passed baskets of dirt to one another down a long line and dumped them into a pile. Once empty, they handed them back along the same line to be refilled.

"Yer father and mother are worried about ye. They'll be takin' ye to a doctor back home, they told me." Finished packing, Lucy closed the trunk. She tried to force the latch, but it wouldn't close. She silently considered it for a moment, then plopped down on its top. It closed nice and tight and, with a quick flip of the wrist, she fastened the lock. "There, now. I left ye some clothes over here fer the carriage ride back."

Valerie crossed her arms and leaned against the rock and canvas wall. "I'm not leaving."

"I beg yer pardon?" Lucy took a step toward her. "Ye took a harder blow to the head than I thought." She motioned at the cot. "Lay yerself down and I'll fetch ye some nice hot tea and another poultice."

Valerie shook her head. She walked to the chair and slipped off her nightclothes. "I don't need tea or poultices. Will you help me dress, please?"

Lucy hesitated for a moment. "Well, I suppose ye'll have to dress sooner or later." She scooped up the heavy corset and held it out. "Ye know the routine."

Valerie held her arms up over her head and held her breath. As Lucy fastened it tightly into place, she slowly let out her breath, recalling days of short, comfortable stolas. She definitely hadn't missed this piece of torture while in ancient Pompeii.

Next, Lucy placed the crinoline on the floor and Valerie stepped into it. The bloody birdcage, she cursed silently as the older woman laced it into place around her waist. Then came her stockings, blouse, skirt, and jacket, followed by a pair of ankle high shoes. She sighed. Why did Vesuvius have to intervene?

"Lucy, what did you do with the dress I was wearing yesterday when Papa found me?"

Lucy wrinkled her nose. "It was disgustin', all covered in dirt and ash. I threw it away."

"You what?" Valerie stomped her foot on the hard ground. "Where did you put it?"

"What's the worry, girl? It's not as if you don't have plenty of dresses." Lucy finished buttoning Valerie's shoes. "If you must know, I tossed it into the dirt pile out back."

Valerie grabbed her cane and headed out the tent in search of her clothing. Christos had touched that outfit. He had held it close and she wanted it back. Venturing into the street, her heart skipped a beat and she forgot all about rescuing her skirt and blouse. Last night, when it was dark, the town hadn't seemed quite so deserted. Now, in the light of day, the death and destruction was so pitifully evident. The same streets she had walked only a day ago, the streets that teemed with life and activity, were frozen forever in time.

"Valerie. Come here, child," Frederick called.

Wiping the tears from her eyes, Valerie walked to where her father was standing near one of the buildings.

"Look what I found. Signore Fiorelli said I could give this to you. A gift for all of your troubles he said. I thought they'd make lovely earrings." He smiled. "What do you think?"

Valerie held out her hand and her father gently placed two stones in her palm. She turned them over and brushed the dirt away with her thumb. They were pink tourmalines, the exact same ones she had held in Christos' garden, so long ago. Carved intaglio with a woman's head, they had survived the volcano intact. Her sight blurred and her breath came in short gasps. The world was closing in around her. She clutched at her throat. She couldn't breathe.

"Whatever is the matter?" Frederick took her hand. "Come. Sit down."

Valerie shook her head. She looked up at the building standing before her. She took a step, stumbled, and caught herself against her cane.

"Christos," she whispered. Leaving her father to stare after her, she entered the ruins and traced the path to the garden at the back of the house. Here, the fragments of Diana and Athena's hunt scene were still visible. Valerie dropped to her knees and dug her hands in the ash that had yet to be excavated. She raised her eyes to the heavens.

"Why? Why didn't he live?" Her shoulders sagged and she leaned forward. "Why didn't I die?"

She glanced up at the sound of children's laughter. Looking down the corridor, she could see Reggie and a local boy running in the street, playing a game of tag. Life has a habit of continuing, this she knew, even when those you loved were gone.

Valerie slowly stood and walked back through the corridor, moving her fingertips over the mosaics still clinging to the wall. A pain shot through her breast and she clutched the cane to her. Leaning her forehead against the wall, she gently traced the outline of the cool tiles as tears ran freely down her cheeks.

Without looking back, she left the remains of the once noble home and made her way through the street and toward the Necropolis, taking the same path she had taken during the eruption. Valerie stopped again as she spied one of Signore Fiorelli's plaster casts. She crouched down and studied the facial expression. A faint outline of a purse could be seen clutched in the figure's hands.

"Gravia," she murmured.

Valerie wiped at her tears furiously and stared at the sky. Having known the past, having known love, how could she face the future?

She stood and stumbled down the uneven pavement until she reached the gates. Slowly, she picked her way toward the tomb where Papa had found her. Would she find her love among the casts of the other bodies? She searched the area nearby. There it was. The heavy column that Christos had fallen next to.

Terrified of what she'd find, but unable to stop herself, she approached the scene before her. Several people had been uncovered. But, to her amazement, none lay under or even close to the column. She dug frantically in the scattered rocks until her fingers were torn and bloody. Where had his body gone?

"*Buon giorno*, *Signorina* Brooks. I am very glad to see you are doing well."

She looked up, glaring. Fiorelli took a step backward. "Tell me what you have done with him!" she demanded, her voice raspy.

"With who?" He leaned over and followed her digging movements with his eyes. He considered her for a moment. "Perhaps you should come and lie down."

"No. I'm not going anywhere until I find Christos." She looked wildly from side to side. "He was here. I *know* he was. Right near this column."

"If you are speaking of the bodies, *Signorina*, some did not survive the casting process. We had difficulty in the beginning, when we were perfecting our methods, and lost several of the forms." He gestured in the direction of the campsite. "I know of some other statues over there. Maybe you'll find one you'd like just as well."

Valerie got to her feet, tears running freely down her cheeks. "How could you destroy him?" she sobbed. She raised her free hand and slammed her fist into his chest. "He was my life!"

Fiorelli gripped Valerie's arm. "You must come with me, *Signorina*. Your mother will be worried after you."

Suddenly exhausted, Valerie fell against him. Fiorelli steadied her and she followed along next to him, moving numbly. She ventured one last slow look at the debris at her feet then allowed Fiorelli to lead her out of the Necropolis and back to the city.

Chapter Thirty-Five

Valerie watched in silence out the window of the carriage as it pulled away from Pompeii and headed north to the harbor. After visiting the Necropolis and finding no trace of Christos' body, she had decided it *would* be better to leave. She couldn't live with the ghosts that haunted the site. Besides, Christos would always be in her heart, so it didn't really matter if she was in Pompeii or London, did it? At least, that's what she tried to tell herself.

Jacqueline considered her daughter. She was so pale and drawn. She had hoped this trip would do the girl some good, not depress her. But, after everything that had happened with Thomas Smythe and then being trapped in the tomb, it probably would have been for the best if they had all stayed home. She looked at her child. "Tell me, Val, what are you thinking?"

Valerie glanced at her mother, then looked back out the window. "Nothing," she murmured.

"The look on your face tells me otherwise. Is it Thomas?"

Valerie's head snapped up. "Heavens no."

Jacqueline leaned back as the carriage bumped and swayed over the dirt road. When Valerie returned her attention to the passing countryside, Jacqueline patted her husband on the shoulder and whispered, "I tell you, Frederick, she's not right. Something's terribly wrong with her. It's almost as if she's pining away."

"She's had a terrible fright," he answered, keeping his voice low. "Trust me. She'll be fine in a few days."

"Well, I think she's gone crazy!" Reggie declared loudly. "And I think she should be locked up until her mind comes back!"

Valerie glared at her brother for a moment, then relented with a smile. She ruffled his hair and tweaked his nose. "You know something, brother? I missed you, even if you are a little lizard." Valerie closed her eyes and leaned back into the padded leather coach seat.

Reggie grinned widely and went back to working on his sailor's knots. "I want to be ready for our trip home," he declared. "Just like a real sailor." While he worked, he glanced out the window. "Papa! I think that other carriage is going to hit us!"

Valerie and Jacqueline both ignored him but Frederick dropped his book and leaned out the window. The driver of the other coach waved at him. Frederick sat back into his seat and tugged at his jacket to straighten it. "Nothing to worry about."

Reggie poked his sister in the side. "Take a look, Val! I say we're going to wreck for certain!"

"No we're not because I know who it is," their father reasoned. "And because I know who it is, I know precisely where they'll be stopping so there's no chance of an accident."

Valerie opened her eyes, her curiosity stronger for the moment than her sorrow. She looked at her father. Always one for a good mystery, he was. "All right, Papa. How about you share your information with the rest of us?"

"Yes, Papa," Reggie chirped in. "I demand to know what's going on." He slammed his fist into his thigh the same as he'd seen his father do a hundred times.

Frederick chuckled. "A friend of Fiorelli's, one of the locals, asked him if her nephew and his daughter could travel with us. Seems the man has business in England but has never been there. She was hopeful we'd show him around." He shrugged. "So I agreed. Seemed harmless enough to honor the old woman's request. Besides, I understand the man's something of an expert in Roman antiquities. Should make for some interesting conversation for you, daughter."

Valerie nodded slightly and closed her eyes again. Let the man talk all he wanted to, she wasn't about to have anything to do with him. Once she got on that ship, she was going to lock herself in her cabin for the rest of the journey home. She struggled to rein in her thoughts. If she didn't quit thinking about losing Christos, she was going to start crying again. Her family was going to lock her up for sure if she didn't stop weeping at the drop of a hat.

Jacqueline smiled and patted her husband's hand. "Your father does have a soft spot, you know, hidden beneath all that gruff."

Valerie opened her eyes as their coach drew up and halted. It listed as the driver stepped down and opened the door. Frederick eased out the narrow door and went to greet their new traveling companions.

A small woman, bent with age, was the first to leave the other carriage. Frederick offered her a hand and she smiled gratefully as she disembarked.

Valerie froze. "Pencia," she whispered.

"Did you say something?" Jacqueline asked.

Valerie motioned toward the window. "I — uh -- I know that woman."

"And how do you know her, Val?"

"Yes, Val. How do you know her?" Reggie echoed.

"I, um, I met her at the site, before the accident." Valerie opened her mouth to say something else, then forgetting her words, quickly shut it again. A tall dark haired man was climbing out of the carriage after Pencia. Her breath caught. It couldn't be! She grabbed the latch and threw the door open. "I'll tell you all about it later, Mama," she called behind her as she lowered a foot to the first step.

Cane in hand, Valerie hurried as fast as she could to where her father and the other travelers were standing. She stopped short of bumping into her father when the man traveling with Pencia raised his eyes to her. Valerie's free hand flew to her throat. Her vision blurred and she struggled to keep from fainting.

Pencia turned and clapped her hands together. "Ah, Valerie. It's nice to see you." She patted her chest and winked. "You listened to the heart, didn't you?"

"You two have met?" Frederick asked.

"Around the site. I see your daughter. She give me water." Pencia smiled. "She's a good girl."

Before Valerie could say anything, Pencia motioned to the man standing beside her. "This my nephew, Christos Campagne." She pointed to her carriage. "And his daughter, Clare. They gonna travel with you to England." Just then, Clarus climbed down, smiled, and offered a shy wave.

Valerie looked from the girl to Christos and fought back the urge to throw herself into his arms. Her thoughts tripped over themselves. How did he get here? She saw him die! Silent tears swept down her cheeks. She had lost him to Vesuvius. She pulled her eyes from his and looked off into the distance, where the remains of the great volcano loomed on the horizon. After almost two thousand years of eruptions, it didn't look nearly so terrifying to her anymore.

"You are thinking of the volcano?" Christos asked. Numbly, Valerie nodded. "My aunt tells me marvelous tales of lovers whose fate Vesuvius has sealed. Perhaps, if you like, I will share these stories with you on the ship?"

"That would be great fun," Frederick interjected. "I look forward to it, sir."

Valerie smiled through her tears. "Your aunt is a very wise woman with a talent for the improbable." She went to Pencia and hugged her tight. "Thank you," she whispered. "For everything."

Pencia held the younger woman at arm's length. "Love always survive everything, even the mists of time."

Valerie looked at Christos, overcome with emotion. He nodded slightly in understanding. She glanced over her shoulder at her father who was waiting for her to finish with Pencia. She turned her attention back to Christos and her voice quivered when she spoke. "Yes it does, my friend. Yes it does."

Valerie took a step forward, then stopped. Her legs shook so badly she couldn't walk. She remembered the figure she saw bent over Christos' body after he had fallen. She realized what had happened. "It was you, wasn't it?"

Pencia smiled, her dark eyes sparkling. "Everyone needs a little help sometimes."

The rush of emotions of the last few days hit Valerie hard and she stumbled. Christos rushed to her side as she fell to her knees. He took her hands in his. "Ah, my love," he murmured in his ancient dialect.

"How?" she asked, the words barely a whisper. She studied his face. "You're not hurt."

Christos shook his head. "I don't know how it happened. After you left, I heard someone calling my name. I opened my eyes. It was Pencia. She took my hand and the next thing I knew I was surrounded by the ruins of the city. She took me to her home." He glanced up and smiled at the old woman. "She said she'd know where to find you."

Frederick cleared his throat. "Perhaps we should be going now, young lady?" He helped Valerie to her feet as she reluctantly released Christos. "Are you able to walk?"

Valerie nodded. "Please, Papa. Just a moment with Pencia before she has to leave."

Frederick glanced at Christos, then the old woman. "Don't take too long. We're on a schedule here."

"I won't Papa." Her eyes met Christos' as she spoke. She fought the urge to throw herself into his arms and whispered to him, "I thought I'd lost you forever."

"Ah, Valerie, you are my life. I will go to this England of yours and do whatever is necessary to make you my wife." Tears filled his eyes. "By the gods," he whispered roughly, "I swear to you that nothing will ever separate us again."

Valerie smiled through her tears as Clarus slipped a small hand into hers.

"Nothing."

The End

ABOUT THE AUTHOR

In addition to her fiction and non-fiction writing, T.A. Moore is an artist, yogi, and Reiki Master Teacher. Teri also maintains a commercial interior design business in Indianapolis and keeps busy painting, silversmithing, and introducing grandbaby Kayla to the world. You can find her online at http://www.tamoore.net.